THE DOG WITH TWO TAILS

THE DOG WITH TWO TAILS

THE COLDSTONE CASE FILES VOLUME TWO

JASON GILBERT

FALSTAFF
BOOKS
WWW.FALSTAFFBOOKS.COM

This is for my daughter and biggest fan. I love you, kiddo!

D ude, that's like beer number six," the bartender said as he approached James Coldstone. He wiped up a small amount of drink that had spilled on the bar from the last order as he regarded James with a raised eyebrow. "Want me to call you an Uber or something?"

"I'm fine." James finished off the dark, heavy brew he'd chosen for the evening and set the glass down. "This is delicious."

"It's local," the barkeep said. "Place over in downtown. That's one of their imperials. High gravity shit, man. Kind of impressed you haven't fallen off your stool yet."

James smiled. "I'm fine, I assure you. I'd like some breadsticks, though. And let's go for number seven."

The man eyed him and looked him up and down. James knew the look all too well. He'd been sized up many times before. This one was checking to see how drunk he was. In any other situation, James knew he'd have been cut off and seen out to a ride home. Most people would have been stumbling all over the place, slurring their speech, and acting like a frat asshole. In truth, James couldn't recall if he'd ever been drunk.

Insane alcohol tolerance was one of the benefits of being a werewolf.

Once the bartender decided James wasn't hammered, he poured another glass of the rich stout and handed it over, then called out to a waitress for an order of breadsticks. The wolf inside made a frustrated huffing noise and sent an image of raw, bloody meat into James's mind.

Thanks, dickhead, James thought. *Seen enough of that. You can deal with bread tonight, and you can like it.*

The thoughts in his head began to slow down again and take on some painful lucidity as he sipped the beer, staring at the rows of liquor bottles behind the bar without seeing them. He shifted every full moon, giving the wolf the hunt it always so desperately desired. He didn't have to wait until a full moon to change. In fact, he could change at will. James had slaughtered plenty of deer in his time. He'd seen animals ripped to pieces and devoured. And people.

"Dude, do I need to cut you off?"

James blinked. "I'm sorry?"

The bartender was back. He motioned at the beer. James looked down and saw that he'd barely touched it. "You're kinda spaced out, man. You good?"

James shook his head. "I'm fine."

"Huh," the barkeep said. "Right. Just watch yourself, man. I don't need to be calling an ambulance."

James nodded. He'd told Phillip once they had returned from Miami that he would stay at Coldstone Keep. He was still a fairly hot topic, the Wade Anderson murders drudging up the city's memories of the Wolf Man Murders committed by David Coldstone, James's father. James wanted to keep his head down, wanted to make sure that he didn't cause more of a scene than he already had when he'd been forced into a change and ran from the Rock Hill police in wolf form.

Then he got bored. And stir-crazy.

The bar was a small dive just a few miles down Mount Gallant from Hands Mill Highway. James could walk there in just under half an hour, and always planned to walk back the same way, keeping to the woods and paths he knew from his nighttime runs in wolf form and away from the road. Open throughout the week, the place was always crowded on the weekends. James knew the sweet spot of Wednesday night at nine when the place was relatively empty except for the random straggler.

Or the couple that walked in the door. They were young, maybe old enough to be in their senior year of college if not college graduates, both dressed for a nice dinner date. The girl was small, delicate-looking with long black hair stopping just past her shoulders. She wore black jeans, a black denim cropped jacket, and a dark purple v-neck shirt that accentu-

THE DOG WITH TWO TAILS

ated her olive skin. The boy wore a collared polo shirt and jeans, his blonde hair combed perfectly to the side and his loafers clean as if he'd just stopped by the expensive shoe store on the way over. He was built well, lean and muscular.

The look on the girl's face told James that she was less than thrilled to be there.

Weird place to bring a date, bucko, James thought, watching them as they walked past him and sat in a booth along the back wall. She sat where she faced the door and glanced over at James, giving him a small smile. James never had trouble with women, something Phillip often picked on him about. He heard the waitress come over and take their drink order. The guy got a rum and coke. The girl decided on a glass of merlot. James could hear them talking behind him as the waitress put the order in with the bartender. "You've got expensive taste," dude-bro said. James couldn't tell if the asshole was cocky or condescending.

The image of the little girl on the internet asking "Why not both?" flashed in his mind.

"Sorry," the girl said. James detected a British accent. "I can order something else."

"No, no, it's okay," the guy said. "I'm good for it."

James grinned, looking into his beer in a way that still let him see them out of the corner of his eye. *Nice one, dumbass.*

The girl cleared her throat. "Chad, right?"

"That's me," the guy said. James could tell dude-bro was wearing a shit-eating grin.

"Right," the girl said. "So why this place?" She glanced at James, then around the room as she spoke. "It's quaint, don't misunderstand, but it doesn't seem like a 'meet-for-dinner' kind of establishment."

"Best wings in town," Chad said. "And they make a bangers and mash plate that is just unreal."

"Ah," the girl said. James could tell she was wholly unimpressed.

"Oh," Chad said. "Um," He snapped his fingers, biting his lip as he winced a little.

"Molly," the girl said, her tone humorless. "My name is Molly."

Molly isn't terribly difficult to remember, James thought. *He may just be an idiot.*

"Right," Chad said. "Molly." He said it with almost a purr. "Interesting how you don't have the accent."

"How do you mean?"

3

"Most Indian girls sound like an IT person from Microsoft or something."

Damn, James said. The wolf huffed in his mind, equally unimpressed. *I agree. I believe we may need to upgrade him from idiot to fuckwit.*

"Bangladesh, actually," Molly said in a forced pleasant tone that barely masked her irritation. "My parents immigrated before I was born. I grew up in England."

"Oh, okay," Chad said dismissively. "Just want to make sure you don't mind if I get the bangers and mash. It's not kosher or anything."

"Ah."

James sighed deeply, raising an eyebrow as he looked over at Molly. She glanced away immediately as if he'd caught her staring at him. Chad peeked out from around the booth, gave James a warning stare, then turned back to Molly.

The bartender set the two drinks down on the bar next to James. The waitress picked them up and took them over to the happy couple. She took their food order, and James heard Chad start up the thrilling conversation once again. "So, you like wine?"

"I do," Molly said, picking the glass up casually and carefully shaking the wine in a circular motion and taking a sip. "This is surprisingly good. I wouldn't expect a small place like this to have higher-end wine."

"What's your favorite? Merlot, I guess?"

James saw Molly glance at him again, this time giving him a flirtatious smile as she spoke. "I'll settle for a merlot, though I do enjoy a *ménage à tois.*"

Chad turned around and glared at James again. James could see the guy's face flush slightly, his jaw working. He cleared his throat and faced Molly again. "Since you like wine so much, you should try the Barefoot Cabernet I've got when we get to my place."

"I'm...sorry?" Molly said, her tone surprised.

"Yeah, it's good stuff. We can have a glass or two once we get settled in."

Uh oh, James thought, his humor at the situation turning to some concern. He'd seen something like this plenty of times before. The wolf growled low, and James felt the muscles in his body tense slightly.

"I'm sorry," Molly said again, this time more assertive. "But I'm going to need you to back up to the part about going to your place?"

"Yeah," Chad said as if surprised that this girl didn't understand the standard protocol of sex on the first date. "We eat, go back to my place, I bring you to your car in the morning. Pretty simple. I mean, we can go now if you want. Food's not here yet."

"Do you do this with all of the women you meet?"

"Why not? We met at work. What's a one-night test drive? If it's good, I'll call you."

James watched as Molly gathered up her purse. "I assure you, this has been lovely."

"Where are you going?" Chad said, surprised that she would dare to leave him at the table. "We haven't eaten yet!"

"I'd rather not eat," Molly said, giving him a disgusted glare. "And you certainly won't be eating anything later, either."

James couldn't stifle his laugh fast enough. Chad glared at him. "You find something funny, pal?"

James let his laughter die down. "I am not your pal." He took a sip of his beer. "And apparently, neither is she."

"Mind your own business, asshole," Chad said. He spoke to Molly next. "Sit down."

"Fuck you," Molly snapped. James watched her throw a couple of bills at Chad. "For the wine." She turned on her heel and stormed out. James saw Chad get up and go after her.

The alarms in his head blared as he watched the dude-bro stalk to the door and plow through it, Chad's face red and his gait angry and determined. The wolf growled again inside, and James felt all of his alarms go off at once.

He sighed. "And here we go." He dropped enough cash onto the bar to cover the beer plus a generous tip and headed toward the door as the bartender called out to him. "Hey, buddy! Leave your keys! Let me call you a ride."

"I don't drive," James called over his shoulder. "But thank you." He went through the door and saw Chad marching through the lot after Molly, who was pressing the button on her keys near a Jeep with flashing lights. James saw Chad catch up to her, then disappear around to the driver's side of the Jeep and out of sight. The wolf stepped forward slightly as James kept walking, his hearing opening up. He heard Chad's voice loud and clear.

"Where the hell do you think you're going?"

"Home," Molly shot back. "Now get the hell away from me."

"Nobody just up and leaves me sitting there like that! You know how embarrassing that is?"

5

"Ask me if I care. Now fuck off before I call the police!"

James slowed a bit and stopped behind the Jeep, just out of sight. He waited, listening as Chad gave a bitter chuckle. He glanced around the corner of the vehicle slightly and saw Chad standing next to the door, blocking Molly from her escape. "Look," jerk-off said, his tone a forced calm. "Let's just forget about this. Let's go back inside and enjoy our drinks."

"I'd rather eat shit than sit at a table eating dinner with you," Molly spat. "Now let me into my car." James saw her body trembling, not with fear but with fury.

"I'm telling you, I'm willing to forget this happened," Chad said, moving closer to her, looming over her. "Take me up on it."

Molly nodded, her tone dripping with sarcasm as she replied. "Oh, thank you so much for that. I can sleep easy now." She pushed past him and went to open the car door.

"I'm not done talking to you," Chad said as he grabbed her arm. Molly started to shout as he pulled her back to him. James stepped out from behind the Jeep, his hands by his sides, thumbs in his pockets, and his stance casual.

"I believe you *are* done, Chad."

Chad stopped and looked at him, his eyes wide with rage and surprise.

Molly jerked her arm free and backed away. "It's alright," she said to James, not taking her glare off Chad. "I was just leaving."

"The hell you are," Chad said. He rounded on James. "Didn't I tell you to mind your own fucking business?"

"I've decided against taking your advice," James said, keeping his tone conversational. He nodded at Molly. "Now, that being said, I'm fairly certain I heard Molly say that she would like to end your evening."

Chad started toward him. The wolf braced. *Easy,* James thought at it. *Last thing we need to do is shift. Let me handle it.*

"What the hell's wrong with you?" Chad said as he drew closer, putting his face inches from James's. He stood only a couple of inches shorter, but he was stockier than James. "You got a hearing problem?"

James kept his stance casual, his body loose, but he stared back into Chad's eyes, not hiding his welling anger. "I do have a problem. I don't like seeing people pushed around. And I don't like seeing a man tell a woman what she will or won't do with him that evening." His mind flashed back to Westenra Island, to what he saw happening on the ship. It was there and gone again in only a split second, but it was enough to heat his blood.

"I think you need to go find your car and drive away, pal."

"Again: not your pal. And no car. I walked here."

Chad set his jaw. "Last time, buddy. Turn around and walk away."

"Oh," James said, mimicking his favorite character from the Rocky Horror movie. "So forceful, Chad. So—" He looked Chad up and down. "*Dominant.*"

James saw Chad flinch, saw him bring his fist up as the wolf moved in just a little closer. He brought his hand up, palm flat as he slapped Chad's right hook even further to the right, causing the dick to overswing and lose some balance. James landed a blow behind Chad's ear and dropped him to the ground. The entire exchange had taken less than a second.

Thanks for teaching me that, Phillip, James thought.

Chad started to get up. "Please stay down," James said, keeping his voice steady and his tone polite. "I'd like for this to be over."

Chad lunged. James side-stepped him, grabbed him by the arm, and used Chad's own momentum against him as he swung him around and slammed him face-first into the spare tire on the back of Molly's Jeep. Chad tried to turn around. Another memory flashed, and he heard Phillip's voice in his mind.

"Right there," he'd said, pointing at his temple. "Land a good one right there, put a motherfucker to sleep."

"Night-night," James said as he plowed his fist into Chad's temple. The blow sent Chad's head into the spare tire again before he went down. James reached down, grabbed him by the shirt, and dragged the unconscious jerk over to the parking spot next to the vehicle. He looked up and saw Molly watching him, her mouth open and her eyes wide with shock. "What?" James asked. "Don't want you to run him over when you leave. Unless you want to? In which case, I don't know that I'd be able to blame you."

"Is he okay?" she asked.

James raised an eyebrow. "Do you care if he is?"

Molly shrugged. "Not really."

James heard Chad breathe, then start to mumble. "Wha...I..."

"You'll have a headache tomorrow," James said, patting him on the shoulder. He stood and spoke to Molly. "You should be able to leave now. And you might want to avoid guys named Chad."

"Um, thanks?" Molly said. "I mean, wow. That's never happened to me before."

"Well, I'm sorry for not stepping in sooner. You seemed to have it under control."

"Then I didn't," she said. "Didn't expect him to grab me like that. He acted so charming at work." She wrapped her arms around herself. "Seriously. Thanks."

James nodded, then winced as his phone chimed in his pocket. He pulled it out and read Phillip's text message.

Don't forget to be at the office tomorrow. We got a case.

"Work," James said, smiling at Molly as he put the phone back in his pocket. "Not important." He waved at her as he headed back toward the bar. "Well, I'll need to be going home. Good night."

"Wait," Molly called to him. "Didn't you say you walked?" James stopped and looked at her. She shrugged, giving him a slight smile. "Let me give you a ride home. Least I can do, right?"

2

L et me make sure I understand," Molly said. "You went to take the light rail train into uptown Charlotte, but the girls got on the train before you could, and you got separated?"

"The platform was crowded, to be fair," James said. "And I had to pee."

"That's brilliant." Molly laughed. "Absolutely brilliant. And you didn't think to catch the next train and try to catch up to them?"

"Oh, we did," James said. "However, they were less than thrilled to see us at that point since we'd forgotten to give them their train passes and they'd been kicked off at NoDa. Unfortunately, we did not know this until we were at Epicenter a few miles up, and had been looking for them. For several hours."

Molly laughed, and James noticed he liked the sound of it. He told her to turn right onto the highway and soon they were on the long drive that led from the road to the front of James's home. Molly stopped the Jeep in front of the house and stared out the window in awe. "Oh my god."

Coldstone Keep was as close to a castle as Rock Hill could get. The mansion boasted a large front porch and double doors with ornate carvings of trees and forestry in them. The top floor had seven gables, which often got James a few jokes from Phillip about having to live in required high school reading. The house stood in the center of over forty acres of pasture and forest, the direct back corner of the property home to the guard house area where Wade Anderson had tried to kill both James and

Phillip months ago. Despite that, it was one of the most beautiful and gothic properties in South Carolina.

James often wondered how long it would take to burn to the ground.

It'd been built with the family fortune amassed by David Coldstone. James hadn't known his father since his mother had killed the man before he was born. Joan Coldstone had told her son over the years about the man who'd made his wealth traveling the world doing god-knows-what, and the horrific murders he'd committed along the way right up to her finally putting him down with a silver bullet. She'd died while James was in college, but not before making sure her son had access to the entire fortune. James Coldstone was worth billions, and he hated every penny of it. He could've lived his life comfortably, paying his bills and keeping his refrigerator in his apartment in Downtown Rock Hill stocked without worrying over it. An incident ending with him being forced to shift into wolf form and rampage through the city running' from SWAT had ensured that his apartment would no longer be available to him. He'd been given no choice but to move back into Coldstone Keep.

"This is amazing," Molly breathed as she stepped out of the Jeep. James was already out and walking up the front steps, the wolf inside urging him to look at her. "You live here? On your own?"

James stopped and turned back to her. "Yes," he said. His sensible side kicked in, and told him to thank her for the ride and wish her a good night. The moon was high, not quite full. He could see her dark brown eyes sparkling as she looked around the yard, the shine on her black straight hair that fell just past her shoulders.

She wasn't Lacy.

"I'm surprised you haven't heard of it," James said. "Most people claim to know everything about me just by my last name."

"I've only just moved here a month ago," Molly said, walking up to him. "Coldstone doesn't ring much of a bell with me. Never heard it around Yorkshire."

"I'd be lying if I said I wasn't somewhat relieved."

"Relieved?"

"That someone doesn't know me through my father." *Way to go, dummy*, he thought. *Go deep and depressed right away. Good job.* "Makes things a little weird sometimes," he said, forcing a grin. He mimicked an old man as he spoke. "I remember bouncing you on my knee when you were just a little boy!"

Molly laughed, and James's sensible side pushed at him again, only to be pressed back by the heaviness in his chest. *Good save, Coldstone,* he thought. He had to collect himself a little before he spoke again. "Well, thanks for the ride." He turned and unlocked the front doors.

"Not at all," Molly said, stepping closer to him. She held her hand out, and he gripped it and shook gently. She stared into his eyes, and James felt his heart begin to beat slightly faster as the wolf panted in his mind. "Thanks for beating up my date."

James laughed a little.

"No, seriously," Molly said, her tone sincere and her face serious. "I mean it. You could've walked away and you didn't. Thank you."

Why won't she stop looking at me like that? James stared back at her, his chest tense as he realized that he couldn't look away from her, either. He glanced down and realized that he still had her hand. He tried to let go, but his fingers wouldn't respond.

Molly stepped forward, pressing her firm petite body into his as she wrapped her arms around his neck, kissing him on the mouth. James went to push her away, his mind in a panic and found his arms around her pulling her closer to him, her musk mixed with lavender, intoxicating as the wolf enhanced all of his senses at once. Her lips felt softer, tasted sweeter. He could feel her heart through her chest, hear it pounding as rapidly as his. He felt the kiss grow more passionate, more intense as he felt his want boiling over. He reached behind him, opening the door as she pushed him inside. The place was dark, and he wasn't concerned with finding the light switch as he kicked the door closed behind them. Molly tugged at his shirt and yanked it open hard enough to send a few buttons flying as James let her push it off his shoulders and down to the floor. She pulled her own shirt off, tossed it to the side. James's eyes wandered her form, her black lace bra all that stood between his eyes and the entirety of her chest and shoulders.

"I don't do this," she said, her breathing heavy as she stared at him hungrily. "I've never done this. I...I don't know what's happening."

"Me either. Not with someone I just met," James said, trying to slow his own heart and breathing, his pants suddenly a bit snug in the front as the wolf writhed on its back in his mind. "Maybe we should just slow down."

Molly nodded. "Nope." She was on him again, this time her legs wrapped around his waist as she pressed her lips against his, her tongue searching his mouth. He returned the kiss, his mind frantically trying to figure out how the hell he was going to get up the stairs into the one bedroom that had a bed in it.

Molly released him, dropping back down onto her feet. She sauntered away from him, unfastening her bra as she went. James watched her toss it to the side, then begin to unfasten her pants as she made her way into the study. His human eyes couldn't see her in the dark anymore. The wolf tried to step forward, give him his wolfen vision, but he pushed it back as he entered the study. He saw Molly move toward the couch, the blue moonlight in the window barely showing her nude form. James moved to her, moved his hands over her shoulders, her breasts, then to her face as he kissed her. He felt her hands working with his belt, opening his pants, her grip firm and needful. He stepped out of his pants as they slid down to the floor, not wanting to stop kissing her, not wanting her to release him. She pushed him onto the couch, straddled him, and leaned forward to keep kissing him. He felt her hair brushing his face, her lavender musk sending his senses spinning as she shifted her hips slightly and let out a deep sigh as she settled her body back onto his, bringing him inside her. She sat up straight, moving gently against him as he touched her body, felt her impossibly silken skin under his fingers as he rested his hands on her hips. She grabbed his right hand, pulled it off of her hip, and pressed it over her right breast as she began to move harder against him, her sighs turning into moans as he began to thrust into her, move with her body. She tilted her head back, her body shuddering as she cried out and tensed, her nails digging into his chest as her body went rigid for a moment before she relaxed and began on him again. James started to sit up, but she pushed him back down, swatting his hand off her breast and leaning forward as she rocked faster against him, her moans and sighs growing louder and more intense as her hair moved over his face and her breasts touched his lips. He kissed them, felt his body tense just as she started to shudder again, her moans turning to cries as her body jerked, sending him over the edge as he pulled her close to him, feeling her skin against his, staying inside her until the throbbing subsided.

She laughed a little as she sat back up. James felt his muscles in his groin twitch slightly as she moved, not letting him out of her. She grinned at him.

"As much fun as the couch has been, you do have a proper bedroom. Right?"

James lay there as the morning sun began to drift in through the window, the room still dark as the morning sky went from black to a deep purple.

And fire in the sky, James thought humorlessly as he watched Molly sleeping next to him. The covers had somehow been pushed down to her hips, exposing her bare back to him, her dark olive skin taking on a slight golden glow as the sun peeked over the trees, its rays moving in through the window. He wanted to wonder how he'd managed to be lying next to someone so beautiful, so breathtaking.

He saw Lacy in his mind, that night on Westenra Island replaying over and over again. He sat up, looking again at Molly, wondering what would have happened had it been Lacy instead. It should've been her. He loved her.

And he'd strayed.

Shit, he thought to himself as he got out of bed slowly. He heard Molly stir as he stood and pulled on a pair of boxer shorts. He found his robe and put it on as Molly sat up, pulling the covers up to cover her chest as she smiled at him. "I haven't slept that well in ages."

James blinked. "We've only been asleep for about four hours."

"Well, four hours restful is better than eight hours of tossing and turning." She gave him a sly grin. "Besides, it was a busy evening."

James laughed. "Right."

"Are you okay?" Her tone carried some concern. "Are you feeling guilty?"

"I mean," James said as he ran his hand through his hair. "I did slap your date around last night because he was trying to get into your pants. And here we are." He motioned at her and the bed. "Well, your pants are downstairs, I think."

Molly smiled at him. "Difference is that I didn't do anything with you I didn't want to do. All three or four times. I lost count." She rubbed her face. "God, I've never done this. Ever. I'm sorry. I don't want you to get the wrong impression. I'm not like this generally."

"Nor am I," James said. The wolf panted inside his head, grinning stupidly. *That makes one of us*, he thought at the animal. He watched as Molly got out of bed, wrapping the blanket around her as she went.

Lacy. It was supposed to be Lacy. Wasn't it?

"Look," Molly said. "You're cute. And *really* good in bed. But I don't want you to think that this instantly makes us an item. I barely know you."

"Of course," James said.

"May I use your shower?"

"It's the door over there. Please, help yourself."

"My clothes?"

"I'll get them."

They stared at each other throughout the whole exchange. James felt he could cut the tension with a knife. Not bad tension. More like both fighting to not end up back in bed again. Molly smiled, nodded, and closed the bathroom door behind her.

James made his way downstairs, his mind spinning as he tried not to feel guilty. He and Lacy hadn't exactly solidified anything. She agreed to come stay with him in Rock Hill and even followed him back to Cold-stone Keep. She'd immediately gone to sleep in one of the closets to avoid the rising sun, and James had slept all day in hopes of seeing her that evening. All he'd found was a note she'd left for him on the desk in the study.

A note explaining that they could not be together.

Yet he still felt as if he'd betrayed her. He'd searched for her ever since. Last night was supposed to be part of his attempt to find her, talk to her. Instead, he'd met a girl. He'd smacked around her asshole date and brought her home.

He'd slept with her.

"I think it was three times," he muttered to himself. "I can't remember, either."

James started picking up the clothing on the study floor when the doorbell rang. He made it to the main hall just as one of the doors opened. Phillip looked him up and down, his eyes stopping on the black bra that hung from James's fingers. "How's Lacy?"

"I wouldn't know," James said, feeling like he'd just been kicked in the gut. He couldn't be angry with Phillip. It wasn't like he'd texted his best friend and explained that he'd brought home another girl.

Phillip shook his head and closed the door behind him. "Well, damn, James. We gotta move."

"Shit," James said under his breath. "Right. Let me run these up to her."

"Go for it."

James started up the stairs, then stopped and turned to Phillip. "Normally you would be yelling at me for doing something like this."

THE DOG WITH TWO TAILS

Phillip held his hands up. "Like what?"

"Bringing a girl home like this." Though James wasn't being actively hunted by the police anymore thanks to the SCU, he'd still been advised to keep a low profile. He figured having a girl over probably did not qualify as keeping a low profile.

Phillip raised an eyebrow at him. "James, you've been moping around for two months. Lacy ain't nowhere to be found, she ain't returning your calls and messages, she's in the wind." He shook his head. "And you've been a real pain in the ass since she left. You needed to get laid. Now go handle ya' business. I'll get the SCU pulled up on a video call after your date leaves."

"It wasn't a date."

"Right."

"We only just met."

"Don't care."

"It just happened—" James started just before Phillip plugged his ears and started shouting: *"La-la-la-la-la-la-la-I-don't-care-about-James's-damn-sex-life-la-la-la-la!"*

James laughed as he turned and continued up the steps. He needed the laugh.

3

James left Molly's clothes on the bed and came back downstairs while Phillip typed on his iPad. While upstairs, he'd changed into jeans and a button-up casual shirt with the sleeves rolled up to his elbows. Phillip spoke over his shoulder. "You gonna take a shower before we go?"

"It's occupied," James said. "I can wait until she leaves."

Molly's voice startled them both. "Oh. Oh, my."

James and Phillip both stood, and James moved over toward her. She was wearing the clothes from the night before, her hair still damp from the shower. Her face flushed slightly as Phillip greeted her. "Hello."

"Right," James said. "Phillip, this is Molly. Molly, this is Phillip."

"Pleasure," Molly said. "I'm sorry, did I interrupt—"

"No," James and Phillip said in unison. James cleared his throat. "No, nothing at all. Work." He shrugged and rolled his eyes. "Boring."

"Well then," Molly said. "Nothing like awkwardness with breakfast." She pulled her phone out and looked at it. "*Shit!* I'm late to work!" She darted past James and headed toward the door, calling over her shoulder as she went. "Dresser! Text me!" James watched her shut the door behind him.

"She's cute," Phillip said. "Seems nice."

"She's quite pleasant."

"And less likely to kill you or your human best friend."

James looked at him and grinned. "I know. Kind of takes the fun out it, not knowing whether a girl you like will eat the people you care about."

Phillip muttered a few of his favorite curse words, ending with "C'mon, let's go." He walked past James, who held up a hand. "What?"

"Are you forgetting something?"

Phillip narrowed his eyes at him and sighed. "You're a dumbass."

James nodded. "There it is. Shall we?"

The morning sun was already up, the sky clear and bright as Phillip parked his blue Honda Civic in the parking lot at the strip center on the corner of Cherry Road and Ebinport. The playground at the school across the street was active, kids running around on the equipment or chasing each other, laughing and screaming as they went. There were at least forty cars in the lot in front of the gym that now operated in what was a grocery store back in the 90s, and a few employees were in and out of the pub and the pizza place at the other end of the strip setting up for the lunch rush. Phillip had parked near the rear of the flooring place that had once been a Blockbuster Video so they could see the majority of the strip center.

He briefed James on the way over.

"You're in luck this morning, my friend. Turns out they want us to nab the were-mouse and bring him in with us. We'll report to the briefing after we get him processed."

James groaned. "Were...mouse? Not him again."

Chuck Creighton was a local supernatural that had the ability to shift into mouse form and cause havoc. Technically speaking, he wasn't a were at all. While some shifters could take on the form of any animal, some were only able to adopt one form. Chuck fell under the latter of the two, though he liked to refer to himself as a were. He wasn't particularly dangerous, but his habit of running up women's skirts and dresses had earned him the moniker of "Cooter Critter" from Phillip.

He was also known for trolling people with computer viruses that would do minor things like erase hard drives or replace their bookmarks with Korean internet porn.

Phillip sighed. "He's a slippery shit, but orders are orders. He skipped out on parole again."

James shook his head as he looked out at the area through the window in Phillip's car. "He's never actually hurt anyone."

Phillip looked up from the iPad. "Dude, he's sexually assaulting women."

"Fair point."

"He keeps that shit up, and people are gonna figure out supernaturals are a thing real quick." He grunted. "Hell, you'd know about fucking up in public, wouldn't you?"

James nodded, remembering his romp through downtown in wolf form. Rock Hill seemed to have moved on, the local news writing it off as some kind of advertising stunt for a movie.

But there was the even bigger question of why a Federal agency was interested in spending time and resources on a pervert for no other reason than to detain him as a supernatural.

In the weeks since James, Phillip, and Lacy had brought down the child sex trafficking ring run by the vampire house Wangenheim, the Supernatural Crimes Unit had kept James and Phillip active on small cases. Some of them, to James, seemed unnecessary. There was a guy who had robbed the local Best Buy by using his vampire suggestion to have a warehouse employee open the bay door and load three large televisions into the back of his pickup so he could take them home and watch three football games at once. There was also a woman who used her witchcraft to turn the gasoline in her cheating husband's fully restored 1965 Shelby Cobra 427 sports car into sugar syrup, then hexed his penis to only achieve any kind of arousal when he watched videos of people popping zits and cysts on the internet. The more graphic, the harder he got. The Cooter Critter was a different story and a particular pain in the ass for the SCU, mostly for James and Phillip. They'd managed to bring him in once, but he'd been released shortly after pending a parole hearing.

In fact, all of them had been released shortly after. It was as if the SCU was bringing them in just to make a point. James found it odd, though Phillip had written it off as standard for first-time criminals. But none of these people had caused serious harm to anyone. Even Chuck Creighton once made it clear that he did what he did for laughs, and not for any kind of sexual gratification. James was cooperating, but by force. Agent Smith had given him a choice: work for the SCU or get doxed and exposed. Why not just offer him the job? Phillip may have even been able to talk him into at least a small role if it meant helping people.

All of it gave James a bad taste in his mouth.

"Anyway," Phillip continued. "Once we get back, we're supposed to get briefed on something going on in Savannah."

"Why on earth would I want to go to Savannah?"

"Because we have a case there."

"I'm busy."

"Don't start with me, James."

"I have better things to do."

"I'm sure you do. Call her from the hotel. You're going."

James's phone chimed. He looked down and saw a text message from Molly responding to the test text he had sent earlier based on the note she had left.

Sorry to rush out this morning. Call me later. I'm off around 4. It was followed by her phone number.

The wolf moved in his mind, panting as it flashed images at him from the night before. *I need you to focus. The faster we get this done, the faster we can tell them we're not going to Savannah.*

The wolf huffed and stepped forward. James's hearing opened wide, and he cracked the window slightly. His ears were met with the sounds of people chatting as they walked toward the gym, the conversation mixing with traffic moving up on Cherry Road. He saw a waitress step out of the bar at the other end of the strip and heard her lighter snap open as she lit a cigarette.

She apparently didn't hear the woman's shriek from behind the building.

"I believe he's here," James said. He pointed at the escape room that was located almost in the corner of the shopping center. "Behind there."

Phillip put it in gear and zipped through the parking lot, taking the corner just hard enough for his tires to squeal on the asphalt as he whipped the car into the back area and sped toward the shopping center elbow. He hit the brakes, and James saw a heavy-set woman out behind the escape room flailing around, smacking at her skirt as she shrieked and screamed. She spun on her heel, dancing around as she put her arms out to the side and threw her head back.

"She's so excited," James sang under his breath as she began to run in place, her feet moving in almost a blur. "She just can't hide it."

"Would you shut the hell up?" Phillip muttered. His eyes widened as the woman's body stiffened and she began moving backward, her feet still shuffling on the ground as she let out a long high-pitched howl. "Damn, he made her Moonwalk?!"

James rolled his eyes. "You're no fun."

"Got your fuckin' fun right here," Phillip muttered as he unfastened his seatbelt. "Let's go stop him before he has her break-dancin'."

"To be fair, I can see some talent here."

"Yeah, she does move well for a big girl."

James got out of the car and started toward the woman, who'd already begun running around the area leaping into the air every few steps in an impressive series of ballet jumps. He paused and saw Phillip standing by the car. He looked at James. "What?"

"You're not going to help?"

"Let's see," Phillip said, his tone sarcastic. "A black dude and a white dude wrestle a screaming white woman to the ground in an alley trying to get something out of her skirt. Gee, I wonder what that'll look like on camera, and who's more likely to catch a damn bullet if the police show up?" Phillip pursed his lips and jabbed an index finger at his head.

James sighed. "Fine." He approached the woman as she stopped in front of him and did a perfect series of pirouettes. He glanced up and saw the camera pointed right at them. "Chuck," he said, turning his attention back to the woman. "We know you're in there. Let's go."

The woman staggered, breathing heavily as she stopped spinning. "Wait, what? I'm Katie."

"Hi, Katie," James said. "Chuck is the mouse in your skirt."

Before she could respond, Katie's leg shook and twitched. She screamed and slapped at her thigh, and James saw the small field mouse drop out and hit the ground running faster than he'd ever seen a mouse run before. The back door of the escape room opened, and a man stepped out. James saw the Cooter Critter zip underneath the man's legs and into the building. Phillip was beside James in a flash, his gun drawn. "Shit, *damn!* Little motherfucker's fast!"

"He went inside," James said.

"The hell is going on back here?" the older man asked. "Katie, who are these people?"

"Federal agents," Phillip said as he flashed his ID. "Sir, I'm going to ask you to stay outside. We're after a fugitive who just went into your establishment."

"It's just a mouse," Katie said, her tone panicked. "Jesus, a gun?"

Phillip looked at her and spoke low, his tone dark. "That mouse is no joke. He bit an old woman on the neck, and she went insane, killed several people in a diner, and infected more. A whole town got wiped out in one night, and the only survivors won't ever go near a lawnmower again. Now stay out here."

Katie backed away, her eyes wide with horror. "Daddy, do what he said."

J ames glanced around the back room as Phillip shut the door behind them. It was quiet, the walls painted with different murals depicting brick walls as if they stood outside a castle or wooden planks that led to a door that looked like something from a pirate ship. He turned and looked at Phillip. "That was an interesting story you told back there."

Phillip shrugged. "Not everyone's seen *Dead Alive.*"

"It is truly a masterpiece of our time."

Phillip pulled his phone out and sent a text message. The reply came immediately, and he looked up at James. "Okay, the SCU just hacked in and disabled the camera system. Fetch."

James stripped and tossed his clothes into a nearby chair. He breathed out as the wolf came fully forward in his mind, settling in at the forefront of his consciousness just enough to still allow him control. His muscles expanded, his bones growing and shifting as bluish-silver hair grew over every inch of his changing body. His fingers ended in long claws, and his mouth and nose stretched forward into a muzzle, his teeth sharp and his canines elongated.

He crouched down when his ears brushed the ceiling, a subtle reminder of the difference between being a six-foot-four man and an eight-foot-tall werewolf. He caught a glimpse of his massive form in the mirror, his arms now the size of tree trunks, his shoulders broad and his muscles rippling under his thick fur. Every inch of his body was warm, radiating raw and feral power, strength beyond what any human man was capable of, and speed only matched by vampires. His claws were sharp, capable of ripping through steel. His jaws were powerful enough to mince bone or crush a car.

Everything he would need to hunt down a perverted field mouse in an escape room funhouse.

James went to all fours, sniffing the floor as he moved. He smelled the bleach and floor cleaner before he noticed the shine on the tile. They'd just mopped. He stopped and sniffed again, the scent of Clorox and Mr. Clean not quite covering the tiny trail of Cheetos and Mountain Dew. He heard Phillip ready his gun, then moved forward down the hall past different doors advertising escape rooms with varying themes. A pirate ship. A haunted house. The office of some famed fictional archeologist with a hang-up on mummies. The trail stopped and cut sharp to the left, the space under the door just enough for a small mouse to fit through.

"Oh, hell no," Phillip said behind him. James looked up and saw the warped, grotesque grins matching the large red noses and colorful hair. One of the figures in the mural was handing a child a balloon from the cluster he held in his other hand while another snuck up behind the kid with a rolling pin held high in one hand and a recipe book in the other. The title of the book read: "The Joys of Children and How to Prepare Them."

"I fuckin' *hate* clowns," Phillip said behind James. "What?! 'Cannibal Clown Circus?!' No. *Hell* no."

James rolled his eyes and pushed the door open slowly, carefully looking around to make sure Chuck didn't use the opportunity to slip by. He heard Phillip speak again. "I'll stay here and make sure he doesn't come back under the door."

James moved on in, letting the door shut behind him. The lighting in the room was low, the faux brick walls on either side depicting a fictional alley in Sometown, USA. There were two electrical panels on the wall to the left next to a pay phone, and a bin on wheels at the end of the room that sat under a large chute. A pre-recorded clown laugh came over the speakers every now and then accompanied by the desperate cries of someone begging them not to eat them. The chemical smells outside were replaced with paint and WD-40. James tried to move, but the room was small, cramped, and obviously not designed with werewolves in mind. He stopped when he picked up the Cooter Critter's scent again and followed it to a door marked "Funhouse Buffet."

Right, he thought. He gently tried the door, but it wouldn't budge. *Okay, so do I solve the puzzle to get in?* He looked around again and saw one of the panels standing open with several breakers flipped. A wire stretched from one of the lugs to a light, and he was able to see scrapes on the floor where the laundry bin had been moved a few times. He sighed. *I think I'll do it my way.*

He smacked the door and sent it flying into the next room, frame and all. The wolf barked in approval inside as James moved into the next room. A large table dominated the area and was surrounded by several high-backed dining chairs. The table was laid out with a pile of waxed fruit, various desserts and sides, and empty wine glasses. A mannequin dressed as a generic schoolboy from the 1950s sat in the center of the table on a large platter, the thing positioned on its knees and bent over with its hands tied behind its back and a wax apple in its mouth, a look of utter fear plastered on its plastic features.

Subtle, James thought. The wolf huffed back in response.

James's ear twitched. He stopped, listening for the sound again. Small, tiny claws scratching. A desperate squeak. The scent of Cheetos and Mountain Dew mixed with a sense of primal fear.

James heard the latch release just before the secret door opened in the wall behind him, releasing the knife-wielding clown mannequin as fiendish pre-recorded laughter howled in the room. He heard the scratching behind him this time, turned, and saw the mouse running away from the roasted kid doll and scurrying toward the open door. James went for him, knocking chairs aside and shoving the killer clown back into its cubby as he charged after the mouse. Chuck darted left, and James slammed his fist down in front of him, blocking him off. He maneuvered himself in front of the door and snarled, the sound more like a roar as he challenged the rodent. The Cooter Critter stood up on his hind legs, and James heard a sound come from him that sounded more like a graveled squeak than a snarl just before he charged. James rolled his eyes and leaned down as the mouse darted again, this time running up the back of the chair and kicking off, flying through the air toward the door. James turned his head lazily, opened his mouth, and slammed his jaws shut. He felt the mouse scurrying inside, screeching as it clawed at his gums and the back of his teeth in panic. Phillip stepped in, shuddered at the sight of the clown portraits around the room, and looked at James.

"Where the hell is he?"

James pointed at his mouth.

"Again? Shit, James. You're gonna give him a complex." He held his hand out. "Out. Now."

James spat the now-soaked mouse into Phillip's hand. Phillip put the mouse onto the table, made a disgusted sound as he flicked the drool off his hand, and spoke to the pest. "Okay, Chuck. It's over. C'mon."

The mouse quickly grew, and it was less than a second before James was towering over a short, balding, overweight naked man cowering back against the table with his hands in the air. "Fuck! God *damn*, Coldstone, is that really necessary?!"

"Turn around, asshole," Phillip said. He went over and had Chuck in zip cuffs in seconds as James moved down the table, looking over the décor, searching. There was something else.

"I hate clowns," Phillip said, his face close to Chuck's. "I'm gonna make you *pay* for this shit, you little cretin!"

Chuck looked over his shoulder at James and grinned. "Apple."

James poked the apple in the kid's mouth with his claw and sat back to watch the show as another clown dummy, this one armed with what may have been a functional chainsaw, erupted from its hiding spot in the room and launched at Phillip.

4

James wiped the tears out of his eyes, trying to calm his laughter when Chuck began howling and snorting from the backseat, which brought James back to laughing so hard his face hurt.

"Both y'all can kiss my ass," Phillip muttered, his face dour as he glared out at the road ahead. "Punk-ass motherfuckers."

"Dude," Chuck said from the back, out of breath and trying to stop his laughing long enough to talk. "Dude, I'm sorry. I did *not* know you were that scared of clowns."

Phillip jabbed his finger at James and shouted. "*That* motherfucker did! *That* motherfucker right *there!*"

"I believe it's called coulrophobia," James said, calming down. "An irrational fear of clowns."

"It's a serious condition, James," Phillip snapped. "Sweats, fear of death, paralysis..."

"Right," Chuck said, his serious tone downplayed by the obvious laughter he was stifling. "And it makes grown men scream like Mariah Carey."

Phillip grumbled and cursed at them as he took the corner at Oakland and Black Street and made his way into downtown Rock Hill. The SCU office was inside the office and recreation complex where the Bleachery once stood. It'd been a central part of the city's economic growth and industry back in the early part of the twentieth century as a textile finishing plant, then was left to ruin until 2009 when a massive fire wiped the remains of the facility out. New buildings were constructed on what was left of the original offices, and a restaurant was opened in the bottom floor of the main building. Several companies and agencies had moved in, including the Supernatural Crimes Unit of the FBI, which encompassed an entire floor of the building and also had space in the lower sub-levels for holding cells.

Phillip pulled the car into the parking garage and parked on the end nearest the elevator that exclusively led up to the SCU offices. Though it did stop on other floors, a badge scan was required to have it stop on the federally-owned floors.

Cooter leaned forward from the back. "So...just wanted to throw something out to you guys."

"Shut the hell up," Phillip grumbled at the same time James said, "Do tell."

"Yeah. You're about to take me up to the offices for processing, right?"

"Yeah," Phillip said, looking over his shoulder. "This ain't your first rodeo, Cooter. You know the drill."

"Oh yeah, for sure," Chuck said. "Just wanted to point out that I had clothes the last time I was here, so I wanted to know what the plan would be to haul the naked guy in for booking." He sat back with a smug grin. "I'll wait."

James and Phillip looked at each other. "He makes an excellent point," said James.

Phillip groaned and rubbed his face in his hands and mumbled to himself. "What the hell did I do to deserve this shit? Attacked by damn clowns and now I gotta deal with a naked man in my damn car."

"The seats are nice and clean," Chuck piped up. He grinned devilishly as a loud, wet-sounding fart rumbled from beneath him. "Well, they were."

"When I scan my badge, the elevator will take us straight up to the office without stopping," said Phillip. He opened the car door and nudged James. "Get him the hell out of my car, and you're paying to have the seats cleaned."

James got out, helped Chuck out, and they made their way over to the elevator, making sure to move close to the other parked cars to avoid being seen. Phillip ran ahead and scanned his badge while James and Chuck waited in a small space between a large SUV and the concrete wall.

"I'll be back out in a day, you know," Chuck said.

"Right," James said, looking down at him. "Don't all the bad guys say that?"

"They don't really do anything," Chuck said. James picked up the sincerity in his tone. "I mean it. They take me down to holding, I sit there until they're ready for me, then they ask me a bunch of questions and let me go."

"Interesting," James said. "Perhaps this time will be different?"

Chuck shrugged. "Doubt it. Though the first time I came through they put this barcode on me." He shifted around and showed James his right shoulder. A small barcode had been tattooed into the man's skin, barely the size of a dime. "Guess it makes it easier to pull my shit up when they want to look at my records."

Phillip's voice echoed out before James could respond. "Elevator's here. Let's go."

James walked Chuck the short distance from their hiding spot to the elevator doors. Phillip held them open as the two got in, then stepped inside and scanned his badge. An older man and a middle-aged woman walked up as the doors began to close. They stopped, their eyes wide as they looked at the scene in front of them. Phillip held up a hand and spoke in what James liked to call his "Cop Voice."

"Official business, folks. Nothing to see here."

Chuck snorted. "Says you."

James and Phillip dropped the Cooter Critter off at booking and headed over to the SCU briefing room. The only description James figured he would ever be able to give the office was summed up in one word: beige. The carpet, the walls, everything was some kind of earth tone that all mixed together into the kind of work environment that would make someone with any sense of life outside a cubicle want to bungee jump off a bridge before hooking up the giant rubber band. The entryway was a glass wall with glass double doors embossed with the FBI insignia. The room was populated with desks all pushed together into clusters, each home to a human staring diligently into the large computer monitors in front of them as they worked on reports and filing for the various cases in the Southeast. There were four offices total in the country, one for each quarter of the US.

The southeastern office in Rock Hill tended to be the busiest.

James followed Phillip into the briefing room, sitting down next to him at the conference table. The room was dark, with one wall and a window overlooking the rest of the office. A large flatscreen television hung on the wall opposite the door, the FBI logo floating in the center of a blue screen. An elegant, sharply dressed black woman sat at the other end of the table typing furiously on her laptop. She glanced up at them, as they sat down. "Agent Smith will be here in a moment."

"Thanks, Darlene," Phillip said casually.

"Agent Kimble is just fine," she shot back.

"I've always preferred Agent myself," James said out of the corner of his mouth. "Got a ring to it. 'Agent Coldstone.' I could get used to that."

"You're not an agent, Mr. Coldstone," Kimble said. "You're a consultant. Please remember that when you are in the field."

"Right," James said, forcing a polite tone. "My apologies. I often forget the office terminology here."

"James," Phillip said under his breath, his tone warning. "Don't start."

"Job? Blackmail?" James shrugged, ignoring him. "Tomato, to-mah-toe."

"Oh goddammit," Phillip breathed as he shook his head. "Here we go again."

"Your terms of employment are between you and Agent Smith," Kimble said, her eyes flashing at him. "If you have an issue, you'll need to take it up with him."

James opened his mouth to shoot off another smart remark when Smith walked into the room, a tablet in his hand and his usual smug expression on his face. "He has no issue, and fully understands the terms of his agreement to assist the Supernatural Crimes Unit. Don't you, Mr. Coldstone?" His British accent gave the statement a sharper, more pointed tone.

James sat back in his chair. "Whatever."

"Very good." Smith nodded to Kimble. "Agent Kimble, if you please."

Kimble stood, picked up a remote control, and pointed it at the television. The image changed, and James was only able to tell it had once been a woman by her hair and the name on the report next to the image. Something stirred in his memory, and the wolf let out a short growl in his mind. "Kathleen Wilson. Twenty-two, Charleston University graduate. Moved to Savannah, Georgia for work in her field." Another image popped up, a South Carolina driver's license photo of a pretty, happy college girl accompanied by her personal information.

"Says she was an accountant," Phillip said, nodding at the screen.

"She took on employment as a personal accountant, but we don't know who."

Phillip leaned forward, resting his elbows on the table. "What about her computer? Emails? Texts?"

"All gone," Kimble said. "Our computer forensics team in Savannah obtained her computer, but the drive was destroyed with a military-grade program that also physically destroyed the hardware."

"Her face," James said, not taking his eyes off of the crime scene picture onscreen. The skin was gone, the lidless eyeballs staring into the camera, exposed teeth keeping the body locked in a lipless skeletal grin. "It's missing. Just like on Westerna Island."

"Excellent," Smith said from his spot next to the television. "I was hoping you would notice that small detail."

James gestured at the screen. "It's a little hard to miss. I'm assuming the body was not intact?"

"Quite the opposite," Smith said.

"The body was fully intact," Kimble said. "Large stab wounds and lacerations. The medical examiner determined her death to have been caused by exsanguination."

James looked at Phillip. "Eh?"

"She bled out," Phillip said, not looking away from the screen.

James rolled his eyes. "She could've just said that."

"This murder is too close to the MO used by whoever killed our agents on Westenra Island," Smith said. "This is why you two will be going to Savannah before more bodies turn up."

"Where was she killed?" Phillip asked.

"Her body was found at Butler Island Plantation," Kimble said.

"Why take the faces?" Phillip said, sitting back in his chair. James knew that tone. He was talking to himself, not directly addressing anyone with the question.

He couldn't resist.

He leaned forward and whispered at Phillip. "It's bad if you answer yourself. Though, if you tell yourself the answer, that will be impressive."

Phillip looked at him. "Shut up."

Kimble looked at Smith. "Are you sure you want to send these two?"

"It seems we have no choice."

Kimble huffed. "We could send in intelligent people. There's an option."

"Touché," James said.

Smith cleared his throat. "I've informed the local FBI and ME offices that you two will be in Savannah this afternoon. Please do not dawdle. Once you find the unsub, use any measures necessary to either bring them in or take them down." He looked at James. "Obviously, one of those is a more permanent solution, which is easier on the paperwork."

James sat back in his chair and stared at the TV as Kimble switched it back to the FBI logo and set the remote down. "I've emailed the information to both of you. Drive safely." She and Smith both left the room, the air heavy for James as Smith's words moved around in his mind, jumbling in with the images of dismembered bodies with their faces torn off their severed heads. It'd been one of the most gruesome things he'd ever seen. He'd caught a vampire in the act, but when he'd run the man down, fang-face had had no idea what James was talking about when he mentioned the murders.

"You only act like a child when something's got you fucked up," Phillip said, turning to him.

"That's not true," James said. "I typically act like a child for all kinds of reasons. Sometimes no reason at all."

"What the hell is it, James?" Phillip asked, his tone firm. "Not havin' the bullshit. Spill."

"Why send us?" James nudged his chin at the screen. "It's one dead girl. Not that I don't think she deserves justice. She absolutely does. But to send in a werewolf?" He looked at Phillip. "It seems a little overkill."

"And sending you after a dude who turns into a mouse and makes a big girl manage perfect grand jetés in a back alley by running up her skirt isn't overkill?"

"This kind of case seems like something a normal detective would look into," James said. "As in a normal police department."

Phillip nodded. "Yeah, not gonna lie. Seems a little much that this would come across our desk. A pattern, sure. One woman?" He shook his head. "Still, it's on us."

"I don't like it," James said.

Phillip gave a laugh. "It doesn't matter if you like it or not. Orders are orders." He shook his head. "Look, I didn't want Smith to bring you in like this, either. But you're here."

"I don't trust him," James said, simply. "I don't trust the agency. Something is off."

"It's a top-secret agency specializing in highly unusual cases and black-ops against things that go bump in the night." Phillip shrugged.

James looked at him, noting the sarcasm. "You make a valid point. What isn't there to trust?"

"Now you're catching on." Phillip stood. "I'm gonna go double-check my night bag. We're on the road in an hour." He left the room, and James stood and went to the window overlooking the rest of the office.

He wasn't opposed to working. Not at all. His family fortune made it unnecessary for him to work, but he still saw value in it. He always told himself that if he could find something he wanted to do, something he was good at, he'd take it on. Months ago, he'd found out that he was good at detective work. He'd discovered that he'd been paying more attention to Phillip than he thought. They had traveled the coast, solved murders, and brought down a drug trafficking operation *and* a child sex trafficking operation. If Phillip had offered him a chance to work for an organization that specialized in helping people, protecting them from crazy shit like that, he would've been all over it.

But Smith rubbed him the wrong way. He was oily, snide. James could sense that the man had an agenda. But what? And why bring James in by force? A government agency?

That didn't fit. Not at all.

But Phillip had been with them all this time. He'd been fired from the Rock Hill Police Department shortly after they'd returned to Rock Hill from Florida because of the SCU.

And Smith had been fairly forward about wanting James to kill whoever had killed Kathleen Wilson. Previously, Smith had always been clear that they needed to try to take the bad guys into custody. Why was this one different?

Before the trafficking incident, James had never killed a human being. Animals, sure. He ate a deer every full moon. He'd torn a few apart by accident in his early years when he was figuring out how to control his strength. He'd killed vampires, zombies, even a demon. He'd killed Wade Anderson, the shapeshifter who'd used Dracula's ring to free the wolf inside his mind and force the change.

It wasn't until later that he learned that a few of the crewmen on the ship he'd raided in search of Mindy Robertson hadn't been vampires. He'd thrown up when he learned about it, certain that he'd killed at least four people that night.

Four people who wouldn't be going home, possibly to someone waiting on them.

The wolf sent an urge at him. *Mercy.*

He looked across the office and saw Smith and Kimble down on the floor talking. He glared at Smith as he spoke out loud under his breath.

"I do hope you enjoy paperwork. Asshole."

5

I think you're reading too much into it," Phillip said as he passed a slower driver on the interstate, then ended up being passed by someone doing at least a hundred miles per hour. Interstate 95 was only moderately crowded, and it usually let up a little the further it went. James personally hated it because it seemed like endless flat, barren terrain with the occasional spots of trees and a gas station or fast-food place off the seemingly random exits.

Then again, unlike most dogs, James hated riding in the car.

James used the opportunity to talk to Phillip about his thoughts and observations at the SCU. "Look," Phillip said. "People say shit all the time. Maybe he was joking."

"Have you known him to joke before?" James asked, looking at Phillip. "I don't quite get the comedian vibe off the man."

Phillip gave James a sidelong glance and sighed. "I'm kinda surprised you're fighting this so much."

"Really? Do tell."

"You got your rocks off hunting down that little girl." Phillip paused. "Okay, let me try again because that did not come out right."

"Agreed."

"You enjoyed yourself. Lookin' for the bad guys, solving the mystery, saving the girl. Hell, *all* the girls. You kept Lacy from being a pile of dust a few times."

"It was a hunt," James said. "And, if you'll remember, Mindy is half Fae. It's in my nature to be her protector."

"How is she these days, by the way?"

"They moved."

"Sorry, man."

"I'm glad they did." James looked out the window. "Last thing they need is to be tracked down by whoever might be pissed off enough at me to go after them."

"Right," Phillip said. "Good point."

They chatted on and off about other things as they crossed over into Georgia. They were soon parking in a lot in front of the Olde Harbor Inn on Old Factors Walk. They checked into the room, then sat down in front of Phillip's laptop for their video call with the medical examiner. He was in his mid-thirties, had black straight hair that went past his shoulders, and tan skin. He wore a necklace that James was sure had something to do with Native American lore, and James could see the word *Nechochwen* across the top of his t-shirt at the bottom of the screen.

"Hey, Dr. Blue," Phillip was saying, "you told me to video call you before I came. What's up?"

"Sorry about this," the ME said over the computer speakers, "says your clearances haven't checked out yet. I'm not gonna be able to get you guys in here to see the body. Can't give you the report, either."

James saw Phillip's brow furrow. "They should've done that before we even left Rock Hill." He looked at James. "This is weird."

"Nah," Blue said. "Probably just slipped up somewhere in the system. Hit the wrong key or something. It happens. If you come down here, they can get it straightened out. Oh, and you can just call me Hoyt."

Phillip nodded. "Thanks. See you soon." Hoyt's face disappeared from the screen, and Phillip closed the laptop and looked at James. "Well, shit."

"It sounds like you may have to go speak to a manager," James said.

"Shut up," Phillip muttered. "C'mon, let's go get this clusterfuck fixed so we can get a look at that body." He stopped and closed his eyes, rubbing his temples as if he was warding off a migraine. "Again, not how that was supposed to come out."

"I'd rather not," James said. "If it's all the same, I've had enough of the office view for today."

"James, you'll need to see if you can get a scent."

"I'll likely not get much beyond bleach and hydrogen peroxide if she's already been cleaned and sterilized."

Phillip sighed. "Yeah, you're right. You would've needed to see her at the scene. Damn." He pulled his phone out and tapped on the screen. "Shit. Looks like you're not even on the list for clearance approval at all. I'll call Smith about it while I'm out. See who dropped the ball." He looked up at James. "I'll be back in an hour or so. Try not to hump anyone's leg while I'm gone."

"I make no promises."

James walked around the park for about an hour, looking out over the water as various boats and cruisers went by. There was no point in staying in the hotel room. He knew he'd get stir-crazy and sitting alone made his mind wander to things he didn't want to deal with anyway. He was outside looking out over the water within ten minutes of walking from the hotel. Joggers and tourists passed by, some of the walkers stopping to take in the view while others commented on how warm it still was despite the Fall season.

He pulled his phone out and looked at the time before reading Molly's text again. The wolf sent an image of Lacy to him, and he felt a pang of guilt in his stomach. *She's gone,* he thought to the beast. *Besides, this girl is probably about to tell me we can't see each other and last night was weird anyway.* Another thought occurred to him. *Or that she's in love with me and wants to get married and she's staring at me from down the walk now. And thinks I'm cute when I sleep.* He sighed. *At least the latter would be easier to deal with. Witness protection is a thing.*

The wolf made a chuffing noise and shook its head before laying down and putting its paws over its eyes.

James turned to head back to the hotel when he saw a woman standing next to the Waving Girl statue. She wasn't as tall as him, maybe just shy of six feet. She had long, wild blond hair hanging past her shoulders, and she wore a plain brown skirt and a bright orange sleeveless top with spaghetti straps. She had a scarf tied on her head, holding her large mane out of her face, and her skin was sun-touched and rough-looking. She eyed him, putting a cigarello to her mouth and taking a draw before blowing the cloud into the air as if trying to seduce him from across the room at a jazz club in some Roarin' Twenties murder mystery.

Merry Christmas, ya filthy animal, James thought in his best Cagney voice.

"Ahoy," the woman called to him, her tone welcoming, her voice carrying a slight husk likely brought on by smoking. "The waters are smooth this day."

Must be "Talk Like A Pirate Day," James thought. Phillip often kept him in the loop on the social media-born holidays. *Or she's a tour guide.*

"You can come closer, mate," the woman said. "I'm not gonna bite." She moved her eyebrows up and down once as she grinned at him. "Much."

"I gather you're offering tours?"

"Only if you're takin' them, sweet," the woman said. "People in these parts call me Agatha. I come here in the afternoons to get some peace and admire the scenery."

James held his hand out. "James Coldstone. Pleasure to meet you, Agatha."

"Coldstone?" Agatha said as she shook his hand. She closed her eyes and breathed deeply, opening them again and flitting them about as if she were trying to track a dozen flying objects at once. "A surname that carries some history, I see."

"No relation," James said, comfortable with the lie. The less he had to hear about his father, the better.

Agatha laughed and wagged her finger at him. "No lyin', handsome Coldstone. Lying isn't in your nature. You'll never be good at it."

James raised an eyebrow. "And why would that be?"

"Because dogs are the most loyal of Gaia's creatures. They only know the truth."

James's heart skipped a beat. The wolf sat up in his mind and bristled. He did his best to not let it show on his face and in his voice. "I have no idea what you're talking about."

Agatha smiled sweetly. "Of course not. Walk with me." She moved up to the walk where James was and started to stroll casually, running her hand over the rail as she looked out at the water and hummed a tune James had never heard before. James fell into step beside her, his curiosity peaked. "You're wondering how I know so much about you," she said, her tone conversational.

"I see you can also read minds."

She laughed. "Hardly! I'd be in a wealth of trouble if I could. Know too many secrets. Be forced to ask for mercy from Davy Jones right in front of him in the depths of his locker if the wrong people found out. No, I'm no mind reader. I'm an Earth Witch." She looked up at him and smiled. "I

36

can hear the spirits of nature, feel the hum of the earth under my feet. It's where I draw my power."

Okay, James thought. *Why am I not surprised that a woman who talks like a pirate and dresses like she was at Woodstock tells me she talks to plants and dirt?*

"I can hear the spirits all around us," Agatha said, holding her hands out slightly as if calming a gaggle of chatting children and then letting them down by her sides again. "All I needed was your name."

"My name?"

"Be careful who you give your name to, James Coldstone," Agatha said. "It invites that person in, gives them power." She nodded. "You'll not have to worry about my telling a soul about your feral nature. This would be a betrayal, which would do me as much harm as it does you."

"I appreciate it."

"You're not just here for a vacation and a pleasant walk with a pretty lass," Agatha said. "What brings you to Savannah?"

"They didn't tell you that?"

"They be cheeky bastards sometimes, the spirits."

James chuckled. "I'm here about the murder at Butler Island Plantation. Kathleen Wilson. Did you know her?"

Agatha shook her head. "I can't say that I do. Even with a name, the owner has to be among the livin' for me to hear the wind in their sails." She clasped her hands behind her back, the breeze off the water picking up slightly and blowing her hair back enough for James to see her neck. He caught a glimpse of a small tattoo in the shape of a shield with a few smaller symbols inside the shape before she rubbed her neck, covering the tattoo with her hand.

Had he seen that shape before? That symbol? He couldn't place it. *Probably saw it tattooed on someone else's neck or in a book or something,* he thought. He shrugged it off. The wolf grunted on the inside, and he swore for a second that he saw the thing's yellow eyes flash.

"Bad business, though," Agatha continued. "Murder. Heard somethin' happened there but no details."

James felt suddenly guarded. How much information did he want to give her?

"I see. I'm not sure that any details have been released."

"I do know that David Coldstone spent a few nights there many years ago."

James stopped walking, the mention of his father's name bringing that small amount of anger he held onto to a low boil. It infuriated him that he couldn't go anywhere without someone knowing who his bastard father was. It infuriated him more that the sonofabitch had given him so much access in circles that he wouldn't otherwise be able to move around in.

That wasn't what drove his hatred the most.

James could shift at will. He maintained his humanity during the change, could think rationally, and communicate without having to rely on talking. He'd always thought that set him apart from other weres. It was Angel the werecat who'd filled him in. Were families had made a pact with druids generations ago to keep their humanity when in form and keep the beast from taking their minds.

Which meant that David Coldstone knew what he was doing every time he'd killed. Every man. Every woman. Every child. No one had been safe. It was James's mother who'd brought David Coldstone down, but not before he'd impregnated her.

She'd died in James's first year of college. Cancer. And now he had access to a fortune made up of blood and lived in a house that only served as a reminder of his dark family history.

Just the essentials a man needs to lead a healthy and well-balanced lifestyle.

It all ran through his mind in the seconds it took Agatha to walk a few steps ahead before she stopped and turned to look at him. "You look vexed. What's sinkin' you?"

James shook his head and tried to regain control of his expression and tone. "Nothing. Bad memory."

"I'll wager that's not entirely true," Agatha said. "You didn't look like that till I mentioned your father's name." She shrugged. "I didn't know the man, so don't worry about any stories from this lovely lass."

"This is a good thing."

She stepped forward and grabbed his hand. Her skin was rough and cold to the touch as she lifted his hand and turned it over, tracing the lines of his palm. "You got a lot going on here, James Coldstone." She smiled. "Such a long lifeline."

"I work out."

Agatha looked up at him. "You're on a path you can't turn away from. Can't set a course in these new waters and go against the wind. And you're gonna have to make a choice. And no matter what you choose, you're gonna hurt one who you love."

The theme song from the movie *Police Academy* sounded from James's pocket. He pulled his hand away and pulled it out of his pocket. "Thank you for your insight. I have to take this. I'll be right back."

"Of course," Agatha said with a small curtsy.

James turned away from her and answered the phone. "Hello, Phillip."

"You done sightseeing?" Phillip said. James could hear the telltale sounds of the inside of Phillip's car.

"I've yet to check out the fudge shop."

"Which one?"

"Yes."

"Gonna have to put it on hold," Phillip said. "They're working on the clearances, but I did get to look at Kathleen Wilson's body. You were right about the scent. Hoyt confirmed that once a body is cleaned up as part of the autopsy, a K9 wouldn't smell cocaine cut into rows right there in front of him."

"See? I'm smarter than you give me credit for."

"Delusions of grandeur? What's next? I've already seen you play fetch."

"I can roll over."

"Seen it."

"Sit?"

"Old. Anything on your end?"

James started to turn back to Agatha as he spoke. "Actually, I've met someone wh—" He stopped as he stared at the empty spot where Agatha once stood. He looked around the area, trying to see if he could see where she'd gone. He hadn't turned away from her for more than a few seconds. He would at least see her walking away.

Nothing.

The wolf growled low in James's mind as he turned his attention back to the phone and Phillip calling out to him. "James? Met who? Hello?"

"I'll tell you when you get here," James said, still looking around. Had he missed her? She didn't strike him as someone who could blend in, a barefoot hippie chick wandering the park and smoking. "How far out are you?"

"Five minutes. We're gonna head over to Butler Island and check out the spot where they found Kathleen Wilson."

"I'm in the park. See you in ten."

6

James told Phillip about Agatha as they drove down Interstate 95 toward Butler Island, making sure to include the symbol he'd seen tattooed on her neck and her disappearing act while he'd been on the phone.

"I've seen that symbol before," James said. "I can't remember if it was in a book, or a movie, or on another vampire."

"A shield with something inside it?" Phillip snorted. His degree included a minor in History, and he'd taken a few graduate courses online through Winthrop University during his first years in law enforcement. "That narrows it down to, oh, *most* of Europe and the European colonies. You took a couple of history classes with me. There's no tellin' how many family crests and shit we saw in those books."

"Right," James said. He shook his head and rubbed his eyes as he focused his mental attention on the wolf. *What about you?*

The wolf flashed an image of Bela Legosi as Dracula. Then another rendition of the vampire from one of the many video games James had watched Phillip play.

"What about Dracula?" James said. "We did destroy his ring a few months ago."

"Dracula's dead as hell," Phillip said. "Remember? After that cat-girl you were drooling over filled us in, I had the SCU trace things out on him. He got staked back in the eighteen hundreds. A couple of his cult followers managed to grab some of his shit, and his ring ended up with Wade Anderson."

"A two-bit thug shifter working for a pedophile vampire running a trafficking ring." James looked at Phillip. "If I were Wangenheim, I don't know that I would've trusted one of my low-level grunts with a magic relic from the father of all vampires."

"You think Wangenheim didn't know Anderson had it?" Phillip raised an eyebrow. "Damn. That means that someone else was involved. Someone who wanted to stir the pot." Phillip glanced at James, then back to the road. "And cause some serious fuck-shit for you, in particular."

"Then it ended up with that girl in Charleston," James continued. "Rebecca. We never questioned how. But she knew who we were from the moment we walked into that restaurant. She targeted us."

"And damn near killed you."

James furrowed his brow. "This is connected somehow." His phone started ringing in his pocket. He pulled it out and felt a pang of guilt when he saw Molly's caller ID on the screen. "Shit."

Phillip glanced at the phone, then at James before looking back to the road. "Go get her, handsome."

"It's not like that." He stared at the phone, letting it ring as memories of his night with her meshed with his memories of Lacy. He shook his head as the call went to voicemail.

"Are you serious right now?" Phillip said. "Did you seriously just let that girl go to voicemail?"

James looked at him. "I'm conflicted."

Phillip snorted. "You're a dumbass."

"I need time."

"Call that girl back."

"I will later."

"Call her back."

"In time."

Phillip glanced at him sidelong before reaching under the seat and pulling out a rolled newspaper. "This is the Sunday edition. Means extra content for added heft. Funny papers are in color. Took the ads out to improve handling and balance. That rubber band around it is high-grade, not the wimpy-ass ones they send with it. A little tape in the right places to keep the shape for an easier grip."

James raised an eyebrow. "You *customized* your newspaper?"

"I *customized* my newspaper." James held his hands up and shrank back

41

in the seat against the passenger-side door as Phillip wailed on him with the paper, never looking away from the road as he emphasized four of the blows with: "Call! That! Girl! *Back!*"

"Alright! Alright!" James said. "Christ. You're going to give me a complex." Phillip set the newspaper down in his lap as James dialed Molly back. He felt his stomach flutter a bit as her voice sounded over the phone.

"Hello? James?"

"Yeah, hey," James said. "Sorry, I didn't get to the phone in time." He heard a car horn in the background accompanied by the sound of a radio being turned down.

"No worries," Molly said. "Stuck in traffic. Funny how a twenty-minute drive in the morning translates to an hour and a half drive in the afternoon."

"Five o'clock rush," James said. "Always fun."

"It's only just after four."

"It's a figure of speech. Doesn't have to be five o'clock to be five o'clock traffic."

"Americans are weird."

James smiled a little. "You have no idea."

"Look, I wanted to talk to you," Molly said. He heard her take a deep breath and let it out slowly. "About last night."

And there it is, James thought. "Right, that. I hope you enjoyed your evening." James closed his eyes. Phillip made a noise next to him, and James cracked open an eye to see him purse his lips to stifle his laughter.

"Oh, no worries," Molly said, sounding equally as awkward as James felt. "It was great. I mean the…well, you know. The sex."

"Ah. Yes."

"Especially that third time."

"Third time?"

"Or fourth. Maybe?"

"I lost count."

"Same." She laughed on the other end before clearing her throat. "Look, I just wanted you to know that I've…I've never done that before. Like ever. I'm not like that."

James wasn't about to fill her in on his sex-capades during his college years, but he'd only had one or two one-night flings. He decided the smart thing to do was to keep his mouth shut for a change.

"I just…I'm mortified that you may have gotten the wrong impression of me," Molly continued. "And I just...I mean, I enjoyed chatting with you. You know, in between."

Say something intelligent, James, he thought to himself. "Well, I'll not argue the effective conversation starter." He closed his eyes and rubbed them to ward off the oncoming headache. *That was not something intelligent, James.*

Molly laughed at the joke. "Right? Look, I just wanted to clear the air."

"Right," James said. "Of course."

"Are you at home? I could drop by."

James felt a sudden wave of panic. "No, I'm not. I'm out of town for work. I'll only be gone a couple of days."

"I see," Molly said. He could hear the skepticism in her tone. "Right, well—"

"I'll call you as soon as I'm back," James said, cutting her off. "I promise. It's only a few days."

"Okay," she said, her tone still wary. "I'd better run. Traffic. See you in a few days?"

"Yes, definitely."

"Ciao."

James put the phone away as it signaled the end of the call. He looked at Phillip, who was staring ahead obviously trying not to laugh. "Something funny?"

"You tryin' to be smooth."

"I thought I did well."

Phillip gave another snort. "Shit was funny as hell."

James made a mental note to shit on the hood of Phillip's car the next time he shifted. The wolf panted in his mind, its way of laughing as it winked at him.

They stopped for dinner before heading out to Butler Plantation. The sun was just setting when they finally pulled up to the house. The last of the tours had just ended, the families and couples headed back to their cars as Phillip found a parking spot in the lot. James got out and breathed in the air as the wolf moved in to enhance his senses, shifting the glands in his mouth slightly into their wolfen state so he could run the scents over them. The dense smell of mildew and soil wafted in from the woods, mixing with the gasoline and oil from the surrounding cars cranking up and leaving for the day. The October air was still warm and muggy despite the darkening sky. He caught something else, something more akin to the stench of hamburger meat left in the fridge for too long, but it was too faint to tell where it came from.

"I already phoned in to management that we were coming," Phillip said. "No need to check in." He gestured at the house. "There are some walking trails down behind the house that go through the woods. That's where they found the victim. No real trace of the unsub other than footprints that could've been made by any of the hundreds of people who were on the path throughout the day."

"And no one saw anything?"

"No, they found her first thing in the morning. Hoyt placed time of death at around midnight."

"What the hell was she doing out here at midnight?"

Phillip pulled his phone out. "According to the police, she was meeting her boyfriend. She was a tour guide here on top of the accounting gig she'd landed. Call came into her cell around close to midnight. He canceled on her. Come to find out he was seeing his other girlfriend." Phillip put the phone away. "Broke up with her on the spot. She probably was too upset to see the unsub coming."

James nodded. "Very well. Let's go." He and Phillip made their way around to the back of the house as employees moved around the yard picking up any trash they found as they prepared to leave for the night. Some of them nodded and waved at the two of them in brief hurried greeting, exercising the typical Southern style of acknowledging another human in sight. It wasn't long before Phillip was leading James down onto one of the walking paths, his phone out as he used the map on it to navigate. He pulled a flashlight out of his jacket pocket and turned it on. The path was neat and clean, the walk paved over and the foliage trimmed away just so as to give the scene a photogenic appeal. Moss hung from the trees in tendrils, and cicadas whirred and chirruped in their nightly chorus.

The smell of rotten meat and dried blood grew stronger. James felt the wolf tense inside, felt his own body go on high alert. He sensed something, the feeling making the hairs on his neck stand up. The feeling of being watched out of curiosity and being hunted were two different things. The gaze of the curious could either be empowering or cause paranoia. The leer of a hunter gave the prey a sense of danger.

James did not take kindly to being prey, human or otherwise.

He reached out and tapped Phillip on the arm, stopping him. "I do not believe we're alone."

Phillip put the phone away and pulled his gun from the shoulder holster. James looked around the area, both to see who was watching them and to make sure no one was around to be a problematic witness for later. He stripped quickly, putting his clothes near a tree before shifting into wolf form. His yellowed vision moved past the darkness, allowing him to see everything clearly. He huffed again, this time pulling the scents and smells in over fully formed glands. He could taste the rot, the flavor having a curious sweetness that came with the promise of poison and sickness. He turned his head, the scent growing weaker at first, then stronger as he picked up the smell of old soil and mold, dry and decrepit, not rich and damp like the trees and brush around them. He growled low, clenching his jaw.

"Over there?" Phillip whispered, nudging his chin in the direction James stared. James let out a low *woof* and went down to all fours, moving carefully toward the thick growth of trees, slowly so as to not startle his hunter.

Now his prey.

He heard the long croak just before he saw the large scythe swing at him. He dodged out of the way, the blade slicing the air only inches from his face. The wielder lunged out onto the paved walk and swung again, James jumping back to avoid the second blow as Phillip shouted at the attacker. "*Freeze! FBI!*"

The man stopped, and James was able to get a good look at him as he stood in place. His clothes were rags, rotted pants and a long-sleeved shirt made of what appeared to be burlap. His skin was partially rotted away, what was once flesh was now dried, pale, and discolored particularly around where bone was visible. He gripped the large two-handed scythe tightly, his skinny arms hiding the amount of strength needed to swing the tool the way he had. He turned his head slowly to look over his shoulder at Phillip, the sound of creaking joints and bone rubbing together mixed with his rasped breathing. James could see the movement of dried and rotted lungs through a section of exposed ribcage.

"What the fuck?" Phillip breathed, blinking at the sight. The man turned fully to Phillip and stepped toward him. "I said freeze, goddammit!"

James barked at him. *Shoot!*

Phillip's gun roared, and the man's head snapped back, making him stagger as if he might fall. He straightened himself, shook it off, and made a gurgling sound as he broke into a run toward Phillip, readying the scythe for another swing as Phillip sent more rounds into the thing.

James charged the zombie and swung at it, his open hand connecting with the thing's head and sending it spinning into the trees. He pounced as the body tried to get back up, picking it up and tearing it in half easily. It'd dropped the scythe when he'd knocked the zombie away from Phillip.

When the creature's arms finally went still, it all turned to dust. Dried meat powder sifted between James's claws.

"What the hell was that?" Phillip said. "Zombies don't fucking run and use weapons. They don't dry out and turn to dust like vampires, either."

James moved back to the paved path as Phillip picked up the scythe. "Jesus *fuck*," he said. "James, this thing is old as shit. I can have the lab try to date it."

James shifted to human form as something caught his eye. "The handle. There's some sort of bag." He took the scythe from Phillip and plucked a small pouch from the handle right below one of the two small grips. It was damp. Phillip shined his flashlight at it, and James saw the dark patch of blood that had soaked through the burlap fabric. The wolf came forward, and his vision yellowed as he untied the drawstring and opened the pouch. He held the pouch out to Phillip.

"The hell's in there?" Phillip said.

"I believe we've just killed our killer."

7

Phillip laid the backseats in his car down, and James broke the tool in half, but they made the scythe fit into the Honda Civic for the trip back to Savannah. They dropped the scythe off with the Georgia Bureau of Investigation lab the FBI and ME worked with, then drove back to the hotel. They bounced ideas back and forth, discussing the zombie and coming up with no ideas.

"Might ask your new girlfriend about it," Phillip said.

James looked at him. "Molly is not my girlfriend."

"I mean the other one. The one you met earlier."

"Agatha is also not my girlfriend. It's the pirate vernacular. And the smoking."

"You said she said she was a witch." Phillip shrugged. "Maybe she knows something about raising the dead."

That was how James found himself back out on the walk, leaning on the railing and staring out over the Savannah River, the Waving Girl statue just a few yards from him. The night breeze was cooler, the temperature down just enough to cause a chill but still be too warm for a coat. He let the wolf enhance his senses and sniffed the air, trying to pick up a scent before remembering that he hadn't locked on to Agatha's. He tried to remember what it was. He knew he'd smelled her when they'd met. Cigarettes? That narrowed it down to half the population. Some kind of spices? His mind fogged a little as he tried to remember.

"Tis a late night to be wanderin', bucko."

James looked in the direction Agatha's voice came from and saw her leaning against the statue. She still wore the same outfit and was still barefoot despite the cool air. She lit a cigarello casually and blew the smoke into the air before waving her hand. The cloud took the shape of a large bird and flew off into the night.

"Impressive," James said.

"The albatross," said Agatha. "Leads men to salvation. Unless they kill it. Then it leads them to death." She leveled her gaze at him. "What brings you to the waters this hour?"

"Looking for you," James said. "I've got questions."

"I can oblige," Agatha said. James told her about the run-in they had with the zombie on Butler Island. Agatha listened intently, her expression growing stoic before it changed to fear. She backed away from him. "God," she muttered, crossing herself. "Was no zombie you killed this night, James Coldstone. Thing of evil, it was."

"What was it?"

"Nothin' I'll speak of," Agatha snapped. "You want answers on that dark sin against Gaia, you go to Alma. She deals in that. Abercorn." Agatha turned and began to walk in the other direction, calling over her shoulder as she went. "You'd do best to walk away, James Coldstone. Leave it to rest. That kind of magic only brings death and darkness."

James started after her but stopped as he saw her fade into the dark.

———

I really hate your ass for this," Phillip grumbled as he got out of the car and closed the driver's side door. James got out and looked across the street at the large house that faced Abercorn Street and was large enough to also be considered both on the corners of Abercorn and East Gordon *and* East Wayne Streets. The winding front steps led up to a terrace-like porch with old wrought-iron railings. No lights shone on the house, meaning that the porch itself was too dark to see the front doors. The gabled window at the front looked like something a ghost would peer out of in the early acts of a haunted house movie, and the place stretched down the property a bit, giving it the appearance of an old residence that could've been a functional inn at some point were it not considered the most haunted house in Savannah. A construction fence encircled the place, the front gate locked with a large padlock.

Phillip stepped up beside James. "It only makes sense to come here now," James said. "Agatha said they practice dark magic. Visiting them at lunchtime might not be conducive to our goals."

Phillip glared up at him, his eyes narrowed. "James, it's damn near midnight, and my black ass is standin' outside what looks like an empty house with an idiot when I should be layin' down to get a few hours of sleep before we go into the bureau tomorrow."

James raised an eyebrow. "Why do we have to go there?"

"There's a meeting."

James sighed. "I hate meetings."

"Too bad."

"It could probably be an email."

"It's not."

"Make it an email."

"You never check your email." Phillip turned to him. "Get with the program, James. You gotta do what you're told now. If they say you gotta be at a meeting, you gotta be at a meeting. In this case you'll be fine, it's just a debrief."

The voice came from the pitch darkness on the porch, loud enough to be heard but quiet enough not to echo in the empty street. "You two realize people are trying to be at peace?" James saw a figure emerge from the dark, the shape of someone in a hooded robe moving purposefully down the front steps. The woman approached the fence with a gait Phillip often referred to as someone's "cussin' walk." She flipped the hood back to reveal herself as a young black woman, maybe in her mid to late twenties. She had fair-colored brown skin, long hair tied back in a braid that draped over her shoulder and still reached down to her midsection, and full lips that would probably have looked seductively pouty were they not pursed in anger. "Why do I have two grown men bickerin' like children in front of my house?"

"I apologize, ma'am," Phillip said, clearing his throat and adopting his more "official" tone. "I'm Agent Ph—"

She held her hand up and cut him off. "Uh-uh. Stop."

Phillip blinked. "Excuse me."

"Don't give your name. Ever. Not during these times. I will call you agent. And that is all I will call you." She looked at James. "You, on the other hand, have already been a damn fool, James Coldstone. Gave your name to someone who communes." She shook her head. "All the pretty ones really are stupid."

49

"Agatha," James said. "Right."

Alma shook her head. "I don't know no Agatha. Probably not her real name. But if she can talk to the spirits around her, then that means you're already a foot in the grave."

"Why is that?" Phillip said as he pulled his small notepad and a pen out of his pocket. "Um…"

"You may call me Alma," the woman said.

Phillip jotted it down. "Last name?"

"I've told you what you may call me." Alma raised her eyebrow at James. "Does he listen?"

"Intently," James said, pressing forward. "I'm assuming since you know who I am, that you also know what I am and why I'm here."

"And that is exactly why I'm not allowing you into my house," Alma said.

"You live here?" Phillip asked. James could tell he was trying unsuccessfully to not show some disdain for the abandoned dwelling in front of them.

Alma put her hand on her hip and eyed him. "You got a problem with that?"

"No, ma'am."

"Good." She looked at James. "You're here about that poor girl they got a few blocks away. Got herself killed out there at the Butler place. Missin' her face too."

"How do you know about that?" Phillip asked. "We haven't released any details."

"Spirits," Alma reminded him. "Since Mr. Coldstone let your Agatha in his front door, the spirits follow him and gather the information. All we need to do is ask, and they'll tell us." She looked back at James. "That girl likes you. That pretty little olive-skin one. But you better get your house right because she's not the only one."

"I'll keep that in mind," James said, both Molly and Lacy being the last two subjects he wanted to add to the clusterfuck that was his mind palace. "The victim's face was removed, not just torn off. And it was preserved. The thing that killed her seemed like it was on its last legs when we got out there."

Alma closed her eyes, breathed deeply, then opened them again, her features relaxing a little. "I see. You killed a dead man. But his spirit was tormented. He was a good man. Died a slave. Brought back as a slave."

"He attacked us with a weapon," Phillip said. "We want to think he's a zombie, but we've never known a zombie to be that coordinated or fast."

"Because he wasn't a zombie," Alma said. "He was a draugr. Nordic, but that doesn't mean the spell can't be used on anyone but Norsemen." She crossed her arms in front of her. "You two have come across something we've been dreading for a while now, me and my coven. A necromancer."

"Necromancer?" James said. He remembered a few years back when Phillip was trying to teach him how to play Dungeons and Dragons. The necromancer had the ability to summon the undead and control them. "I wasn't aware that was a real religion."

"Not so much a religion," Alma said. "It's a practice. An evil, dark, twisted magic. It corrupts the user, turns them into a shell of a human being. Makes them hate the living, want to see anything that can draw breath draw its *last* breath."

"So, it's safe to say that we're also dealing with a psychopath," Phillip said, looking at James. "Wonderful."

"Why remove the face?" James asked.

"To see through another's eyes," Alma said. "It's an evil spell. You can see the memories of the original wearer. Recognize people. Ed Gein used it to hunt down his victims in Texas back in the sixties. It's a form of Necromancy. Only practitioners of that black magic use such a spell."

James paused. "But don't you practice black magic?"

Alma stiffened. "I practice *dark* magic. There's a difference, asshole!" She took a breath, making a motion in front of her face as if pulling her sudden anger from her lips as she breathed out. "Insinuating evil like that to a witch is truly offensive. Please do not make that mistake again."

Phillip and James looked at each other, then back at her. "I apologize," James said.

"Dark spells have to do with death, it's true. We live in the shadows, and commune with the spirits who cannot pass on. Help them find peace and how to cope with having to stay here as wanderers. We channel our power from shadow."

Phillip crossed his arms. "No offense, but how is that different from necromancers?"

"Necromancy is a sin against nature," Alma said, glaring at him, biting the words off through gritted teeth as she spoke. "Black magic. The *blackest* of magic." She took a breath and adopted a calmer tone and demeanor. "Necromancers derive their power from the dead. They use them, enslave them in every way."

"How?"

"They force their victims back into their flesh, living or not. If there is no flesh left, they create it from the fresher dead around them. The husk takes just enough form of the spirit's original body to be functional. That's why this draugr looked the way he did. He's been dead since the Civil War era, but he had a form. Could've been from animals, insects, whatever was around him and dead in the earth where he was buried and conjured."

James nodded, his mind going back to the fight with the dead guy. The draugr had enough strength to wield that scythe, but he ripped apart like a cardboard doll when James had gotten hold of him. But the thing also acted with intent. "Do draugrs ever act on their own?"

"Never," Alma said. "If they aren't given purpose, they don't rise. They can only be given one purpose, though. That's what makes a necromancer so dangerous. They don't have to keep their concentration on them."

James felt a small chill as a realization hit him. "I'm then to assume that the possibility of a necromancer raising an army of the dead isn't unrealistic?"

"Not at all." She looked at the sky. "The moon is almost in position, and we have a ritual we're trying to perform. If you're looking for someone who wants control of the dead, I might suggest talking to Noble Jones. Good night." She spun on her heel and stalked back to the house, climbing the stairs and slamming the front door behind her.

"I like her," Phillip said.

"Indeed," said James, mulling over the information Alma had just given them. "The agents on Westenra Island that were murdered. Their faces were never recovered."

"Nope," Phillip said as he and James started back toward the car. "But now it makes sense how whoever was killing them off was able to find each one and stay ahead of us."

"And how they knew Lacy and I were there," James said. "And why." He stopped at the car as Phillip made his way around to the driver's side. "Phillip, that night went far too easy."

"How do you mean?" Phillip asked. "Lacy almost died, you both crashed a pedophile auction, and managed to wipe out a vampire criminal master and his entire crew. We brought down an entire trafficking ring that night. And it led to a few more after the fact."

"Wangenheim knew I was coming. He acted as if I was sent there specifically to kill him."

Phillip shrugged. "You went there to save Mindy, but don't lie about the fact that you were there to kill him too."

"Oh, I was *definitely* going to kill him. But he knew about me specifically."

"James," Phillip said, shaking his head. "You followed that mother-fucker all the hell the way to Jacksonville, Florida. And you're surprised he knew who you were?"

Something else fell into place, but James didn't want to say it out loud. Not to Phillip. Not to anyone. Not until he could mull it over more. Lacy had known exactly where Wangenheim would be. She'd been able to take the time to fill a water cannon with holy water and bring it with her to kill him. He remembered that night in the captain's cabin, to his fight with the old vampire. Lacy had saved his life. Hadn't she?

The more he replayed the memory, the more sense it made that she'd kicked the door in with purpose. That she'd targeted Wangenheim specif-ically. He thought back to the auction. She'd known when to strike. But her niece was the one for sale that night. It made sense that she was tracking Wangenheim down to save the girl. That's what she'd told James back in Charleston.

But Wangenheim had been far older than her. Which meant that he was stronger. Using holy water made sense in that case. She wouldn't have won a direct fight.

The wolf flashed the night she and James had almost slept together into James's mind, specifically to the point where James had moved her hair back to kiss her neck.

"James," Phillip said, snapping his fingers. "Hey, you awake?"

"Yeah," James said, shaking his head a little to clear the memory. "Just something on my mind."

"It's called sleep deprivation," Phillip said. "C'mon, let's head back."

James nodded and got into the car as the wolf sent the memory of Agatha to him again, showing her hair blowing in the breeze coming off the water that day.

That symbol on her neck. Where had he seen that symbol?

8

P hillip hadn't been wrong about the sleep deprivation. James slept hard, his dreams vivid and, at times, hellish. One involved Molly and Lacy. James had been poisoned with silver and made to watch as a shadowy figure rammed a stake through Lacy's heart, turning her into dust before she could let out a scream. It turned and gutted Molly, dropping her lifeless body in front of him. James woke up in a cold sweat, and it seemed like hours before he went back to sleep only to have the dream again. The wolf intervened the second time and took down the shadow person before he could harm either of the two women. And the third time. And the fourth.

Thanks, James thought to the beast as he woke up, the sun shining in through the windows of the hotel room and directly onto his face.

The wolf groaned a little in his mind, rolled over, and got some well-deserved rest.

James picked his phone up and saw the time. It was past nine in the morning. There was a text message from Phillip on his notification screen.

I'm at the bureau. Smith wanted a meeting with me and the director this morning. Figured it would be better if you weren't there to provoke him. Be back soon.

Good call, James thought. He got up, showered, and headed out to grab something to eat at a nearby café before calling a Lyft driver to take him over to Calhoun Square. He didn't want to be cooped up in the room until Phillip got back, and the day was far too nice to stay indoors anyway, the sky already blue and the air mild with an easy continuous breeze that brought in the clean smells of the gardens mixed in with the slight aroma of whatever the restaurants nearby were cooking up that morning.

Admittedly, it was more about seeing Alma's house, 432 Abercorn Street, during the daylight hours.

He sat in the park facing the house, the sunlight revealing the more worn and aged nature of the building that the night had been able to hide. The construction fence was still up, but no workers toiled around the lot. James checked his phone again. It was a weekday. No holiday (though Phillip would likely know what internet holiday was going on), and just after ten in the morning. People walked by, paying no attention to the house as they went, some making sure to put space between them and the fence.

A necromancer. That was a new one. He thought back to Westenra Island, to the different cabins he'd found in shambles. He tried to remember more details about the body parts he'd found, particularly the heads. The more he thought about it, the more he remembered thinking that the faces had been torn away, not cut. *That doesn't make sense,* he thought. *If the killer had torn the face off, it would've torn up the skin. It wouldn't be viable, would it?* James had slaughtered enough deer in his wolf form to know that skin was a lot more fragile when it was separated from the muscle. It could tear easily, dry out in a short amount of time. The guy who owned the bookstore near Winthrop University in Rock Hill worked with leather and had once talked to James about how leather could be a challenge at times if it wasn't preserved correctly. He'd said that he wouldn't want to be the one processing the skin for leather because the fresh skin was far too delicate.

The wolf joined in with its own memories, and James saw the vision of the severed, faceless head at Westenra more clearly. The skin was neatly cut, not tattered. Not torn.

James had second-guessed his memory, doing the human thing of adding missing details. James trusted the wolf to be more accurate.

But that meant that the killer on Westenra hadn't been some feral supernatural. That meant that the faces there had also been removed with enough care to make them useful to whoever was hunting down the agents of the SCU. Which meant that a necromancer could've been on the island. Could have been the same one? Kathleen Wilson hadn't been an agent. She'd just been a recent graduate working for the Butler Plantation tours. She had no record.

James's phone rang. He pulled it out of his pocket as a middle-aged man jogging by pointed at him and nodded approval at the ringtone. "Classic movie, man!"

James waved at him and answered the phone. "Good morning, Phillip. And thank you for sparing me the pain of a meeting."

"Yeah, well, I'm starting to think you should've been there," Phillip said. James could hear the frustration in his tone.

James raised an eyebrow. "Do tell."

"Smith killed the case. We're to report back to Rock Hill today."

P hillip picked James up from Calhoun Park and drove straight back to the hotel. James felt as if he'd been slapped across the face. The wolf had sat up immediately in his mind when Phillip had broken the news, cocking its head to the side in confusion.

James, on the other hand, was struggling to keep his frustration from igniting his already fragile temper as he and Phillip went back to their room. "Please fill me in as to what the hell is going on. Why did they kill the case?"

"No real suspects, no real clues," Phillip said, mocking Agent Smith's British accent. "It's a dead-end case for the local authorities to worry on, guv-nah!" He defaulted back to his normal mutterings of "punk motherfucker" as he sat down at the desk in the room and took his jacket off. He rubbed his face and muttered a few more of his favorite sentence enhancers.

"That's crap," James said, pacing. "He knows it's crap. We haven't even been here twenty-four hours." He stopped and faced Phillip. "Even I know this kind of thing takes time. It took us over a month to get Mindy back." Most missing persons have little to no chance of being found alive after twenty-four hours or so. Phillip had talked to James about what a miracle it was that they'd beaten those odds and found Mindy Robertson so long after her abduction.

"He wants us to walk away from it," Phillip said. "Look, James, I don't like it either. But we don't have a choice."

James started pacing again. He took a deep breath and exhaled, the image of Kathleen Wilson's driver's ID photo in his mind. She was pretty, smiling, and happy. She'd had a future. She'd just made it through college, working at her first real job. And she'd been killed for no apparent reason. James's frustration boiled over, but he fought it back and kept his calm. "I'm not leaving."

"James, don't do this," Phillip warned. "These people are not ones you wanna fuck with."

"The murders won't stop," James said, stopping again as he faced Phillip. "You know this as well as I do. Whoever sent that thing after Kathleen Wilson wasn't done with it. It still had her fucking *face* in a bag."

"I know," Phillip said. "But it's not our problem anymore."

"So, you're just going to give up?"

Phillip's eyes flashed. "It's the fucking *job*, James. You do what the fuck you're *told*. I'm already burned with the RHPD, and I'm a Federal agent. I don't have a choice. And, frankly, *you* don't have a choice either—"

"I'm not going to just sit here and let this go," James snapped, talking over Phillip's last few words. "Maybe it's a normal day at the office to let people get murdered and the killer walk away, but not for me. That girl deserves justice, and no one else deserves to die." He paused, his tone calm again. "Wait, what do you mean no real clues? We just turned in a scythe from the Civil War days that was used to kill Kathleen Wilson and was used against us by a guy who's been dead for close to two hundred years."

Phillip pulled his phone out of his pocket, showed it to James, then powered it down. James took the hint and powered down his phone as well while Phillip did the same to his laptop and iPad. He motioned for James to wait a minute, then pulled a small device out of his jacket pocket and placed it in the window. It looked like a small speaker with an antenna on it. Phillip switched it in, and a low static sounded from the box. It wasn't particularly loud, more like a white noise machine one would buy to keep at their bedside at night. "Now we can talk."

"What is that?"

"It's a scrambler," Phillip said. "That static is actually an audible code that makes it impossible for audio devices to pick up anything else in the room. I'm not supposed to have it, and we'd better be quick before someone figures out we're chatting on deaf ears."

James nodded, not surprised that the room was probably bugged. "I'm listening."

"No, *I'm* listening," Phillip said. "You said the murders won't stop. I agree with you, but I wanna hear why you think it's not over."

"Very well," James said. "Alma said that a necromancer, or anyone who practices black magic, can use a person's face to see what they saw in life. Wear it like a mask and see memories. Someone was using that technique to hunt down the SCU agents on Westenra Island, and they almost wiped all of them out except for Tiny Tim."

"The agent that helped you get cleaned up and onto the ship," Phillip said. "Yeah, he said hi, by the way."

"Hi," James said dismissively. "What did Kathleen Wilson do at Butler Plantation?"

Phillip moved over to the bed and pulled a file out of his suitcase. He opened it and leafed through a couple of pages while speaking. "Tour guide." His brow furrowed a little as he stopped on a page. "No, my mistake. She kept the books and was a volunteer in the research and record-keeping there. So that tracks for the accounting gig she picked up."

"Wouldn't that mean that she would have some knowledge of the financial and business history of the place?"

Phillip nodded. "Yeah, or at least know where that info is. They would keep it on the property in an archive somewhere. If she was part of the archive team, she would know exactly where to look." Phillip closed the file. "But why would that be important? What would a necromancer want with Butler's old records? The dude was broke. Squandered away his entire fortune, held the largest slave auction in history to get it back, then blew it all again and ended up dying a pauper in a big house with shit crops."

James rubbed his chin. "Someone knows something we don't. Something even the history books don't know about."

"You're thinking Kathleen Wilson was specifically targeted?"

"Yes. It's looking more and more like that."

"Which makes it a premeditated homicide. And since that thing was under someone's control, it's technically a murder weapon."

"That I destroyed," James said, sighing. He rubbed his eyes and cursed under his breath. "I'm an idiot."

"Not gonna argue."

"Fair," James said without missing a beat. "My point is this: we intercepted the draugr before its master could come get Kathleen's face."

Phillip nodded. "Which means our unsub didn't get what they were after."

"Which means they'll try again. And if they hunted Kathleen down, they probably got information on everyone there to determine the best target." James froze as another realization hit him. "Which means that they'll try again. More than likely, tonight."

Phillip stiffened. "James, we can't go back there. The place is being watched by the SCU, I promise you that. The Federal government gives an order, they're going to do some surveillance to make sure you follow that order. Both of us could find our asses in jail right next to the damn Cooter Critter."

"We don't have a choice," James said. "If we do nothing, whoever dies next will be blood on our hands." He looked at Phillip. "I can't live with that. Can you?"

Phillip sighed, the sound accompanied with a groan. "I hate your ass sometimes, you know that?"

James shrugged. "I usually only take issue with my ass the day after taco night."

Phillip rubbed his face in what he often referred to as a "woo-sah" and glanced out the window before looking at James again. "Okay, dumbass. We're about to disregard orders from the higher-ups. That shit is called 'insubordination.' They don't play around with that shit. That's on top of breaking the damn law. Once we're called off a case, anyone else we question can call harassment, and going back out to the crime scene is trespassing. If this case is suddenly part of something bigger that we're not officially on, that's obstruction. Given that it's a Federal case, you can chalk those up to felonies along with anything else they decide to charge us with. That's jail time, fines, you name it. And, considering the SCU is all about the cloak-and-dagger bullshit just like her FBI mama, we'll be debriefed and made to sign a non-disclosure. We blab anything we know, and we're fucked. And they'll be watching. The only thing that could *maybe* save our asses from possible jail time is if we find something that gives the SCU a slam-dunk and ties their hands into having to re-open the case. And that is a *big* fuckin' maybe. And the time window is tight. We'd have to do it right now. Tonight. We don't show back up at the SCU first thing in the morning with not even a 'fuck-you' sittin' in Smith's inbox, that's it for both of us."

James smiled. "At least we won't be bored."

Phillip narrowed his eyes at James and grumbled. "I hate dogs."

"I'll arrange us a different room."

9

The streets were empty, the moon high in the sky. James knew he'd be looking at a full moon shift in the next few days. *Lovely,* he thought. *Timeline just got a little shorter.* Even though he could shift at will, like any other were-creature, the full moon complicated things. He would be forced into the change once the moon was fully visible in the sky, and he wouldn't be able to shift back until the first sign of dawn. It was when he usually hunted, letting his savage side have an evening of fun. He had a particular taste for deer meat and still maintained his human side while in that form. Once the wolf had been separated from his consciousness and made its own entity within his mind by Dracula's ring, he'd had to form an understanding with the animal. An understanding that they both agreed on.

Humans were not food. Nor would they ever be.

James began to undress as Phillip popped the trunk of the car and opened a small box he'd pulled from the compartment where he kept the spare tire. He held up a small earpiece as he spoke. "You need to wear something so we can communicate."

James tossed his clothes into the trunk and looked at Phillip with a raised eyebrow. "Something that small is going to do one of two things once I shift. It will either fall out and be useless, or it will fall deeper into my ear canal, and I won't be able to shift back without a surgeon present to remove the device and tell me that I will never be able to hear out of that side again."

Phillip rolled his eyes. "I'm smarter than that, you idiot." He pulled a collar from the box and showed it to James. "This is what you're wearing. It's got a low enough frequency to where only you can hear me talk to you."

"SCU gear?" James said. "Won't they be able to track us?"

"I made this," Phillip said. "Been working on it since we got back from Florida. This stuff is mine."

James smiled. "You don't trust them, either."

Phillip gave him a look and kept talking, avoiding the statement. "They can't track this thing without the Mac address. I made sure it communicates on a private channel. The earpiece I've got is the only thing the collar will talk to. You'll go on ahead since you can get there faster. I'll stay here and keep up appearances. Once you get there, get inside the house and try to find the archive. It's probably in one of the locked rooms the tourists don't get to see. I'll be able to track you with the app on my tablet. It's ghosted, so the SCU won't see me using it."

James gave the collar a disdainful look. "A collar? I feel degraded."

Phillip glared at him. "Just shift so I can put this on you."

James shifted into wolf form and crouched down. Phillip fastened the collar around his neck and stepped back as James reached up to fidget with the new accessory. It was made of Kevlar, the stuff snagging his fur in places and pulling it just enough to be annoying. He tried to detach some of the hairs from the thing but managed to cling to more, the hundreds of tiny tugs registering as both pain and itching. He sat down on his haunches and scratched at it with his foot.

"Stop that, you moron," Phillip spat, still keeping his voice down. "You break it, we're fucked. Quit being a baby." He tucked his earpiece into place and pressed against it. He spoke again, his voice also coming from the collar. "Can you hear me?"

James stopped scratching and woofed once. *Yes.*

"Good," Phillip said. "The idea is stealth. They'll have off-duty cops watching the place, so try not to fuck this up."

What if Lacy texts me? James suddenly thought. *Or Molly? Probably not her at this hour, but someone will need to answer Lacy.* James reached into the trunk and used his claws to carefully pull his phone out of his pants pocket. He handed it to Phillip and gave a low *"Woof."*

"What?" Phillip said as he took the phone. "Are you serious? You're worried about your girlfriend calling you at this hour?"

James rolled his eyes and woofed again, this time a little louder. Phillip's eyes widened a little as he tensed. He kept his voice low as he snapped. "Dude! Keep it down! You wanna get the wrong damn attention on us? We're already doing something stupid!" He sighed, groaning at the same time as he tucked the phone into his pocket. "Fine, I'll be your damn secretary. I'm sure they have a doggy kiss emoji somewhere."

James remembered Phillip giving him hell about Molly earlier, and recalled his planned retaliation. The wolf began panting in his mind, laughing. It was too good an opportunity to pass up, and they'd eaten dinner only a few hours ago.

Phillip headed off to the hotel as James moved to the front of the car. Directly on the vehicle would be overboard, and time was ticking. He heard something down the way, the sound of hooves on the street and a horse sighing loudly through its nostrils.

He panted and grinned, looking at the spot on the ground next to the driver's side of the car.

James moved through the dark brush on all fours, stopping long enough to look around the area with his yellowed night vision to make sure that there weren't any security guards or police watching the place. He saw two cop cars parked in the lot facing opposite directions and heard the low chatter from the officers as they talked about sports and the occasional political headline.

"Yeah, there they are," Phillip said, his voice coming from James's collar. "Probably hired off-duty to watch the place after Kathleen Wilson's murder. Depending on who's doing the hiring, that gig can pay pretty well. Remember those times I went and played security at the movie theater?"

James gave a soft woof.

"Yeah, you *should* give a shit," Phillip said. "If they have two there, that means they're also making rounds inside the house. They have keys. Wait for 'em to start walking around, then get inside once they get the door unlocked. Oh, and do it without causing a shit circus."

I've already accomplished that feat, James thought, fighting the urge to pant with laughter. He knew Phillip would probably try to one-up him later, but it was worth it. He didn't doubt Phillip's prowess with practical jokes. Having been best friends with a werewolf for years, the man was capable of one-upping at a giant pile of werewolf poo. In fact, James looked forward to it. They were overdue for one of their joke wars.

The two officers got out of their cars, turning on their flashlights and checking their gear as they continued to chatter. James focused in on them as they spoke, letting the wolf take control of his hearing.

"You said your kid knew that poor girl?" one said as he locked his squad car.

"Yep," said the other. "Went to school with her before they graduated. Sweet girl. Straight A's. My daughter told me Kathleen was into history and research. Apparently was looking into some old records here the courts sealed back in the day."

Interesting, James thought. *Why would they have sealed documents in Butler's archive?* Sealed court documents were usually held by the authorities, not turned over to a private citizen.

The officers chattered more about kids and how they grow up too fast as they began making their rounds around the house and property. They eventually split up, one walking outside of the house while the other checked the edges of the yard near the woods and trails. James waited until they were out of sight, then moved from his vantage point toward the house. The ground was damp from the dew that formed in the grass, the soft earth making it easy for him to move quietly. He'd have to make his own plan on getting in once they unlocked the door. As much as James hated to admit it, he'd have to take one or both of the officers down and take their keys. He could knock them out easily, get it done before they knew what hit them, and leave them with nothing but a major headache when they woke up in the trunks of their cars. He still didn't like the idea of smacking people around who didn't deserve it. On the other side of things, they wouldn't be able to do much to him since it was highly unlikely they were using silver bullets. Still, regular bullets hurt like hell.

At least no one would get killed.

James froze in place as a scream overpowered the sound of the cicadas in the area. He heard the other officer shout the screaming officer's name, then heard the scream get cut short. He took off around the house and slowed a bit as he saw one of the cops enter the trail into the woods, gun and flashlight raised as he called out his partner's name again. The wolf growled inside, forcing a low growl from James as he heard another sound come from the trees and brush. A low, scratching rasp.

Like someone trying to talk with rotted vocal cords, James thought. *Shit. So much for not being seen.* He ran to the woods as the second officer's shouts were followed by the gun reports. James began to pick up scents instantly as he hit the trail. Rot. Mildew. Dust. Cologne, likely from one of the cops. He saw the second cop aiming into the woods and firing as several figures closed in on him. The guy was older, balding, but in good enough shape that he probably wouldn't have to worry about taking multiple people acting as assholes and holding his own.

Then again, a gang of dead things attacking with yard tools would probably make even Batman crap his cowl.

"*Stop,*" the officer shouted. He aimed low and fired another round, kneecapping the nearest draugr. It went down, rasped at him, and started to crawl forward. He fired at the thing, the round smacking it in the face. James charged as the group closed in on the cop, snarling as he slammed his hand down and smashed the crawling draugr's skull against the asphalt walking trail. The cop screamed a stream of profanity as he aimed at James and tried to fire. A draugr rushed him, swung a shovel at his hands, and sent his gun into the trees. James attacked it as the cop fell back onto the ground holding his hands and trying to backpedal away from his attacker. Two more draugrs came at James as Shovel the Magnificent raised his tool to deal a death blow. James plowed through the draugrs, sending them flying into the dark as he made for Shovel, the scent of dead, dried bone and meat acidic in his nose, mixing with something else.

Vanilla. Blood.

James's heart skipped a beat as a blur zipped by Shovel, his body jerking before it fell to the ground without its head. The two draugrs from the woods rushed at James again, both wielding hatchets. He pounced on one, picked it up by the face, and used it to bludgeon the other into pieces. The body snapped free of the head and flew into a tree hard enough to shatter like dried wood. James tossed the crumbling head aside and made for the officer, putting himself between the terrified man and the things moving around in the woods. He braced himself, taking an attack stance as he growled at the movement, his teeth bared as three more draugrs stepped onto the trail, all three of them dressed in the clothing of their former slave days. They stopped, staring at him. One held a freshly severed arm with a large watch on the wrist. Another held a handgun, looking it over as if it'd never seen one before.

The one standing in between them was wearing the face of the police officer they'd just butchered.

It looked at James, then glanced around him at the cop he guarded. It pointed at him and said one word in a graveled rasp. *"Keys."*

James made to attack when Phillip's voice sounded from the collar. "Shit, James! What the hell is going on?!"

Nothing unusual, James thought as the wolf grunted at the sarcasm. *Just a regular Tuesday.* He charged the three draugrs, snarling as he lashed out at the one in the center and took the head clean off with enough force to send the body sideways. The other two pounced, and James tried to shake them off as they grappled onto him with unexpected strength. He felt jagged, broken teeth latch down into his bicep, going through his thick silvered coat and into his skin just enough to break the surface. The thing tried to pull its serving of werewolf steak away in its mouth, but James rolled and slammed his arm down onto the ground underneath his body, crushing the hungry ghoul under his eight hundred pounds of were-weight. The draugr on his other arm tried to bite him but couldn't get through his fur before he reached over and peeled the thing off like Velcro and smashed it on the asphalt. Both draugrs were piles of dust by the time James was on his feet. He wasn't surprised when he found himself staring down the barrel of a Glock 40-caliber pistol.

I don't have time for this, James thought. The wolf huffed in agreement. James turned away from the cop and looked around the path while the cop whimpered and kept his pistol pointed at him.

Lacy. He'd smelled Lacy. Was it in his mind? No. Couldn't have been.

Phillip's voice came back in his ear. "How many?"

James shifted to human form. "Four, maybe five. I wasn't counting."

"I heard gunshots," Phillip said, his tone strained as if holding back the urge to scream. "You need to Google the definition of 'stealth.' It's a real easy concept, James."

"I wasn't given much choice," James said. "One of the officers is dead." He turned his attention to the cop still sitting on the ground with the Glock pointed at him. He smelled something else in the air, the scent strong enough that the wolf was able to step back and let James handle this one on his own. "The other one no longer needs to use the bathroom."

"Nice. In other news, the red flags went up. Looks like something tripped the alarm in the house. There's a legion of cops on the way. You need to get the fuck out of there *now*."

"Right," James said. He moved over to the guard and crouched down in front of him. "Might I trouble you for the keys to the house? It's important."

"Relax, Jimmy. I already got in."

James felt his heart jump into his throat as he stood and found Lacy Faulkner walking casually toward him, a large manilla envelope in her hand. Every one of the things he'd been wanting to say to her, every question, every emotion he had hit him at once. He tried to form words, but too many things tried to come out. He finally managed all of it down to one word.

"Lacy?"

10

J ames stood in place as the wolf barked and yipped happily in his mind. It rolled over onto its back and wagged its tail furiously as if inviting Lacy to rub its belly.

Lacy smiled as she approached James, looking him up and down. "Nice collar. Leash laws?"

"Something like that," James said, trying to hold back the tidal wave of questions he wanted to ask her, all of them some variant of asking where she'd been and why she'd left.

Lacy motioned at the guard. "Somebody needs a diaper change. Give me a sec." She moved over to the man and crouched down. He whimpered, turning his gun on her as her ice-blue eyes glowed a little. James couldn't take his eyes off of her, couldn't stop watching her long thick brown curls flowing over her shoulders like chocolate curtains, her pink t-shirt moving up slightly to reveal the flawless skin of her lower back. "Hey, sweetie," she said. "You really need to go inside and take a shower. You stink."

The cop's face slackened a little as he lowered the gun, his eyes locked on hers. "Yeah," he said, his speech slurred. "Thanks for letting me know." Lacy stood and stepped back as the guy got to his feet and headed toward the house.

James fought to calm the hand grenade that had just gone off in his mind palace. *Keep it business for now, Coldstone.* "What's in the envelope?"

"Dunno," Lacy said, holding it up. "Didn't get a chance to look. I did grab the log, though."

"Why are you here?" The wolf chuffed loudly in his head. James kicked himself mentally. *Way to fuck that one up, James.*

Lacy blinked. "Wow, Jimmy. Missed you too."

"You know what I mean," James said. "You show up out of the blue, and you obviously knew to grab what I was after from the house."

"Got a phone call from that Agent Smith guy," Lacy said. "He told me to come down here and grab this envelope. Said he'd pay the shit out of me for it too."

Huh, James thought. *He blackmails me, but he offers her money? Maybe she mind-jobbed him.*

"No distant relative?"

"Nah," Lacy said, shaking her head. "Marianne is safe. I was actually just taking a night on the town in Charlotte when Agent Smith called me."

The wolf sat up in his mind and stopped panting, cocking his head to the side. *You're right,* James thought. *She's acting...different?* Something was off. He couldn't put his finger on it. Why hadn't she been answering his texts? And neither James nor Phillip had shared their trip to Butler Plantation with the SCU. How did Agent Smith know about it?

Lacy was acting the same way she'd acted when he'd first met her in Charleston what seemed like eons ago. She'd been evasive, not willing to share much information, and had even lied to them about some details of who she'd been hunting and her reasons for being there. James had written it off back then, not blaming her for not wanting to share information with two men she didn't know. But now?

Sirens sounded in the distance. James expanded his hearing and heard Phillip's voice over the collar. "Oh, fuck *me*, James."

"What's going on?" He said as he glanced at Lacy, who looked at him with some confusion. He pointed at the collar and mouthed "Radio."

"It's the goddamn calvary," Phillip said. "I've got the police band pulled up. They're sending in the damn SWAT team. Get out of there!"

James looked at Lacy as the sirens grew louder. Lacy clutched the envelope to her chest and nodded. "Lead the way, Jimmy."

James opened the door to the hotel room to Phillip cursing and grumbling as he stood. "Fuck. We're done. *I'm* done. I had to know this would turn into a shit-circus."

James stepped aside and allowed Lacy in first as Phillip turned to them, still ranting. He stopped mid-curse word, his eyes wide and his mouth open at the sight of Lacy standing in the hotel room. James closed the door behind them and moved next to her. "Phillip, you remember Lacy."

"Hi, Bacon," Lacy said cheerily.

Phillip blinked. "What the hell?"

"It's complicated," Lacy said. She handed him the folder. "All I know is that I was supposed to grab this and jet. Heard Jimmy outside having a hard time making some guys re-dead and stepped in before both cops got killed. Cue the sirens, and here we are."

"She said Smith called her," James said.

"What? How?" Phillip said. "I sure as shit didn't tell them we were going out there." He glanced around the room. "I checked for bugs while you were out there."

"I don't know," Lacy said, pointing at the folder. "He said grab the folder that Kathleen Wilson last logged and get it to Noble Jones."

Phillip sighed and looked at James again. "We don't have time for this. If the SCU knows what we were up to, then we're cooked. Asses will be fired for damn sure." He motioned at Lacy. "If he's callin' her in on it, that means we've been replaced and they're trying a different approach."

"It probably means vampires," Lacy said. "Not really likely a human and a werewolf would be able to march right into Wormsloe House and interrogate Noble Jones without a party happening."

Phillip rolled his eyes. "This just keeps getting better." He went back to the desk and sat down, opening the envelope and sifting through the contents. "Just give me a sec with this. Let me see if I can salvage this damn nightmare."

James looked at Lacy as she moved over to the window and stared out into the night. The initial shock of seeing her again began to fade. He remembered the night they'd kissed on Westenra Island, remembered how they'd made no real secret of their feelings. She'd pulled away, frightened. He'd almost given his life to save hers when she'd been attacked by the vampire he chased down and eventually killed. James remembered the first time he'd fallen in love. The first morning in Rock Hill, he realized that it didn't hold a candle to what he felt for Lacy. He'd gone downstairs to the study to figure out what he wanted to say to her when she woke that coming night only to find her letter.

Another feeling hit him as Molly's face flashed in his mind, images of her on top of him, the two of them wrapped in each other's arms in the heat of sex only an hour after he'd saved her from her disastrous asshole of a date.

Guilt.

What would he tell Lacy? Did she need to know? They weren't exactly together. Or did she feel the same way he did? That they still had something there? Phillip sometimes ragged him about his loyalty, but James knew that it was his wolfen side that made his loyalty to others so intense and powerful. She'd proven trustworthy to him, put her own trust in him. And he'd betrayed that trust for a night of what? Releasing pent-up sexual urges?

Or was it something else?

He set it all aside as he moved over to Lacy. "Hey," he said, his voice low. "What happened?"

"What do you mean?" Lacy asked.

"Why'd you leave?" James shook his head. "All I found was your note."

Lacy looked down, bit her lip, then looked up at him and smiled. "I had some things to take care of. Now I'm here in Savannah helping you, thanks to your boss calling me." She shrugged. "Not real complicated."

James started to speak, his heart pounding as he tried to form words. "Lacy, I—"

"Do me a favor," Lacy said, cutting him off. She touched his arm, her smile shrinking a little, her eyes pleading, her voice small. Not the girl he'd met in Charleston. "Don't complicate it."

He didn't look away from her until he heard Phillip curse.

"What. The. *Shit*."

"What is it?" He moved away from Lacy, the wolf settling down in his mind reluctantly. *We'll come back to it later,* James thought to the animal.

"Check this out," Phillip said as he handed one of the forms in the file over. "And be careful. It's old as hell."

James took the page from him, handling it with care as he looked over the handwriting. It took him a moment to make out what it was saying, the cursive penmanship unique to whoever had written the document ages ago. It wasn't unlike reading the Constitution or the Declaration of

Independence. All he needed was a few seconds to adapt to the writing style.

"What's it say?" Lacy asked, stepping away from the window.

"It's a legal agreement between Pierce Butler and Noble Jones." James read over the text again to make sure he was seeing it right. "It grants all of Butler's properties back to Jones's family in the event that no Butlers are left to run it."

"What a lot of people don't know is that Butler and Jones were close," Phillip said. "Jones helped him set up the two plantations he had here in Savannah: Butler Island and Saint Simon's."

"I know Noble," Lacy said. "Of course, it was well after the Civil War when I met him. Never thought I'd see a black guy running a vampire house in the South."

"Jones is black?" Phillip asked. "That can't be right. If you were black back then, you were out in the fields. Not running the place."

"Noble's father had a slave mistress," Lacy said. "Good news was that his father, Noble Senior, loved his son and had a change of heart where he was concerned."

James shook his head. "I'm not sure I understand why this is significant," he said, indicating the document in his hand. "Why would this make Kathleen Wilson a target?"

"Money's out of the picture," Phillip said. "The Weeping Time, remember? Even after selling off all those slaves and getting his fortune back, Pierce Mease Butler ended up squandering it away again and died broke as hell. Butler Plantation became useless as a functioning plantation. Outside of being a historical landmark and tourist attraction, the place has been worthless since right after the Civil War. Around the time Butler died." He grunted and muttered under his breath. "Damn place is useless now, truth be told."

"So, Jones already owns the place, then," James said. "Which begs the question as to why this is a conversation. Why kill a kid for snooping around in this? I assume that this is what the necromancer is after."

"Necromancer?" Lacy said. James saw a slight glimmer of panic on her face before she was able to mask it away. "This is a new one."

"It's who's responsible for our draugr friends," Phillip said. He told her about their visit to Alma's.

"Jones wouldn't mess with that shit," Lacy said, shaking her head. "Vampires don't dabble in magic. We don't need to, and too much of it can be dangerous to us anyway. It's kind of an unspoken law, especially if it's magic that gives a vampire control over other vampires like that. And even if we did, Jones isn't the type. He likes to keep things simple and bringing magic and witchcraft into the mix would rock the boat too much for him."

"Well, there's one way to find out," Phillip said. "You two need to go have a chat with Noble Jones."

Lacy crossed her arms in front of her. "Not a good idea. I'd better go alone. Vampires and werewolves don't usually mix well." She looked at James and winked. "*Usually.*"

Phillip stood and faced her, moving in close enough to where James had to step back as he watched Phillip square off against someone who could snap his spine with her pinky finger. "I don't care. James can handle himself, and you ain't goin' out there alone."

"Don't trust me now, Bacon?" Lacy asked, blinking innocently at him. "Kinda hurts my feelings."

"Well, I have a hard time trusting a girl that walks out on James without so much as a fuck you, then shows back up after just so happening to get a phone call from my boss with intel that we didn't even give him."

"I didn't have a choice," Lacy said, getting back in Phillip's face, her tone sharp and defensive. "It was either leave or stay and risk him getting hurt."

"Oh, and leaving him high and dry wouldn't hurt him?"

"I had to make a choice. He'll get over a broken heart, not death."

James raised his hand slightly. "I'm still here. In the room. Right here."

"Guess who got to pick up the pieces when you dipped out," Phillip said, ignoring James. "That's right: *me.* He's been mopey as shit ever since. You could've at least answered his text messages."

"Well excuse the *fuck* out of me," Lacy spat back. "Maybe I had my reasons, and *maybe* I don't have to share every-damn-thing with you. What's next, Bacon? Wanna know my bra size? What kind of conditioner I use? How about my menstrual cycle while we're at it?" She paused. "Nevermind on that one. Dead girls don't do that."

James raised his hand again. "If I could interject?"

Lacy and Phillip both looked at him and shouted in unison. "Shut up!" They looked back at each other, and Phillip turned away, rubbing his face in another of his "woo-sah" moments before speaking again. "Okay, we don't have time for this shit. You two need to go talk to Jones." He spoke over Lacy as she began to protest again. "*Yes,* James is going with you. I'm not fired yet, and he's still technically working in an official capacity for the SCU. Since Agent Smith called you in, you're also working in an official capacity. As the only one here who is an actual agent, I'm in charge. Don't like it? There's the fuckin' door. Feel free to dip out. Again. But you risk being arrested by the SCU if you do anything else in regards to this case once I boot your ass out." He paused, narrowing his eyes at her. "Any questions?"

Lacy looked sidelong at James. "Is he always like this?"

James shrugged. "Only when he's awake."

"Don't start your shit with me, James," Phillip said. "I'm already up to my ass here trying to keep this going before the SCU finds out we're going against direct orders."

James nodded. "Understood, and I apologize. I just hate it when mommy and daddy fight."

Phillip flipped him off.

"What about the folder?" Lacy asked, pointing at the open file on the desk. "I'm supposed to get it to Noble."

"Let me go over it some more," Phillip said. "I want to see if I can suss out why Smith called you and wants it to go to Noble Jones besides the obvious. When you talk to Jones, bring up the Butler property deal and see how he reacts."

"You think our Agent Smith has some sort of ulterior agenda?" James asked.

"He's a Federal spook," Phillip said as he sat down at the desk and began going through the papers again. "Of course, he does. But if I can try to figure out what he knows and find something he doesn't know and needs, then that might just take us off the hook." Phillip looked up at James. "*Might.*"

"And if it doesn't?"

Phillip shook his head. "Just go and pray it does."

11

***

Leaving the hotel after midnight was easy enough for Lacy. She'd be able to simply stroll by the front desk and out into the night with no questions asked, no raised eyebrows, and only a little judgment from people who liked to assume things they knew nothing about.

James always wondered how nice it would be if he could stay clothed while doing supernatural things.

He looked out the window and saw her waiting in the street, the backpack she had with a change of clothes for him slung casually over one shoulder. He tossed his clothes on the bed as he opened the window. "This sucks."

"Well, it beats the shit out of answering awkward questions," Phillip said. He still sat at the desk pouring over the paperwork from Butler Plantation. "Besides, for all we know the front desk guy is an agent, and Lacy is the only one of the three of us who could get by him without him noticing. Or remembering. We can't take any risks here. Same reason you're not wearing that collar. Lacy said this guy is a little on edge when it comes to strangers. Last thing we need is him thinking we're recording him."

"Yet I'm still jumping out of a window."

"Just try not to land on your head," Phillip said, as he read a form. "Looks like they just repaved the sidewalk down there."

"What's your problem with Lacy?" James asked abruptly.

Phillip looked up from the paper in his hand and shook his head. "You serious?" he asked. "You're okay with her just showing up out of the blue again?"

"She's helping."

"James," Phillip said, setting the paper down. "You ever stop to think that maybe that girl has secrets for a good damn reason? That maybe she's not being entirely honest with us? You haven't known her more than a month if you add up all the time you spent together."

"We went through a lot together in that month," James said. "All three of us."

Phillip shrugged. "Not gonna argue that. But it's weird as all hell that she just so happens to get a call from Agent Smith, who wasn't all that thrilled with her being around in the first place when we were hunting down the traffickers. Double-weird-as-shit that he just so happens to call her with intel that we didn't send him. As far as the SCU knows, we're packing up and heading home."

That means they knew from the beginning, James thought to himself, not wanting to say it out loud and start another argument. The wolf grunted in agreement.

"Just go with her and talk to that vampire," Phillip said. "Get it done. And be careful."

"I'm about to jump out of a window."

"I mean after that."

"Your concern is touching."

"Kiss my ass."

James shifted, rushed Phillip, and licked the side of his face. Phillip screamed and cursed, swatting at James as wolf drool hung off his jawline. James was out the window and on the street before Phillip could swing at him, his laughter coming out as panting as he approached Lacy. She nodded and took off into the night with James close behind.

J ames and Lacy made the ten-mile trek to Wormsloe in less than ten minutes. Since Lacy was slightly faster, she kept her pace down enough for James to keep up as she led him down the Harry S. Truman Parkway and main roads until the trees were thick and the traffic lights were no longer a necessity. He'd barely broken a sweat by the time they reached the closed front gate. It was tall, wrought iron and framed by a stone archway large enough for cars to come in and out of. He saw parking for tourists beyond, the lot empty except for two cars: an old-fashioned Buick station wagon complete with wood-paneling and another vehicle parked next to it, some sort of black sports car. He stood and was about to shift into human form when Lacy turned to him and held a hand up. "Wait a second, Jimmy. Just in case."

James chuffed and motioned to her. *Okay, your show.*

Lacy approached the gate and looked around before moving over to the small intercom set at the perfect height for someone to use from their car window. She pushed the button and waited while it beeped at her before a gruff-sounding and annoyed voice came from the small speaker. "We're closed."

"I'm here to see Noble Jones," Lacy said. "Open up."

"Lady, I said we're closed," the voice said, sounding more annoyed. "And I don't know who that is."

"Right, and I'm a werewolf," Lacy cracked, winking at James.

There was a pause, then the voice returned, the annoyance replaced with dead serious authority. "State your business."

"I already told you: I'm here to speak with Noble Jones."

"Concerning?"

"Concerning nothing you need to worry about. It's private."

"This is your last warning. Turn and walk away."

Lacy rolled her eyes as she muttered. "I fucking *hate* vampires." She moved back to the entrance and kicked at it right where the two ten-foot-tall iron gates met. They swung open as if they weighed nothing, and James heard the mechanism that controlled them on the other side break and hiss as the hydraulics were forced back. Lacy walked through and into the lot, motioning James to stay back in the dark as two large men in black got out of the station wagon passenger area. A short man emerged from the driver's side front, his hair slicked back like some nineteen fifties greaser, his leather jacket open to expose the tight white t-shirt underneath. The two goons were both bald, both wore sunglasses despite the dark, and both looked like their shirts would shred under the strain of trying to contain the muscles underneath. Their faces were hard like they'd been chiseled from granite, stoic as they followed behind their boss.

Shorty sauntered up to Lacy, looking her up and down as he smirked at her. "Evening, gorgeous." He took off his shades and used them to motion at the gate. "You know you're going to pay for that."

"I have a rich boyfriend," Lacy said. "And I'm here to see Noble Jones. I'm an old friend."

Boyfriend? Again? James thought, remembering the times on Westenra Island when Lacy had referred to him as her boyfriend. At the time, he'd figured she was just playing the part and cracking wise. Typical Lacy behavior. She had no reason to mention him now. Did she? She'd made it pretty clear they couldn't be a thing.

And, of course, there was Molly.

James pushed away the thoughts, annoyed with himself for acting like a teenager. Now was not the time to mull over his lady issues.

"Everyone is an old friend of Mr. Jones," Shorty said, puffing his chest a little. The effect looked less like he was dominant and more like that one short kid everyone went to school with who would act like he was the biggest badass on campus only to get an atomic wedgie from his kid sister later. "Got a name, sweetie?"

James saw Lacy bristle, but she calmed it back down quickly enough for it to be barely noticeable. "Not your sweetie, sweetie," she said, her tone short and warning. "Now you either back the hell up, or I do a repeat performance of what happened to that gate on you and your two boyfriends here."

Tweedle Dee and Tweedle Dum tensed, both moving forward as Shorty stepped back. "See, I'm pretty sure that these two guys would take issue with that, baby girl. One little girl vampire versus two heavyweights from the twenties? This should be rich."

The two meatheads rushed Lacy. James darted from the shadows and charged in as Lacy ducked a punch from Tweedle Dum and hit him hard enough in the chest to send him flying. James took down Tweedle Dee, the man surprisingly strong enough to take the impact and roll until he was on top of James and swinging. James bucked, and the vampire lost his balance enough for a solid right-handed blow to land against his head and send him sideways. James was on him again, this time on top as he pinned the guard down and clamped his jaws on the bloodsucker's neck and ended Tweedle Dee's nighttime career. He was up before Dee's head stopped rolling away, running down Tweedle Dum as Shorty ran by at full speed back toward the Buick. Tweedle Dum tried to intercept the blur following Shorty, but James grabbed him by the head and smashed the skull onto the ground like a ripe watermelon before he could get to Lacy.

A loud, piercing scream filled the night. James turned, ready to kill Shorty for whatever he'd done to Lacy to make her scream like that. The wolf urged him to charge, but James braced against the beast, resisting as he thought to the beast. *I think she's got it.*

Lacy had Shorty pinned against the car and lifted off his feet until he was a head taller than her. Her left arm was braced against his chest, and her right hand held him in place in the one area that was apparently a weakness for even vampires. He sputtered, his eyes wide and his face whiter than it'd been before. "Am I still your baby girl?" Lacy asked.

Shorty spoke, giving away his talent for imitating Minnie Mouse. "No, ma'am."

James shifted to human form and walked up to the pair. Shorty's eyes got wider. James nodded at him. "I believe my friend would like to speak with Mr. Jones."

"No way," Shorty managed, his voice straining as it lost some of its Disney mouse tenor. "A werewolf? He'd kill me for it!"

Lacy squeezed again, and Shorty let out a scream at an octave James didn't think was possible. "Hey, Mariah Carey! Mr. Jones and I go way back. Tell each other fairy tales and shit."

"Good reference," James said to her. *Mariah,* he thought to himself. *That's great. His name is now Mariah.*

"Jimmy here is house trained, and shit's going down Jones needs to know about," Lacy continued. "Get in the car, take us up there, or we see if gelding a vampire is really a thing."

It was too dark to see what the tourists normally saw when visiting the Wormsloe Historic site during the daytime, but it wasn't long before they pulled up to a large white plantation house. A gazebo sat at the bottom of the hill and acted as an entryway for a staircase that led up to the front porch, low-emitting LEDs giving just enough light to keep someone from tripping up if they decided to come up for a visit without using any sort of supernatural dark vision. James climbed out of the back of the station wagon, turned, and help Lacy do the same. "See, Jimmy? The trunk seat in these things was great!"

James was just thankful he'd been able to put on clothes before having to sit so close to her for the drive.

"While I live and breathe, if it ain't Lacy got-damn Faulkner!"

James and Lacy both looked to the source of the booming, baritone voice. A tall, slender, handsome black man stood in the gazebo, smiling at them as he held his arms open. He had a low-cut goatee and wore black denim pants and a black button-up dress shirt with the top button open and the sleeves rolled up. "Welcome to my home."

"Thanks, Count Dracula," Lacy said. "Good to see you too."

Noble Jones laughed as James and Lacy made their way over to the gazebo. James swore he could hear Mariah in the Buick, and gave a quick glance to see the vampire bent over in the driver's seat and crying while he mentioned something about how much pain he was in.

Jones stepped up to Lacy and shook his head at her, still chuckling. "That's *Blacula* to you, missy." They both laughed and hugged like old friends.

Another good reference, James thought. He also felt a slight pang of... jealousy? He pushed it away, irritated with himself for being childish again as Jones turned to him and looked him up and down. "Huh. I thought I smelled a wet dog." He gave Lacy a hard sidelong glare. "Known you a while, Lacy, but how're you gonna bring a damn werewolf on my property and think I'm gonna appreciate that?"

"It's okay, Noble," Lacy said. "He's with me. Noble Jones, meet James Coldstone."

Jones's eyes flashed at James's name. James pushed the growling wolf in his mind back as he offered his hand. "It's a pleasure to meet you, Mr. Jones."

Jones took his hand reluctantly, giving it a firm shake. Almost too firm. James kept his face stoic despite the urge to wince at the vampire's grip. "You can understand my hesitation in allowing you to be here, Mr. Coldstone."

James shrugged. "No offense taken. I've always found Southern Hospitality a bit forward, myself."

Lacy shot James a look and mouthed "Jimmy, don't."

Noble Jones just chuckled as he let go of James's hand and spoke. "It's not just you being a werewolf, Mr. Coldstone. My family is familiar with your father's work."

James bristled at the mention. "Do tell."

"Let's just say he had a way with words, negotiation, and politics," Jones said as he clasped his hands behind his back, giving James a smirk. "And people."

James clenched his fist as the wolf tried to surge forward, forcing a change. He pushed the beast back again, gritting his teeth as Lacy moved in between them. "Okay, you two. Enough with the dick-size contest." She faced Jones. "Noble, we need to talk."

"Then talk," Jones said, crossing his arms in front of him as he kept his glare on James, trying to stare him down.

James didn't budge, keeping his eyes on Jones as he spoke. "The murders at Butler Island Plantation. It started with a young woman working there and ended up in a second murder tonight."

"I heard about the first one," Jones said. "Poor girl. Troubling business."

"Indeed," James said. "She worked in the archives. Looking over historical documents pertaining to the Butler family's holdings and wealth."

"I'm sure she found a goldmine of incompetence and stupidity starting around the time Pierce Mease Butler took over." He paused. "So, what does that have to do with you coming here to question me?"

"I spoke with Alma at the Abercorn House. Apparently, we're dealing with a necromancer." James raised an eyebrow at Jones. "Do you have any familiarity with the craft?"

Jones's lip curled in disgust as he gave Lacy a furious glare. "Are you kidding me, Lacy? It's been what? Twenty years since I've seen you?"

Lacy started to speak. "Noble—"

"And how *dare* you, sir," Jones said, turning his ire to James. "Your kind is not welcome here, your family name is *certainly* not welcome here, yet here you are asking me accusatory questions about blasphemy?" He spat on the ground at James's feet. "*There's* what I think of your Alma and your necromancer. Now get the hell off my land before I kill you and leave you in a ditch like the damn dog you are."

Lacy moved up to Jones, putting her face close to his. "Noble, back off. He's here to help you." She looked over her shoulder at James. "And Jimmy, *cool it.*"

I'm not going to get anywhere like this, James thought as the wolf braced inside, still ready for a fight. *And you're not helping. I'd like to be able to keep my temper in check. If you don't mind.* The wolf snorted at him and turned away to show his rump. *Better.*

James cleared his throat. "I do apologize. I didn't intend to insult you. But there's evidence that could point to you being responsible, and Alma isn't hiding her dislike for vampires in general, which could send people after you that you might not be able to handle. Lacy seems to think you're innocent, and I trust her. I'd like to have a calm, rational conversation about this."

Jones didn't lose the steel in his eyes as they flashed red before he nodded. "Come inside."

12

Noble Jones led James and Lacy into his home, waving at his guards to stand down as they passed through the large front doors. Some of them were dressed like the two he'd killed at the gate, but there were also some on patrol dressed in full heavy SWAT gear and armed with assault rifles. The stormtroopers glared at James as much as the plainclothes guards did, their body language making it clear that it was Jones and Jones alone keeping them from attacking James and making him a permanent resident six feet below the property grade.

James kept his discomfort off of his face. He didn't doubt that he could hold his own if things went south, but that would only last a short while. He would take down a decent number of the plainclothes men and women, but the stormtroopers outside were likely firing silver bullets. He needed to tread carefully.

Jones led them through the house and into his study. Portraits of men and women hung on the walls, some of them painted rather than photographed. It looked like the kind of homes James had been on during tours, but without the roped-off areas and locked doors. Jones brought them into his large study. He motioned to a couple of ornate chairs in front of a giant oak desk as he closed the double doors behind them, then took his place in the large chair behind the desk as James and Lacy sat down.

"I'm not sure how you manage to keep yourself secret here," James said. "Seems like a lot going on for a museum."

"This house isn't on the tour," Jones said. "The house the tourists see is elsewhere. I own the property, and Mr. Barrow and I have a mutually beneficial arrangement. Now what is going on, and why are you on my property insinuating that I would have anything to do with blasphemy against nature?"

James filled Jones in while Lacy sat back, only interjecting in her role once James got to the fight at Butler Plantation from earlier that evening.

Of course, he left out the contents of the file Lacy had found.

"Huh," Jones said, rubbing the stubble on his chin thoughtfully. "So, all of this over some old documents? It's a shame such a young person got caught up in something like this. What was she researching?"

"My partner is going over it now," James said. "We'll know soon." He saw Lacy shoot him a look out of the corner of his eye.

"I can call you once we get it all together," Lacy said.

Jones nodded. "Please do."

James leaned forward, clasping his hands in front of him and resting his elbows on his knees. "Please pardon my forwardness, but I have to know how a black man got the namesake of a former slave owner and ended up owning the plantation."

Jones shrugged. "My father was Noble Jones, a physician and statesman back in the day. He led the Georgia patriots during the Revolutionary War and was one of the original settlers in Savannah. He took a slave mistress at some point, and I was born."

"And he didn't push you aside?" James asked.

"Sure didn't," Jones said. "In fact, he was an excellent father to me and provided for my mother."

James raised an eyebrow.

"He was a white Southerner who'd sired a black son," Jones said. "It wasn't uncommon, but he'd also been turned shortly after I was born. He had power and influence, and he knew that he could control the narrative. It was better for him to have the history books stay consistent and his peers stay ignorant than it was to invite vampire hunters to kill him and white men to kill me as an abomination."

"Fair point," James said.

Jones looked at Lacy. "What evidence do you have pointing to me as the suspect in the murder of that girl?"

"Noble, I don't think you did it," Lacy said. "I know you. I wanna make sure that you're clear. Jimmy's here to help."

"That is not what I am asking," Jones said, his tone hard.

"Your father gave the Butlers that land," James said, stepping in. "Pierce Mease Butler squandered the fortune away and almost lost the property before he died. No one gives someone the gift of wealth out of kindness."

"True," Jones said, his attention back on James. "My father got a percentage of the profits from Butler. That was prime real estate back then. The soil was rich, and the crops were plentiful."

"Would it make sense to have a clause that reverted total ownership back to your family in the deal?"

Jones paused and sat back in his chair before speaking again. "If there was such a clause, I'm not aware of it. But Wormsloe would benefit greatly from that."

"How so?"

"Wealth. Power. Particularly politically." Jones shook his head. "A vampire house with that much in assets could become the most powerful house in the Southeast. But let's be honest, right? There's no way House Tepes is gonna allow some marsh-dweller to take over the Southeast. Especially not a black man. If such a clause did exist, they'd do everything they could to make it disappear."

House Tepes? James thought to himself. *As in Vlad the Impaler? Why would that matter?* The wolf growled again, this time sending him an urge of wariness. He sensed some tension from Lacy at the mention and noted it in his mind for later. "I would think something like that would be beneath the vampire community," he said, taking a glance at Lacy.

"We're still people," she said. "And people can be assholes."

"Racism isn't a human issue," Jones said. "It's much deeper than that. It's ingrained into the culture. Vampires are no exception to that. Just like there are vampires who still celebrate Christmas and Hannukah, there are also vampires who spend a lot of their time and energy making sure that brown people stay under heel."

James and Lacy got back to downtown Savannah while the sun was still down, stopping in the park next to the water. James changed into his clothes while Lacy checked the time on her phone. "We've got a couple of hours before sunrise."

James looked up at the window of his hotel room across the street. The lights were completely out. "I believe Phillip has called it a night."

Lacy snorted. "Humans. Sleep is for the weak."

James felt his heart flutter as she looked at him, and he started to wander into her impossibly blue eyes. His guilt over Molly was just as strong, not only because of what'd happened with her, but because he was interested in getting to know her as well. "Lacy," he said. "I—"

Lacy stepped up to him, looping her arm through his and nodding toward the water. "Walk with me, Jimmy. Been a while."

James nodded and led her down to the walkway, the sound of water lapping against the concrete soothing. The wake was small, the water calm. He took the night air in, opening his mouth slightly as the wolf unwrapped his senses and brought the scents over his tongue and glands. He felt his heart beat a little harder as Lacy's familiar vanilla scent hit him, mixed in with the coppery scent of blood.

"I guess you kinda figured Jones and I used to be a thing," Lacy said.

James shrugged. "Hadn't crossed my mind."

Lacy laughed. "God, you suck at lying, Coldstone."

"I know."

"Yeah, we ended it about fifty years ago or so. Just wasn't working out. We're better as friends."

"I gather that you're trying to tell me something."

Lacy stopped and looked up at him. "No, Jimmy. I'm not." She paused. "Or I am. God, I don't know." She rubbed her face and pushed her hair back, holding her hands to her head as if to prevent a headache.

"I don't want to push you," James said. "You said no. I have to respect that."

Lacy put her hands down and turned to him. "Jimmy, I'm going to level with you: I do care. I promise I do." She held her hand to his face, and he looked into her eyes and tried futilely not to lose himself in the icy blue pools. "You barely knew me in Charleston, but you risked everything to save me from dying in the sunlight. You could've died on Westenra when you made me feed from you, but you did it anyway. No one's ever done something like that before. Not for me."

James shrugged. "You would've done the same for me."

"Most vampires wouldn't," Lacy said. "The first one? No. But over and over again? It's not just that good old 'werewolf loyalty.'"

"No, it's not," James said, reaching up and covering her hand with his. His stomach knotted as the wolf flashed the memory of the other night with Molly at him. The beast wasn't trying to be vindictive. He could feel the same guilt coming from it as well. "Lacy, I met someone the other night. It was a mistake. I just..."

Lacy smiled as she pulled her hand away. "Jimmy, we're grown-ups. I don't care who you sleep with. We're not a thing." The smile faltered a little. "We can't be."

"Why?" James felt the frustration rising and fought to push it down. He didn't want to run her off again. "Can you at least tell me that?"

Lacy breathed deeply before she spoke, her tone even. "Racism isn't just about skin color, Jimmy. And the vampire world is just as savage, if not worse. The older ones, the ones who make up the Elders of Night, are the worst. They wouldn't just kill me. They'd kill you." She swallowed. "And Phillip. Mindy. Everyone you've ever cared about or is even remotely connected to you."

James shook his head. "That doesn't scare me. I wouldn't let anything like that happen."

"You wouldn't have a *choice*," Lacy said, her tone suddenly hard. She covered her face with her hands, took another deep breath, pulled them away and looked up at him. "Jimmy, these people run the show. Don't you get it? You're outnumbered. You've only ever really tangoed with Younglings. The vampires that would come after you are much older and way stronger." She paused. "What's her name?"

James blinked, caught off-guard by the sudden subject change. "Uh, Molly."

"Cute," Lacy said with a small grin. "You should call her when this is over. See if it was more than a one-night thing." James could see some pain in her eyes, his thoughts and emotions swirling with the sounds of the water, cicadas, and breeze in the air mixing in with the noise in his head.

And something else. A small voice. Weak. Female.

"Help. Me."

They both looked in the direction of the sound. The lights in the park were mostly out, only just enough to keep the place from being in total blackness. The sound came from the shadows. Somewhere near the

Waving Girl. James pulled the wolf forward and pushed everything aside as Lacy stepped back. "Jimmy, your eyes are yellow. You see something?"

His senses were wide open. He opened his mouth slightly, took in the scents as he listened and searched the area with his eyes. Blood. Spices, maybe sage? The scent was clear, different from the other smells that usually permeated the walk. The light posts were bright in his vision, but not so much that it hurt. The darker areas were clearer. He saw the statue several yards up, the bronze girl waving with her handkerchief at the nonexistent boats traversing the river. Something was draped over her feet, a brown mass of cloth. Bloody, torn, moving.

Clinging to the symbol of welcome and safety.

Lacy turned and looked in the same direction as James ran to the statue. The figure fell away from her cold and inanimate savior, and James caught her before she could hit the ground and eased her down. She was young, maybe in her mid to late teens, her black hair done up in braids and her bronze-colored skin covered in beads of sweat and blood. Her lower lip was split, her eyes heavy, and her nose bloodied. James pulled his hands back and saw them covered in her blood. Lacy was beside him in an instant as he looked the girl over, his eyes resting on the large splotch of blood on her drab brown robes, the spot tattered and torn. He moved the pieces of cloth away. A sizeable chunk of meat had been ripped from her side, two of her lower rib bones exposed. The girl's breathing was ragged, her body starting to shiver.

Lacy knelt down next to the girl and spoke gently to her as she stroked the dying teen's forehead, pushing a few of the braids away. "It's okay, just relax, sweetie. We've got you."

"You...You're one of them," the girl breathed, her voice weak and hoarse.

Lacy shushed her. "I won't hurt you, sweet. You're safe." She looked at James. "Jesus, Jimmy, she's just a child."

James could hear the girl's heart struggling to beat and smell the telltale scent of a living thing beginning to let go. He looked at Lacy and shook his head, not wanting to put words to what was already understood. "Can you tell us what happened?" he said to the girl, keeping his tone calm and gentle.

"All...dead," the girl struggled. "At...Abercorn. Alma...sent me...spirits in torment."

"Who did this?" James asked, leaning closer. The girl's eyes began to drift as her body relaxed. "Who hurt you?"

"Miss...Alma," the girl breathed, her voice weaker. "Said he...was... no..." She went still, a small breath of air leaving her in a sigh as her eyes stared blankly into the night sky.

James, saw the tears running down Lacy's face. He stood, stepping away from the dead girl, his fists clenched, his teeth grit as raw fury boiled under his skin as he pulled his shirt off. He was stripped nude and in wolf form in seconds, loping down the street toward Abercorn. He heard Lacy behind him, calling to him, but he ignored her as he rounded the corner and charged up the front steps of the Abercorn House. He stopped when he saw the front doors in ruin, one hanging off the hinges. Blood was splattered on the walls, pieces of meat on the floor. He moved in and pulled the scents into his mouth and nose. The wolf growled inside, pushing a low growl from James's throat. He smelled the blood, the rot, the stench of vampire on top of the herbal scents and the fresh coppery tinge of the now cold blood that painted the walls and floors. He saw the sitting room immediately off to the right, and saw the body of another of the Abercorn witches slumped in a corner. Alma's body lay splayed out in a high-backed chair in front of the fireplace. James didn't have to get any closer to see that her ribcage had been pried wide open, her heart torn away, her lungs destroyed. Another body lay at her feet, mangled beyond recognition.

"James?"

James looked over his shoulder at the sound of Lacy's voice and saw her standing on the porch behind him. His body was tense with rage as the dying girl's face showed up in his mind. The wolf snarled, the realization that it was him who'd made the hellish sound not hitting him until the wind was in his face, the world blazing by him as he charged into the night, his blood red hot and his mind a jumbled wire coil of murderous rage.

A child. She'd only been a child.

And Noble Jones was going to pay.

13

James was on the highway in minutes, ignoring the dryness in his lungs from the unusual amount of running he'd done in the past few hours. The road was empty, the night air still and flooded with the loud whirring of the cicada legion in the brush.

He could barely hear it over the blood roaring in his ears as he moved on all fours back toward Wormsloe Plantation.

Miss...Alma...said he...was...no...

Noble. Alma had called him by name.

Noble was going to die. This was going to end. Tonight. Now.

James felt something blow by him, moving even faster than he was. He almost stumbled when Lacy appeared in front of him, slowing down to keep pace as she shouted over his shoulder. "Jimmy! Jimmy, *stop!*"

He pushed harder, let his rage drive his body and fuel his muscles as he ignored Lacy's shouting and made for the exit he needed to get to Wormsloe. Lacy turned and shot at him, plowed into his midsection hard enough to knock the wind out of him, jarring him hard enough to make lights flash in his yellowed eyes. He rolled backward and hit the asphalt hard, the rough stone scraping away skin from his face, arms, and knees. He got to his feet again, his wounds healing as Lacy stood her ground, her arms out as if to block him.

He barked at her, growling and snarling. She set her jaw, her eyes hard as she stared back at him. "Try that shit on someone who can't kick your ass, Jimmy. Now slow your damn roll!"

James shifted to human form and stalked toward her. "Get out of my way, Lacy."

"Wait just a minute," Lacy said, dropping her hands to her sides as he approached. "You don't even know that Noble did this. Not for certain."

"She said his name," James shot back. "Enough for me." He stopped inches from her, glaring down into her eyes. "Now move."

Lacy stood firm, looking back up at him as she kept her tone even in spite of her words being clipped. "James Coldstone, I did not think you were the type of man to try to intimidate a girl by looming over her."

James blinked, his heart skipping a beat. He found his mouth moving, but no words forming, the accusation hitting him hard in the chest. He backed away from her, shaking his head as he spoke around the lump in his throat. "I'm...I apologize. I didn't realize I was...I'm sorry."

Lacy nodded. "Two things: First, I forgive you. Anger makes people do stupid shit, and you don't exactly have the most even temper. Second, whether you know you're doing it or not, if you ever step up on me like that again I'll kick your ass so hard your *ancestors* will feel it and make sure to include it in historical documents. You're better than that, and no amount of anger is worth turning into a complete asshole."

James felt a headache coming on, his anger shifting to upset. He breathed out slowly, imagining that he was blowing his fire out of his system to make room for the coolness of calm. He looked at Lacy and took another breath before speaking again. "The girl at the park said Alma had called him by name."

"She said 'no,'" Lacy said, crossing her arms in front of her. "There's no telling what she was going to say. But I can tell you that Noble Jones is no butcher. Anytime he's ever fed, he's always been discrete about it. He's never killed anyone outside of self-defense and he never drinks more than his victim can handle. And victim isn't really the right word since he insists on consent."

"Can you be so sure?" James asked.

"Yeah, I can," Lacy said, nodding and defensive. "I've known him almost my entire vampire life. I lived with him for years. People tend to show their true colors if you spend enough time with them."

James felt another subtle jab to the gut. *I deserved that,* he thought. "Fine. Then we need to talk to him."

"Not until you cool the hell off," Lacy snapped. "You were about to go

THE DOG WITH TWO TAILS

charging into what's pretty much a fucking military compound, and I promise you every one of his men is packing silver bullets. Even if you'd made it, Jones is old as fuck. He'd tear you apart before you got a lick in." She took a breath, visibly trying to calm herself before she spoke again. "What we need to do is go back and wake Phillip up so we can fill him in." As if on cue, Lacy's phone began blasting the theme to *Dragnet.* She pulled it from her pocket and put it on speaker. "Hey, Phillip."

"Phillip?" Phillip said on the other end of the line. "Not Bacon? Shit, what'd I miss?"

"Nothing," James said. "Lacy and I were on a moonlit stroll."

"Well, can the romance and get your asses back here."

Lacy and James looked at each other. "What's going on, Bacon?" Lacy said.

"Someone had a field day at Abercorn. Shit, they're *all* dead. And someone found the body of a teenage girl in the park next to James's favorite statue. Where are you?"

"We're just off the exit," Lacy said before James could answer. "On our way back from Wormsloe."

"Hang up the grab-ass and get back here," Phillip said. "Hoyt just called from the ME's office. He wants me to come look at it."

"I thought Smith killed the case," James said.

"What Smith don't know won't hurt him. Bye." The phone beeped as the call ended.

Lacy pocketed the phone and looked up at James, shrugging. "Okay," she said. "Let's go."

"Wait," James said, holding up a hand to stop her. "I'm sorry. About before. I've never done that. Not intentionally. It won't happen again. I promise."

"I believe you," Lacy said. "Only because you keep your promises. Let's go before Bacon has an aneurysm."

G od *damn*," Phillip said, leaning back against his car. James glanced around him at the action going on at the Abercorn scene. Police had taped off the road, closing it off to traffic and any potential onlookers who might trample the scene. A small crowd had formed just outside the barrier, and the medical examiner unit was parked out front. "So, you knew about this and didn't say anything?"

"You were asleep," James said, not looking away from the scene.

"You could've woken me up for this, you dipshit."

"You're so cute when you sleep, though."

"Here we go."

"Peaceful."

"Jimmy lost his temper and decided to go launch a one-wolf assault on Noble Jones's place," Lacy said.

James spoke over his shoulder. "Snitch."

"Yeah, that sounds more like him," Phillip said, sighing. James turned to him and found him pinching the bridge of his nose as if warding off a stress headache. "Okay, so you two got a look inside. Which means I'm gonna have to figure out how to cover for anything they find that puts you there, and anything they find on the dead girl in the park. Great. That's just *great*." He pulled his hand away and spoke to James. "And what makes you think Noble Jones did this?"

"The girl in the park said his name as she was dying," James said. "Well, she tried to."

"She said 'no,'" Lacy said.

"But you also saw his reaction when I told him Alma was pointing to him as the necromancer," James said, turning to her. "He did not take it well."

"He was offended," Lacy argued. "Jimmy, c'mon. Wouldn't you be offended if someone accused you of something like that?"

"Also, we gotta look at the timeframe," Phillip said, crossing his arms in front of him. "If you two were with Jones when this shit went down, then he's off the hook unless he sent someone after them."

"Which he wouldn't do," Lacy said. "Nobody would. Not even Dracula if he was still around. Vampires are weird about contracts. Anything like this has to be approved, and you have to be able to provide a damn good case to the Elders of Night. It's all part of keeping the community low-key. Break the rules, they'll make sure any trace of you is wiped off the map. Painfully."

Phillip rolled his eyes. "Damn vampire politics. What's next?" His phone rang in his pocket. He pulled it out and answered. "Yeah? Shit. Okay. Yeah, I'm over here at my car. Blue Honda, me, girl with long brown curly hair, tall goofy fucker. Can't miss us." He put the phone back in his pocket and looked at James. "Hoyt's got something."

James turned back to the house just in time to see Hoyt crossing the street. He was shorter in person, stocky, his long black hair done into long braids that hung over his shoulders. He approached them, and James saw the dreamcatcher tattoo on his forearm and the small bird skull necklace he wore on the outside of his band shirt. He offered his hand to James. "Hoyt. Nice to meet you in person."

"James Coldstone," James said, shaking the man's hand.

Hoyt blinked, glanced at Phillip and Lacy, then back up at James. "I guess you wouldn't know about that."

"About what?"

"Giving your full name. Never do that."

"So I've heard. But my middle name is still a mystery, so I believe I'm safe."

"True, but your first and last name are still enough to open you up to some things." Hoyt turned to Phillip. "It's bad in there, Phillip. Real bad. I've never seen anything like it."

Phillip nodded as he pointed at James and Lacy. "Yeah, I heard. Raggedy Ann and Andy already got a look at it."

"Then you know that the hearts are all removed."

"No," James said. "We didn't get that close."

"Were they taken?" Lacy asked.

"No," Hoyt said. "They were splattered all over the place. Whoever or *what*ever did this was pissed off at these people."

James looked at Lacy, pushing the angry wolf back in his mind as it tried to rage again. "He toyed with them."

"That girl probably got let go for a reason," Lacy said. "She didn't just get away."

"Oh, and your boss called," Hoyt said to Phillip. "He wanted the details."

"Okay," Phillip said. "That's weird. He pulled us off this thing. We're supposed to leave out at sunrise."

Hoyt shrugged. "I don't know, man. He sounded like he was still working on it." He glanced over his shoulder, then back to Phillip and James. "I'll be able to tell more when I get everything back to my lab. If you want me to keep you up on things, I will."

"You could lose your job," Phillip said, shaking his head. "Don't do that."

Hoyt grinned. "Yeah, I think I'll be okay. Got something telling me that you and James need to see this thing through." He looked at James. "Call it voices on the wind."

What does that mean? James thought. *Is he a witch too?*

"Just Native American shit," Hoyt called over his shoulder as if he'd heard James thinking. "You were warned to keep your true names to yourselves."

Phillip drove James and Lacy back to the hotel. He sat down in front of his laptop while Lacy went to the bathroom to freshen up. James checked under the bed to make sure it was open so she would have somewhere to sleep that wasn't the bathtub.

"I still have access to the street cam footage through the department," Phillip said. "Lemme see what I can see."

James stood and sat down at the table across from Phillip. "Street cameras? Here?"

Phillip looked over the top of the screen at him. "Just because it's a historic area doesn't mean they aren't with the times. Let's just hope there's a camera near the house and it got a clear shot at our killer."

"Will it show up on camera if it's a vampire?" James asked.

Lacy's voice called from the other side of the bathroom door. "Why wouldn't it?"

Lacy stepped out of the bathroom, drying her hands on a towel before tossing it onto the bed. "We're solid matter," she said as she approached the table. "The whole 'no reflection' and 'can't be photographed' thing is bullshit. It was an easy way to film a scene when Bela Legosi couldn't be there at that moment to be Dracula."

Phillip's phone chimed. He looked at it and sighed. "Okay. So, Hoyt was able to find a body that actually still had a heart that wasn't mauled."

"He could've found that from the girl in the park," James said.

"He did. He placed her time of death exactly when you said." Phillip looked up from the phone and at Lacy. "The one he found at the house? The temp on it indicates that the victim died about two hours or so before you two went to Wormsloe Plantation."

"It only took Lacy and I around ten minutes to get there on foot," James said. He looked up at Lacy. "This isn't looking good."

"Noble would've had to get to the house, kill an entire coven of witches without getting blasted, get back to his place, shower, and change before we got there," Lacy said. "And he would have to know we were coming in order to know he had to be quick." She motioned at the screen. "Even as old as he is, those girls would've been able to get off a shot on him, and damage from a supernatural is harder to heal from. You know that."

James nodded and spoke to Phillip. "That also doesn't explain how that one girl was able to walk several blocks hours later while she bled out until she found us."

Phillip shrugged. "Could've already been dead. Noble kills them all, keeps her intact enough to raise her from the dead, and tells her to get attention on the house." He leaned back in his chair. "Most criminals wanna be caught. They want people to see what they've done. It's a gratification thing."

James shook his head. "I could hear her heart beating. She wasn't dead when she got to us."

"You two need to remember something," Lacy said, her tone surprisingly firm. "You're accusing a Master Vampire, one of the Elders of Night, by the way, of murder."

"The Elders of Night?" Phillip asked. "What the hell is the Elders of Night?"

"It's an ancient vampire council that dates all the way back to Count Dracula's rule over Transylvania and the Carpathian Mountains. They only have one or two original members left. Necromancy is an abomination in the vamp community and an unheard-of accusation when it comes to vampires practicing it. You'd better have proof, and I mean fucking dead-to-rights proof. And even *then*, you might still hit a wall with the vampire houses. It could bring down your agency. Hell, it could bring down the damn *FBI*."

James turned back to Phillip, whose eyes were wide as he stared at the computer screen. He leaned forward, tapped the mouse pad, and rubbed his eyes as he groaned. "Oh, fuck me, sonofabitch."

"What is it?" James said.

Phillip spun the laptop around on the table and looked up at Lacy as he spoke. "Is this him?" He hit the spacebar on the keyboard, and the black-and-white footage filled the screen and began playing. James saw the Abercorn house in the shot as a figure walked toward the front steps, clearly male, his back to the camera. He was a tall, bald black man in black jeans and a black button-up long-sleeved shirt with the sleeves rolled up. He climbed the steps calmly and stood at the doors for a moment before kicking them hard enough to take them mostly off the hinges. He entered in a flash, and the scene was still. Phillip skipped ahead by about ten minutes, then resumed playback just as the figure emerged from the house and calmly walked down the steps, this time clearly covered in blood and gore. He moved over to the camera, stared into it, and raised a human heart into view. He smashed it into the lens and the picture went to static.

James turned and looked at Lacy as she stood there, her mouth slightly open and her eyes wide as she stared at the digital snow on the laptop screen. "Will this work?"

14

The sunrise staved off the return trip to Noble Jones's home for a solid day. James was thankful that he'd have some time to rest before dealing with what could very well turn into a bad situation.

"We gotta worry about you giving Jones a heads up?" Phillip had asked as Lacy retired to her spot underneath James's bed.

"I'd be just as screwed as you," she'd said, her tone flat.

James had kept his mouth shut. He didn't envy her position, seeing a friend commit such a horrific act. He was all too familiar with the feeling of betrayal.

Phillip pulled to a stop at Wormsloe Plantation shortly after ten that evening, his headlights shining on the two vampire guards standing in front of the large gate. Both were armed in full tactical gear this time, and each carried a gigantic, heavy-caliber assault rifle. They stared at the car behind their masks, their round goggled eyes black and hiding any indication as to whether their eyes might be glowing red.

"Holy shit," Phillip muttered, his eyes wide. "James, what the ungodly *fuck* have you gotten me into?"

"Relax, Bacon," Lacy said from the backseat. "I'll talk to them. They know who we are now."

"They're carrying .50 CAL Brownings and you want me to relax?"

"We were just here," James said. "I'm sure things won't escalate should we approach this diplomatically."

Phillip looked at James, sidelong, glaring at him. "I sure hope the fuck not, James. Those assault rifles they're carrying? People don't just *carry* a goddamn .50 CAL Browning. People who *aren't* vampires have to fire the son of a bitch on the ground using a tripod because of the recoil. They brace them on turrets in fucking helicopters for mowing down the enemy from the sky, and the damn things fire armor-piercing rounds that are almost six-damn-inches long. One shot can blow a grown man in half and go through several cars up to a mile away, and those two are holding them like they're fuckin' pellet rifles. But yeah, I'll relax. You got this."

James smiled at him. "See? I knew you had confidence in me."

Phillip shook his head and rested it against the steering wheel as he muttered under his breath. "I'm going to die tonight."

One of the two guards approached the car, moving over to the passenger side. James rolled down the window as Phillip made a whimpering sound from the driver's seat. The large vampire stood still, seeming to take a moment to make sure James had a clear view of his not-inconsiderate machine gun.

This has got to be compensation for something, James thought automatically. The wolf panted in his mind with laughter as Big Easy leaned down slightly and spoke, his radioed voice from his mask giving James a *Star Wars* vibe. "You again? What's your business here?"

"We need to speak with Noble Jones," James said, keeping his tone professional and serious despite his urge to crack wise. "It's urgent."

"Tell me and I will deliver the message to Master Jones."

"Can't do that, sweetie," Lacy called from the backseat. "It's classified intel."

"I'll be the judge of that. Either state your business, or you and Lassie here can leave while we decide whether or not to take you out."

James heard Lacy mutter about her hatred of vampires while Phillip kept quiet, another small whimper escaping his lips.

James nodded, biting his lip. "Lassie. That's cute. Tell me something: let's say that I had some information that only Jones should be privy to, and it could mean the difference between whether or not he gets to keep his status. And since telling you could get me in more trouble than I care to be in, I decide to just turn away. Then when everything escalates and Noble Jones loses Wormsloe, his wealth, his power, and his legacy, he finds out that I had the information he needed to use as a leg in the fight."

"James," Phillip mumbled from the driver's seat. "Please don't get us killed. I'll be pissed as hell."

"I will be forced to tell him that one of his security guards prevented me from giving him the information he needed to avoid complicating an already complicated matter," James said, ignoring Phillip. He gestured at the gate. "Or, you could just let us in, let Noble Jones know we're here to speak with him on a personal matter, and prevent a serious situation that none of us wants to be in."

Big Easy just stared at James with his soulless, goggled eyes, his mask giving away nothing as to what the heavily armed vampire was thinking. He spoke after a few seconds, his tone clipped. "Fine." He called to his partner. "Open the gate. They need to see Jones right now. Tell the rest to stand down. Blue Honda Civic."

The other guard nodded and started to push the gate open. Big Easy turned back to James. "Drive slow, park where they tell you. Someone will escort you in."

James nodded and looked at Phillip, who began to pull forward, his body stiff and his hands at ten and two on the steering wheel as they passed through the gate. James overheard Big Easy's partner on the radio telling the rest of the compound to stand down as he rolled his window back up. "Well then, that was fun."

"I'm impressed, Jimmy," Lacy said from the backseat. "You sounded all official and stuff."

"I do have my moments."

James saw her in the rearview mirror as she spoke to Phillip. "Bacon, you can unclench now."

Phillip let out a long sigh accompanied by a graveled groan, not taking his eyes off the road as he spoke. "Jesus Christ, how the hell are we alive?"

"You act like you've never been in a situation involving guns before," James said.

"Excuse the fuck out of me," Phillip snapped angrily. "I'm the only human on a compound filled with vampires armed with goddamned cannons, and I'm about to go arrest their boss. But that's okay, I might be overreacting."

"I'm glad you can acknowledge that about yourself," James said.

Phillip sighed. "I need a vacation."

They pulled up to the house after a few minutes, one of Jones's guards motioning them to park in a certain spot near the gazebo at the bottom of the steps that led up to the porch. Jones was already standing there, his arms crossed in front of him and his expression unentertained.

"He looks thrilled," Phillip said, his tone dripping with sarcasm. "Great. I get to get killed by a master vampire while cruising with my idiot best friend and the Tick. Just what I've always wanted."

"Let me do the talking," Lacy said. "He's known me longest. I can reason with him."

"Go for it," Phillip said. "Anything to keep my blood *inside* my body."

James and Lacy both got out of the car as Jones started walking toward them. Two vampire SWAT guards were with him, both carrying what James figured were AK-47s. *Keep the heavy artillery in the front,* he thought. *Smart. It's what I would do.*

"Twice in one week?" Jones asked as he approached. "Lacy Faulkner, you either miss me that much or you grew a set of balls I was unaware of when we were together."

James bristled at the comment. The wolf growled hard enough to make a small noise in the back of James's throat. Jones looked at him with a raised eyebrow. *Cool it,* James thought at the wolf. *We're outnumbered.*

"Noble," Lacy said. "We need to talk." She glanced at his guards, then back at him. "Privately."

Jones looked past her and at the car. James glanced over his shoulder and saw Phillip in the driver's seat staring back at them. Phillip crossed himself, and James could see his eye twitch.

"Why did you bring a human here?" Jones asked. "Is it dinner time already?"

"No," Lacy said. "He's actually a Fed. He's with me and Jimmy."

James turned back to Jones, who was sizing him up. Jones stepped closer to him until their faces were inches apart. "And you? I suppose you came back to throw more accusations at me?"

"Fine," James said. "We can do it here."

"*Jimmy,*" Lacy hissed next to him.

"Alma has been murdered," James continued, ignoring her. "All of the Abercorn witches are dead."

Jones clenched his jaw. James saw his eyes glow red slightly as his fangs started to elongate. "And you came here to insult me again? Call me a murderer and a blasphemer?"

"I'm hoping to clear you," James said, standing his ground. "Because right now it doesn't look good, and we're hoping you have an explanation."

Jones blinked in surprise. James kept talking. "Lacy trusts you. She's known you longest. That is good enough for me to give you a chance to explain what we need to show you. All three of us will accompany you to your study." He motioned at the car. "But Phillip is going to leave with us tonight. I want your word, or we turn over what we have to people who are better equipped to deal with you."

Jones stepped back. "Anything you say to me can be said in front of my men. They are bound to me and will not act without my direct orders." He nodded to the car. "And your human is safe."

James turned and waved Phillip over. Phillip's eyes widened again, and he shook his head. James waved him over again, then heard the telltale sound of Phillip locking the car doors. James sighed. "Excuse me." He pulled his phone out and called Phillip.

"There is no way in *hell* I'm getting out of this car," Phillip said as soon as he answered. "Motherfucker looked at me like I'm dinner."

"He's given his word that you'll be safe," James said. "And we need the cam video."

"I'll send it to you."

"Fine. How do I open it?"

"You click on it."

"I don't have a mouse for my phone."

"You have a finger, you dumbass."

James looked at Lacy, then Jones. He walked away from them a bit and spoke low into the phone. "I told him you'd be part of the conversation."

Phillip cursed and grumbled. "Goddammit, James. If this wasn't such a touchy-ass situation." He grunted. "*Fine.*" He hung up and got out of the car. James put his phone away as Phillip approached him. "If I get killed, I'm blaming you."

"I'll sing at your funeral."

"I'll kick your ass from the grave." They started back toward Lacy and Jones. Phillip pulled his ID out and showed it and his badge to Jones as he spoke in his formal "cop voice." "Agent Brown, SCU." Jones nodded, and Phillip put the badge away. "You're suspected of murder, and Miss Faulkner is vouching for you. Can you tell me your whereabouts at approximately 10 pm last night?"

"I was here," Jones said immediately. He paused, and James saw a slight flash of uncertainty cross the man's face. "My men can vouch for me."

"Based on what I know of vampire social norms, these men will also lie for you," Phillip said.

Lacy covered her face with her hands and muttered. "Oh, fuck. Why didn't you just let me handle this?" She pulled her hands away and spoke to Jones. "He's not trying to insult you or insinuate anything, Noble. I promise." She turned to Phillip and whispered to him through gritted teeth. "Easy."

"I apologize," Phillip said, swallowing hard. James could smell his friend starting to sweat. "But it's normal behavior for vampires, and I assure you I am not passing judgment."

"Make your point or leave," Jones snapped.

"Think hard," Phillip said as he pulled his phone from his pocket. "I want to show you this video, then I want you to answer my question again."

James watched him hand the phone over to Jones. Jones took it and tapped the screen. He watched the video play, and James could see his expression change from irritation to disbelief. His mouth opened slightly, his head shaking. "This is lies," he said, thrusting the phone back at Phillip. "I was not there."

"The camera says differently," Phillip said. "I'm asking again: where were you during that timeframe?"

Jones stammered. "I...I was here." He looked down, then back up at them. "Wasn't I?" James could see something in his face that he never thought he'd see in the few master vampires he'd met: fear and disbelief.

"Noble, what's wrong?" Lacy asked.

"It's...all," Jones said, shaking his head and putting the heel of his palm to his temple. "I was here. I *know* I was here." He turned to her. "Lacy, what is this?"

Lacy breathed deeply. "Noble, I need you to stay calm."

"I'm going to ask you to come with us," Phillip said. "We can talk about this at the bureau."

Jones's SWAT guards started at them, raising their guns and aiming them at James while a few more came from the shadows and covered Lacy and Phillip. Noble Jones raised his hands up at them, palms out as he spoke. "Halt! Lower your weapons!"

The guards stopped in their tracks and lowered their firearms reluctantly. James heard Phillip breathe a sigh of relief, and Lacy just muttered under her breath. "God, could this go any worse?"

"These people have evidence against me," Jones said to his men. "If I committed a crime, I need to pay for it. I will go peacefully, and I will not have it reported to the council that I resisted arrest in the face of damning evidence." He turned to Phillip. "It is not necessary to cuff me. I will go peacefully. But I insist you do so anyway because I allow you to as a sign of good faith." He held his arms up, baring his wrists.

Phillip held his ground, maintaining his stoic professional demeanor as Jones stared at him. James looked between the two, then nudged Phillip. "I believe that is your cue."

Phillip exhaled loudly as if he'd been holding his breath the whole time. He pulled a set of cuffs out and addressed Jones. "These are made of silver, just so you're aware."

"I would expect nothing less," Jones said. He glowered at Phillip. "I assume that I have rights?"

"Rights? Yeah." Phillip began reading Noble Jones his Miranda Rights as James looked at Lacy. She shook her head, then motioned for him to follow her back to the car.

"This is a bad idea, Jimmy," she said. "I know you and Phillip have a job to do, but goddamn. Jones is *connected*. The Elders of Night will be all over this."

"You saw the video," James said. "We don't have much choice."

"Jimmy, I wanna see that video again," Lacy said. "Something was off. I can't put my finger on it, but I know there's something that isn't lining up."

"Okay," James said. "I'll have Phillip send it to you."

She looked up at him, and he felt his heart beat a little harder as he gazed into her eyes. "You believe me, right? I know he wouldn't have killed those people."

"I believe that you see something we don't," James said, trying to be careful with his wording. He didn't know if he could handle her not trusting him. "If I can help you, I will."

She smiled and nodded. "I know."

Phillip escorted Jones up to the car and waved them aside as he opened the door to the backseat and helped Jones in. He shut the door and turned to James. "I have a master vampire in the back of my car, a pissed-off vampire militia with enough firepower to level the state staring at me, and I'm not too proud to admit that I peed a little when they rushed us with damn AK-47s aimed at our heads while that big blood-suckin' motherfucker stepped up on me and looked at me like I'm his munchies for the next football game. Can we go now?"

15

The thirty-minute drive to the Savannah FBI Offices was quiet and awkward. James could feel the tension in the small space, including from the wolf as it stayed ready, its ire still directed at the vampire in the backseat next to the only vampire the animal liked. Phillip stayed focused on the road, his knuckles turning white from gripping the wheel, and James could tell it was taking everything in his best friend not to scream.

Baby steps, James thought to himself with a smirk. *He's doing well.*

They got to the bureau without incident or speaking, and Jones cooperated with Phillip's every command as they made their way into the building through the rear entrance. Phillip led them to the interrogation rooms, gave Jones over to the officer guarding the door to Room B, and motioned for James and Lacy to follow him into the observation room next door. The room was dark and plain, with some recording equipment and monitors that displayed the interrogation room from a bird's eye view. A younger agent sat at the desk monitoring the equipment, ignoring them, his large headphones covering his ears. James watched through the two-way mirror as the officer sat Jones down at the table, offered him water, and left the room, shutting the door behind him.

"Is the kid going to be an issue?" Lacy asked, gesturing at the tech.

"Nope," Phillip said. "It's his job to not hear anything but what goes on in that room." He turned to James. "And your big ass is coming in there with me."

James shrugged. "I have no problem with that, but I'm not sure that I have much to add to the conversation."

"You don't," Phillip said. "You're in there in case he decides to stop being so cooperative and wants to make me his chew toy."

"He won't do that," Lacy said, interjecting. "If he says he'll play ball, he'll play ball. But he can't control how the Elders of Night will react to him being here. This could be a major fuck-up if we aren't careful."

Phillip shook his head. "Seems like James and I only operate on major fuck-ups. What would be new about this one?"

James nodded. "He makes a fair point."

Lacy rolled her eyes. "You two really are a couple of dumbasses. I wanna get a good look at Abercorn before I become the thing under James's bed for the day."

"I'll call you if something comes up here," James said. "And Phillip will send the video shortly."

Lacy nodded and left the room. James felt the stress in his chest growing, starting to make his breath shorten. He needed an outlet, needed to lighten the mood before he went crazy from everything weighing in on him.

Phillip spoke softly. "Showtime."

James took the opportunity. "I'm the bad cop."

"What?"

"The bad cop. The one who yells a lot and slams his hand on the table."

Phillip rubbed his eyes. "Oh god, please stop."

"Stop what?"

"Being an idiot."

James entered the room and stood against the wall facing the table, the two-way mirror behind him as he crossed his arms in front of him and watched Jones steadily. Phillip closed the door and sat down at the table, opening a file he'd brought in. He casually pulled several crime scene photos from the folder and placed them on the table in front of Jones. Each one was in full color, showing the graphic detail of the carnage at Abercorn. James kept his eyes on Jones, refusing to look at photos of young girls torn to pieces.

Jones looked at the photos, and James saw a hint of revulsion on the vampire's face. Jones looked up at Phillip. "What is this?"

"This is the little surprise you left for us to clean up at 432 Abercorn Street," Phillip said.

"You seem to have grown some confidence since our earlier meeting," Jones said, giving Phillip a smirk.

"Silver," Phillip said, indicating Jones's handcuffs that were shackled to the table. "Amazing how it pretty much renders vampires useless if they touch it."

"I've noticed," Jones said, the smirk fading. He nodded at the photos. "They don't help with nausea, unfortunately."

"We have you on camera going into 432 Abercorn, then leaving covered in blood shortly after. Time of death was only a couple of hours before James Coldstone and Lacy Faulkner came to talk to you the first time." Phillip clasped his hands in front of him, his elbows on the table. "I've got you on First Degree Murder. Multiple counts. And a Master Vampire at that. I could add in all kinds of other charges to fatten it up, but why? More paperwork for me, and more headaches with lawyers."

"The Elders of Night should be the ones looking into this," Jones said. "Not some human-run law enforcement agency with delusions of grandeur."

"I'll be straight with you," Phillip said. "Never heard of the Elders of Night until a couple of hours ago."

"Does your agency not educate its people on who they're policing?"

Phillip snorted. "Dude, all I know is it goes bump in the night, and we take it down if it's up to some shady bullshit." He tapped the photos. "Nothin' shady about this. Just a plain-old massacre. Still qualifies."

"I have no memory of this. I do not kill. Not like this." He gave a photo of a disemboweled girl a look before averting his eyes from it. "This is disgusting. Please put them away."

Phillip picked up the photo of the girl and held it up to Jones's face. "Azalea Greene. Sixteen-year-old runaway. Traces of heroin in her system indicated that she was a user. They were low, showing she'd been clean for almost seven days. Had already called her parents and told them she was in rehab." He put down the photo and picked up another as Jones grimaced. "Daisey Clark. Twenty-three, disappeared from home after she found her mother dead at the hands of mom's boyfriend, who also happened to have a hobby of sneaking into Daisey's room at night. They found the guy and arrested him, and this is how they found Daisey."

Phillip put the photo down. "You told James and Lacy that Alma was into dark magic and screwing around with evil magic." He sat back and grunted. "Looks to me like she was helping these girls find their way."

James saw Jones cringing at the sight of the photos, trying to look away, his face twisted in revulsion. *That's not the reaction of someone who had no issue slaughtering a house full of people,* he thought. The wolf chuffed inside, seeming to agree. James sighed and stood up from his position against the wall. "You'll have to excuse my partner," he said, speaking a little louder than necessary. He patted Phillip on the back as he sat down next to him, leaning back in the chair casually. "I'd asked to be the bad cop, and he stole my thunder."

Phillip glared at him sidelong and spoke low. "James, I'm warning you."

James chuckled and pointed at Phillip as he spoke to Jones. "Such a kidder."

Jones did not look amused. "First, I am berated with photos of innocent young girls that I am accused of slaughtering, and now I'm being patronized by a mutt?" He looked back at Phillip. "This is not going to end well for you."

"Is that a threat?" Phillip asked, bristling.

"Not a physical one," Jones said. "And no, threats are meaningless. I'm a man of my word."

"Lacy believes you," James said, leaning forward, cutting off Phillip as he was about to respond to Jones again. "That, alone, is good enough for me to question what I saw on that video. But it doesn't negate the fact that we have you on video going into the house and leaving covered in blood. And it doesn't help that you were obviously offended at Alma's accusation that you had something to do with Kathleen Wilson's murder." He paused, waiting to see Jones's reaction. The master vampire sat still, stoic. James could tell he was holding something back. James continued. "Lacy told me that you don't lie. So, tell me the truth. Did you go there to kill Alma and her coven?"

Jones blinked, breathed out, and James saw him relax slightly. "I don't know," he said, his voice almost a whisper. He shook his head. "I don't remember going there. I don't remember being anywhere near there." His eyes moved to the photos of the dead girls from the house.

Phillip spoke up. "What do you remember, Mr. Jones? Can you walk me through your day?" He paused. "Er...night?"

"I woke up as soon as the sun went down," Jones said. "Ordered my men to canvas the property for stragglers who may have lingered past the touring site's closing hour and make sure they were safely escorted off. Bathed. Fed on a new blood donor."

"Blood donor?"

"I refuse to call them slaves," Jones said. "They've consented. They are fully aware of what they've signed up for. I can show you the paperwork."

"Right," Phillip said, waving it off. "Anyway?"

"Shortly after that, Mr. Coldstone and Miss Faulkner came over."

"We didn't get there until after eleven," James said. "You say you got up at sunset, which was four hours prior. At your vampire speed, that gave you ample time to commit the murders and return home to clean up." He leaned forward. "I must ask you: did you kill Alma and her coven?"

Jones looked at him, confused, shaking his head. It wasn't a denial.

The door to the room opened, and a shrewd-looking older woman with large thick-framed glasses and a sharp-looking business suit marched in, her expression terse and her silver hair pulled back in a fierce bun. She spoke with authority and a slight Southern accent, but her tone was enough to give James some pause on the idea of cracking wise at her. "My name is Angela Warren. I represent Noble Jones and his estate. Why is my client being questioned without me?"

Phillip stood and faced her. "He didn't ask for a lawyer."

"As a member of the Elders of Night, he does not have to," Warren said. "The council can impose legal counsel on a member in the event that accusations against the member can and will directly affect the counsel." She turned to Jones. "Do not answer any more questions, Mr. Jones." She rounded on Phillip. "Your supervisor is outside and would like a word. This interview is over."

James looked at the door and saw Agent Smith standing there, his expression hard, his eyes steel and locked on both him and Phillip. *Oh shit,* James thought. *So that's what he looks like when he's angry.*

"Outside," Smith said curtly before turning and walking out into the hall.

Phillip sighed. "This is going to suck."

A s unprofessional as it is, I believe Agent Kimble's assessment of you two is astute," Smith said the second James and Phillip were in the hall. "You two are, indeed, *fucking morons!*" He shouted the last two words, his face twisted in anger. He cleared his throat and obviously forced his calm and cool demeanor back into place. "I will need an explanation as to why Noble Jones is here, please."

"We have him on video at the scene of a crime," Phillip said. "He's suspected of killing a total of four people."

"Do you have him actually committing the crime, Agent Brown?"

"We have him entering the house and leaving covered in blood. And carrying a human heart."

"And did you think to send this over to the agency?" James saw Phillip open his mouth to answer before Smith cut him off. "No, you did not. Because that would reveal that you were working on this issue despite direct orders that the investigation was over."

"We had good reason to keep going," James said.

"Mr. Coldstone, you are the last person who should speak on this matter," Smith said, his tone acidic. "You were brought in to follow orders and to have a leash on you in a capacity that would benefit the agency. Your opinion is not wanted, nor do I care that you even have one."

James felt something in his mind snap, his temper flaring as he clenched his fists. "Brought in? That's what you call the bullshit you pulled with me?"

"James, tone it down," Phillip said, his tone warning.

James ignored him. "You threatened to dox me. Threatened to bring a goddamn war to my hometown. You *forced* me to join. Needlessly, I might add. And I'm supposed to be thankful?" He gave Smith a look as if the man was covered in raw sewage. "I'd tell you to cram it up your ass, but I'm not entirely certain it would fit next to the stick." He heard Phillip mutter "Oh, Jesus, *fuck*," under his breath, the last word stretching out for a couple of seconds.

Smith's nostrils flared, his face turning a slight shade of red as he bristled, staring back at James. He kept his composure, but his tone was ice cold. "I had to know that we could keep some manner of control over you, prove to the FBI director that you could be trusted. Being the first supernatural to work for the SCU, that was a prime element of your employment."

"You pronounced 'coercement' wrong," James said just as icily.

"I admit that thinking a sloppy, entitled, irresponsible little house mutt would be worth the effort and time of the SCU is my mistake," Smith shot back. "I am not perfect, after all. I may need to ensure that my next acquisition can't be bothered with anything beyond playing fetch when some random little *brat* is snatched up because he was too *stupid* to keep her out of harm's way in the first place."

James grit his teeth. "You shut the fuck up."

Smith kept pushing. "Have you ever let it into that underdeveloped canine brain of yours that the entirety of your little jaunt through that innocent girl's yard during one of your moonlit strolls led those people to her in the first place?"

James felt the wolf surge forward, his eyes turning yellow as his body tensed in rage. Phillip stepped in front of him, his arms out as if blocking him from rushing Smith. "James, *stop!*" At his friend's order, James gathered his will and pushed the wolf back just as his muscles and bones had begun to move and shift.

Phillip spoke over his shoulder at Smith. "Over the line, sir." He looked back to James. "You do this here, you fuck us both, and you throw everything we've done for Mindy Robertson and Kathleen Wilson down the toilet. Stand. *Down.*"

James pushed the wolf all the way back in his mind, the beast still growling, longing to come forward again and tear Agent Smith to pieces. He kept his eyes on Smith, his jaw still clenched, his body still rigid and tense.

Phillip turned to Smith. "James screwed up, but it had nothing to do with what happened with that little girl, sir. And he was the one who wanted to keep the case here going because he knew something was up." He motioned at the closed interrogation room door. "We have Noble Jones on camera walking into 432 Abercorn Street. We have him leaving covered in blood. We have him carrying a human heart in his hand. That alone is more than enough evidence."

"Lacy says you called her in," James said, keeping his tone even. "I find it interesting that she knew exactly where to find me and what we were looking for."

Agent Smith glared at him. "I'm quite certain I've no idea what you're going on about."

James stared back at him, and the wolf nudged his consciousness on the inside as it mewled slightly. He felt its worry, its disappointment.

Worst of all, he could tell that Agent Smith was telling the truth.

Smith straightened his tie and brushed off the sleeves on his suit jacket. "Noble Jones is a member of the Elders of Night. They are *the* council. His assistant at Wormsloe notified the council immediately after you two took him into custody. Naturally, a few phone calls have been made, including the chair of the council. And the President of the United States, who was quite irritated at being pulled out of her bed at this hour to have to deal with an issue like this when her plate is already fairly full." He gave Phillip a haughty smile. "The pressure is now back on *my* shoulders, and I am well aware of how to mend this issue."

16

J ames stared out the window, not seeing the other cars in the lot
across from the hotel. His mind kept replaying what'd happened at
the bureau. The engine still ran, the air conditioning set low
enough to still have its steady hum in the quiet vehicle.

"We're so fucked," Phillip said from the driver's seat. James looked at
him and saw him leaning over with his forehead resting on the steering
wheel.

"I feel quite liberated," he said.

Phillip sat up and glared at him. "James, we just got fired. I'm out of
law enforcement completely. You understand what that means?"

"I do," James said, nodding. "It means we'll have more time to catch up
on reruns of Golden Girls."

Phillip blinked. "Jokes? We just got canned, my career is over, and
you're making jokes?"

"It's my defense mechanism. And Dorothy is simply savage."

"It's you bein' a fuckin' child."

"Tomato, to-mah-to."

Phillip sighed and sat back in the driver's seat, covering his face with
his hands as he let out one of his long, signature groans. "Now what the
fuck am I going to do?"

James shook his head, pushing away his urge to make another wisecrack. While he didn't care one way or the other about his employment with the SCU, he knew that law enforcement was Phillip's career. It was all he knew. "I'm sorry. Truly. I didn't mean to cost you your job."

Phillip shook his head, pulling his hands away from his face. "You didn't. Lacy warned us that arresting a master vampire was messy. We didn't listen. Simple as that." He looked at James. "I can probably appeal, but I won't lie to myself and believe that it'll work."

James nodded. "Why does the SCU want to shut down Kathleen Wilson's case so badly?"

"Probably because Noble Jones is connected to it," Phillip said as if it was common knowledge. "Can't say I'm surprised."

James raised an eyebrow. "Interesting."

"It's politics, James," Phillip said. "People think law enforcement is a bunch of heroes out there to make sure there's truth and justice, and that's true for some of us. But leadership is all politics." He sighed. "Smith probably got heat from whoever this council chair is. Chances are the guy, or woman, is also a sitting representative in the House or Senate. Otherwise, they wouldn't have that kind of influence on the director of a Federal agency."

"Enough heat to remove a werewolf he blackmailed into coming on in the first place." James shook his head. "That doesn't add up. He was adamant that I come in. He did everything he could to make sure that I couldn't say no."

"I don't ask questions when it comes to the fucked-up way leadership works," Phillip said. "If there's shit going down behind the scenes, let them deal with it. Not my damn circus."

James's phone chimed. He looked at the message alert and saw a text from Lacy. *I'll be in before sunrise. Heard about you and Phillip being canned.*

James texted her back. *I'm more concerned about Phillip on the matter.*

I'll bet.

Get anything off the video?

James's phone rang instantly, Lacy's photo showing up on the home screen. He answered and put her on speaker. "Sorry, Jimmy. That question is way too loaded for texting."

"Do tell," James said.

"We aren't on the case anymore, James," Phillip said. "We're not even with the agency anymore. This is illegal."

"Hey, Bacon," Lacy said over the speaker. "So's cursing over the phone.

It's a fucking FCC fucking violation and shit." She paused. "See? No one cares. Fuck it."

James smiled a little at Phillip's unentertained expression as he responded to Lacy. "A fourth fuck would've fit nicely in your 'no one cares' statement."

"Fuck that. I'm a lady."

"Touché."

"Just tell us what you got," Phillip said, his tone humorless.

"Okay, so Noble went into the house, and he left covered in blood and carrying someone's heart. I talked to a couple of his human assistants, and there's no doubt: he did it."

James noticed her tone was conversational, a stark contrast to her more forlorn manner back at the agency when they were discussing Jones's involvement in the murders. "I'm to gather from your tone of voice that this is Tuesday?"

"If I thought he was guilty, I'd be a little more upset."

"Wait, what?" Phillip said. "You just damn well said he did it."

"Right, but he's not guilty."

Phillip sighed loudly. "This should be good."

"His eyes when he came up to the camera afterward tell on him," Lacy said. "They didn't look...he just wasn't there. I can't really explain it, but the Noble who looked into that camera was not the Noble I know. I think he was being controlled."

James looked at Phillip. "That may answer our question as to whether or not vampires can be controlled by a necromancer."

"We're dead," Lacy said. "Only difference is we've got enough super-natural spark crammed up our asses to keep us mobile and going. We drink living blood because dead blood coagulates and can't sustain hemoglobin. Everything else functions just fine, including our hearts. That's why a stake through the heart fucks us over but good."

"Then every damn vampire in the city is a potential threat," Phillip said. "No offense."

"None taken," Lacy said. "And you're right."

James felt the urge from the wolf matching the instinct he already felt. "We can't leave."

"Are you nuts?" Phillip said. "James, we're done here. Kathleen Wilson and the necromancer aren't our circuses anymore. Not our monkeys."

"We've come this far," James argued. "We have information now that the SCU doesn't."

"That would make us vigilantes, James."

"If that's what it takes." James sat up straight, crossing his arms in front of his puffed-out chest. "Justice cannot be restricted by the law."

Phillip rubbed his temple and muttered. "Oh god."

Lacy's voice was low over the speaker. "What the hell is he...?"

"Just wait for it."

James pressed on, adopting his best superhero impersonation. "Super Wolf defends the People, not the laws that could protect the unjust and the villainous!" He flinched as Phillip wailed him on the shoulder with his customized rolled newspaper. James started to speak again, but Phillip pointed the end of the paper at his nose, giving him a warning glare.

"At least you two aren't boring," Lacy said over the phone, sighing. "Bacon, you've still got that video. You two watch it again and you'll see what I mean. I'm on my way back to the hotel. Sun will be up soon, so I'll already be under the bed by the time you get here." The call ended.

"Do you still have it?" James said, relaxing as he put his superhero persona aside.

"Yeah," Phillip said. He reached into the backseat and pulled his tablet out of his bag. He opened a file and pulled the video up. "*Fuck*, I'm tired." He muttered as the footage started playing.

"Yet you haven't given up and passed out," James said. "I must say I admire your endurance."

"Blow me."

"And your insistence on being upbeat and positive."

"Just watch the video, dumbass."

They watched again as Noble Jones crossed Abercorn and entered the house. Phillip went to skip the video again, but James held his hand up.

"Just in case we missed something."

He was thankful there was no audio. He saw blood spatter against the windows, and the lights flicker as lamps and candles were knocked over. The girl he and Lacy had encountered at the statue stumbled out the front door, her injuries and blood loss already affecting her. Jones stood in the doorway. She looked back at him, panicked, and staggered quickly off into the night.

"He sent her out," James said. "I thought she escaped."

"Goddamn," Phillip muttered. "Just a kid."

"Here he comes," James said, pointing at the screen. Noble Jones zipped up to the camera. "Pause it."

Phillip hit the pause icon, Jones's face frozen onscreen. James looked closer and stared at the digital image. At first glance, Jones appeared cocky, arrogant. The gesture said: "I did it. Come get me if you can." But there was something else.

"Look at his eyes," James said.

Phillip squinted a little as he moved his face slightly closer to the screen. Jones's eyes were only half-open, the skin around his bottom eyelid dark and sagged. "Huh. He looks tired. Damn, he looks like he's *on* something."

"Exactly. The Noble Jones we met was alert and clear-headed. I'm fairly certain narcotics have no effect on vampires," James said. "No more than they do on werewolves."

"Which is why you can go through a keg of beer without even gettin' buzzed," Phillip said. "And didn't you say Lacy could toss 'em back too?"

"She told me once that she chugged a fifth of whiskey only to find that she had to pee. A lot."

Phillip looked at James. "Vampires pee?"

"They also sweat when the sun starts to burn them."

"Huh." Phillip unbuckled his seatbelt and opened the car door. "Let's go look at something." He got out, and James followed suit, closing the door and falling into step beside Phillip as they made their way over to the Waving Girl statue. James could smell the early morning scents of fresh baked goods and breakfast wafting over from one of the eateries near the hotel. The sun was just beginning to rise, the dark sky beginning a light fade into the dull grayish blue that preceded the sunrise. A small group of blue herons glided in a formation over the river, and seagulls flocked around the walk as they seemed to enjoy the short time they had before humans took it over for the day.

James also caught the scent of blood as they neared the statue. He saw the young girl slumped against her in his memory, blood flowing from her wounds and streaming down the statue's form before pooling at the base. He couldn't get the teen's face out of his mind, her eyes pleading as she struggled to speak, her body giving in to her injuries. The wolf pushed his senses open to get the scent and move beyond the chemicals the police had used to clean up the scene. James started to push the beast back, then stopped himself when he realized that the animal wanted her scent for a reason.

"They found her here," Phillip said as they approached. "You said this was where she ran into you and Lacy?"

James nodded.

"James, that's a hell of a walk for someone who just got mortally wounded by a vampire." Phillip pulled his phone out. "Hoyt's email said she was bleeding internally. Also says she's the only victim still in one piece."

James started to work things out in his head as the wolf continued to process the girl's scent from the unseen traces of blood still on the statue. "She knew to come here. Knew that I would be here."

"It could've been anyone, James," Phillip said. "Playin' Devil's Advocate here. What if it hadn't been you?"

"Who else would be here that time of night? And it occurs to me that Abercorn is a considerable walk from here even for someone who isn't injured and dying."

"You ain't wrong," Phillip said. He held his phone up. "I put it into the GPS here. Says it's a twenty-nine-minute walk from here to the Abercorn house. Someone making that kind of walk, under those circumstances, is doing it for a reason."

"Vampire suggestion could be that powerful," James said. "Remember Cookie from Westenra Island?"

"You think Noble Jones told her to come talk to you specifically?" Phillip shook his head. "Still doesn't answer how he knew you were here in the first place."

"I don't believe he did. But Agatha has seen me here almost every time."

Phillip's eyes widened. "Holy shit."

James nodded. "Indeed." He motioned at the statue. "And the wolf has the girl's scent now. She was terrified, but she was determined enough to walk until she got to me. Either Noble Jones had a moment of clarity—"

Phillip jumped in, finishing the thought. "Or he was told to send her to you to help point the finger at him."

"Agatha may very well be our necromancer." James looked away, his eyes searching the water as if he might see Agatha out there or standing somewhere nearby listening. He turned back to Phillip. "We can't leave. Not now."

"The SCU is wanting these murders swept under the rug in a bad way," Phillip said. "Bad enough to kill the case and fire us for bringing in a suspect, status be damned." He shook his head. "That only happens if there's a good indication that everything is gonna go sideways. It's a political tactic. Smack the hornets' nest and take it out, but only if you can be far enough away to not get stung. Accidentally smack it too close, you better run like hell." He faced James. "We'd be acting on our own. You understand that? If we whack the nest, we'll get stung no matter what we do."

"If we leave, more people will die," James said. "Whatever Agatha's up to, she'll achieve it."

"We don't know if it'll be a catastrophic event if she does," Phillip said.

James bristled. "You're willing to sacrifice someone's life based on that?"

Phillip held his hands up as if fending James off. "Whoa, hell no. Devil's Advocate, remember? Hell no, I don't think it's worth a life. But we've gotta be practical here, James. Like 'em or not, the SCU at least gave us some protection if something went the wrong way. We don't have that anymore. We'd be at this all on our own."

"The last time we acted on our own, we brought down a human trafficking ring."

Phillip sighed. "James, the SCU was involved in that from the word go. And you know that."

James stopped himself from responding. Phillip had a point. The SCU had made sure that the Rock Hill Police put Phillip on the case when Wade Anderson was killing people left and right. They'd made sure that Phillip could travel with him, made sure that contacting and getting support from the local law enforcement in Charleston and Jacksonville, and the Coast Guard. This was different.

"A recent graduate on her first job was murdered for looking at the wrong documents," James said, standing his ground. "A teenage girl walked in the dark while bleeding out to make sure that we knew that Noble Jones murdered her and her coven before she died right where we're standing." He set his jaw, ignored the fatigue that was working its way through his body as the sun slowly rose in the distance. "Leave if you want. I don't want you to do anything you don't think is right. But you know that leaving is wrong, and I can't finish what we started without you."

Phillip sighed and narrowed his eyes at James. "Quit with the sap-talk, Scooby. I'm not leaving. I'm making sure you get that we're about to fuck ourselves sideways with no lube by staying here and figuring this shit out."

James nodded. "I understand."

Phillip paused and raised an eyebrow. "You rehearse that speech long?"

James shrugged. "Once or twice in my head while they were debriefing you."

"Putz."

"I thought it was a good speech."

"It was. You're still a putz."

17

Since they didn't have to go into the bureau office to check in and debrief, James and Phillip opted to sleep in until around noon. James was up before Phillip, his sleep fitful due to his mind trying to make sense of everything. If Agatha was the necromancer, and it was definitely looking like she was, then he'd have to be careful with his approach. He couldn't kill her in broad daylight, and he couldn't exactly have Phillip arrest her, either. Phillip had been abundantly clear about that.

"That shit only happens on television," he'd said. "The two disgraced heroes marching the villain in and demanding their jobs back? Right. They'll turn her loose under technicalities because they'd never be able to convict her, and we'd end up being charged with impersonating Federal agents."

James decided to let Phillip sleep and headed out to walk down to the park. He wanted to take in the sun a little, smell the fresh air, and listen to the river while he tried to clear his head.

He knew that he'd be too busy trying to lure Agatha out to do any of that.

It was bright outside, the sun already high in the sky as he walked along the waterway. He stopped and stared at the Waving Girl statue, the girl looking excited and happy at the sight of whoever she was eternally gesturing to, welcoming a loved one or seeing someone off. She was an inanimate object, completely unaware that a teenage girl had bled all over her and died at her feet.

James turned away from her, unable to look at her without seeing that poor girl's face in his mind. He rested his arms on the railing and stared out over the river instead. The wolf mewled at him. *I know, I can't look at her either,* James thought. *We need to focus on finding Agatha.*

The wolf growled and sent him a feeling of distrust. It flashed the image of the tattoo he'd seen behind her ear at him along with it. The symbol irked him again, stirred him to try and remember where he'd seen it before.

A shield. Bats. A large D in the center. His immediate reaction was to associate it with Dracula. He'd seen similar symbols in old Dracula films or when Phillip was playing video games, but this symbol was a little different.

James didn't doubt that Dracula was real. He'd been subject to the curse of Dracula's ring, the trinket forcing the change in him and eventually separating the wolf from his own consciousness. But Lacy had destroyed it.

And Dracula had been dead for hundreds of years.

"Wow, dude. When you brood, you *brood.*"

James started at the sound of Hoyt's voice as the ME strolled up to him. He was missing his lab coat, but his band shirt was still tucked into his blue jeans, the word *Testify* scrawled across the shirt in angry-looking script.

"I didn't see you there," James said, quelling his irritation at being startled.

"No shit," Hoyt said, chuckling as he stepped up and leaned against the railing next to James, staring out over the water with him. "Heard about you and Phillip, man. That sucks."

James indicated his shirt. "Didn't take you for the religious type."

"Nah, not really." Hoyt pointed at his shirt. "Rez metal, man. Gotta jam with my brothers." He put a hand up, making the metal horns symbol, then went back to staring out over the water. "Been hearing a lot of whispering though. That maybe you and Phillip aren't leaving yet."

"I believe Phillip may have a point about our cell phones."

Hoyt laughed at that. "No, not that. Spirits, man. They're loud as hell." He gave James a wry smile. "Like I said: shouldn't have given your name like that."

"What about you? Are you saying your name isn't Hoyt?"

121

"I said you can *call* me Hoyt."

"How do you work for the FBI and not use your real name?"

"You and Phillip stumbled onto something major," Hoyt continued, avoiding the question. "You can't afford to not have someone on your side who can get things." He looked back at the river. "I don't mind being that someone. I can get things."

"Why?"

"Because I like you guys. I dig what you're trying to do here." He turned fully to James. "I know all about that shit you pulled a few months ago. Tracking that little girl down and taking down a whole vampire house. Someone who's willing to do that has balls." He pulled his phone out and looked at it. "Damn, I gotta get to work."

"So that's why you want in?" James said, cutting him off. "Because you perceive us as some sort of Justice League?"

"I might be onto something," Hoyt said. "Something I'm not supposed to see."

"I'm sure we can't protect you from the Federal government."

Hoyt waved it off. "Not worried about them. Got my own way around those guys. But you could really toss a wrench into a machine that needs a wrench tossed into it. I'll make sure you get it in the next few hours." Hoyt stared past James. His eyes narrowed as if he saw something. "Looks like we ain't alone."

James turned around and saw Agatha sitting on a park bench and glaring hard at them. He felt a cold chill under his skin and heard the wolf growl inside as he tensed. He looked over his shoulder at Hoyt.

Or, where Hoyt had been standing.

James searched the area with his eyes, trying to see what direction the ME went. People strolled along freely, none of them wearing a black band shirt and blue jeans. He turned back to the park bench and saw that Agatha was gone as well.

"Lovely," he sighed.

P hillip was up by the time James got back to the room, sitting at the small table in front of his laptop and typing furiously. He didn't say a word to James, not looking away from the screen as his eyes widened. He sat back, placed his hands on the table on either side of the computer, and breathed out slowly as if bracing for impact. "Oh, *shit*."

"I see you slept well," James said. "Did the Panthers lose again?"

"We're four and zero," Phillip said, his wide eyes still on the screen. He rubbed his face and groaned under his hands. It took James a second to realize that Phillip was uttering *"Goose-fah-bah"* over and over, stretching the sound out as if meditating.

"I've known you for years," James said over the sound. "I thought there were no secrets between us. Yet I find out that our local NFL team's success transforms you into a Yiddish monk."

Phillip spoke through his hands. "This is my *woo-sah*, James. I need a minute."

"For what?"

"To process some real fuck-shit I just got from Hoyt."

James blinked. "That's interesting."

Phillip pulled his hands away from his face and looked at him. "Interesting? Why?"

"I just got done talking with Hoyt. He was out on the walk by the statue just a few minutes ago."

"Not sure how he accomplished that. Man's been at work all night processing the bodies from the Abercorn site."

James shrugged. "Maybe he was on lunch?"

"And he wandered all the way down to the Riverwalk?" Phillip shook his head. "Whatever."

"You don't believe me?"

"I believe something funky's up," Phillip said. "You talked to him just now, I've been getting emails from him all morning."

"Isn't that the SCU's laptop?"

"No, it's mine, the tablet was the SCU's. I was logged into the FBI server with my computer, though, for work emails." He shook his head. "Guess what? No access. Surprise-surprise."

"How is he emailing you?"

"His personal account, and he's somehow got it encrypted so the FBI can't trace it." Phillip turned the laptop around and pushed it at James. "Take a look at the attachment he just sent."

James read over the document on the screen. He was well aware of what his own financial records looked like, and they were complicated. The information on the screen was vastly more complex and in a layout he was completely unfamiliar with. "This appears to be finances, but don't hold me to that. I've never seen anything like this before." He pushed the laptop back over to Phillip. "What is it?"

"It's the financial records for the Supernatural Crimes Unit," Phillip said as leaned over and pointed at different numbers on the screen. "These deposits here are funds to go toward things like payroll, supplies, all the bullshit they need to function, right? Then here's the transfers over to the departments within the SCU." He indicated some text next to a sizeable number. "This abbreviation is for payroll. This one's office utilities. And so on."

"And Hoyt was able to get this how?"

"I don't know," Phillip said. "And I ain't askin'. He wants to break the law, that's his business. But look at this." Phillip pointed to a transaction on the screen. The dollar amount was an even million, but the transaction ID was blank. "This one here? Nothing. Just a cool million to the unit for what? From who?"

"You think someone forgot to enter something in?"

"Nope. It's all done with computer AI and algorithms. The system will assign an ID of some kind to a transaction source if the source doesn't already have one." He tapped the screen. "Nothin'."

"So, we have no idea where the money came from? Or from whom?"

"Almost." Phillip clicked on the transaction, and the spreadsheet changed over to a different layout. "So, you got different banks that manage wealth, right? JP Morgan and Chase, Fifth-Third Bank, Bessemer Trust, and so on. Look at this." He pointed to an abbreviation next to the blank space where the account holder's ID would've been. "This one? I've never seen that one before. I've tried to trace it, but nothing comes up."

James read the abbreviation out loud. "VTDL. I'm curious as to what it stands for."

"All I can get from it is that it's Charlotte-based." Phillip shrugged. "Beyond that, I got nothing."

The wolf heightened James's hearing instantly, and he heard Lacy whispering to herself under the bed. "Shit. *Shit.*" James looked at Phillip, who obviously hadn't heard her. What was wrong? Why was she reacting that way?

Phillip kept talking. "But, based on this, the organization is getting some extra funding that ain't in the FBI budget. And, on top of that, the other transactions that have the FBI ID on them? Yeah, that's not really the FBI bank ID."

James felt like he knew the answer, but he asked anyway. "What does that mean?"

"It means that the SCU ain't part of the FBI." Phillip sat back in his chair. "At least not in an official capacity. Looks like it's a private organization headed up by some mystery man with a shitload of cash and an interest in playing law enforcement over supernaturals." He cursed under his breath. "We've been played from the jump."

"How would you have missed this while working for them?"

"You really think every agent at the FBI or CIA is fully aware of everything the organization does or has going on in the background? Shit. Google the term 'Confidential' sometime. Hell, James. My uncle turned down being a Navy Seal because he wanted to be able to tell his family about his day at work without having to kill them."

Lacy's voice sounded from underneath James's bed, her tone more casual than the panicked whisper James had heard only a moment ago. "Not saying you two are dumb or anything, but I'm wondering if this is a little above you guys."

"Why's that?" Phillip asked with a slightly defensive edge.

"Let's be real for a minute, sweetie," Lacy replied, not missing a beat. "Breaking bones and causing property damage comes a lot easier to you guys than tracking down dirty deeds done desk-jockey style. Besides, how many cases do you two want to work? Didn't you decide to keep on the whole necromancer thing?" James heard her shift under the bed. "I'd leave this one alone."

"I'm wondering if there's some kind of connection," James said as a few things started to fall into place.

Phillip raised an eyebrow at James. "Dude, she has a point on that one. We have enough going on. How the hell is the SCU being dirty connected with a necromancer killing people with dead people?"

James started to piece events together in his mind, the wolf occasionally pushing forward a memory when he was foggy on details. "We're sent here to look into murders that, on their face, look like just a supernatural on a killing spree. We find paperwork giving full ownership of all Butler properties back to the Jones family, and Noble Jones is the primary executor. He kills an entire household of people. We arrest him. Smith shows up and fires us, and this is *after* he threatened to dox me to a lot of people who would love to see the Coldstone name wiped out so he could force me to work for him."

"Yeah," Phillip said. "I've been here the whole time, James."

"How long did it take us to get to Savannah?"

Phillip shrugged. "About three, three and a half hours because of traffic." He paused and looked at James. "Shit. You're right."

"Exactly."

"Didn't even think about that."

Lacy chimed in again. "You two are adorable when you speak in Twin Code."

Phillip rolled his eyes as James sat down at the desk and replied to Lacy. "Agent Smith was on his way here before we ever arrested Noble Jones."

He had barely finished his sentence when the door to the hotel room exploded inward, the air instantly filled with the sound of muffled gunfire and bullets.

18

James remembered when the film *The Matrix* came to theaters. Phillip had insisted they go and watch it the day it opened. And the next weekend. Then there was the double date. And the matinee. And the college student discount day.

It was the sixth weekend in a row when James finally put a stop to it.

There was one night when James was feeling particularly antsy and picking on Phillip was the best outlet he'd been able to think of. They were trading banter, and James started making fun of the slow-motion clips in *The Matrix* to rile Phillip up. He'd make the low *"Voom!"* baseline sound with his mouth as he would do most of his actions in a pretend slow-motion for a second before resuming normal speed. Washing dishes, sitting on the couch, even checking the time on his cell phone.

"You know how annoying that is?" Phillip finally snapped.

"No more than it was the tenth time I saw the movie," James countered with a laugh. "They should've called it 'Slow Motion: The Movie.'"

"It's called 'bullet time,' dumbass," Phillip spat. "They use it to emphasize the action. You might know that if you weren't uncultured as all hell."

"My disinterest in science fiction and action movies has nothing to do with my worldliness," James had responded in his usual, favorite haughty tone when he was really trying to get Phillip stirred up. "I'll have you know that my tastes, much like my humor, are far advanced."

"Right," Phillip said, rolling his eyes. "And I'm a Federal agent. Bone-head. Just knock it off."

"Fine," James said with a slight grin. "I concede."

"Good." Phillip grabbed the remote and pointed at the controller sitting on the coffee table. "Pass me that, will you? Time to kick your ass at Mario Kart again."

James tried not to laugh through his *"Voom!"* as he picked up the controller and slow-motion-handed it to a fuming and growling Phillip.

It was all fun and games until it happened in real life. James never real-ized how slow time could move when one was ambushed, but he'd been through several surprise attacks by now. The idea of mocking the effect to Phillip didn't hold as much humor as it once had when actual bullets were flying. The hotel room door being kicked inward had startled him, but he was in wolf form before the door finished swinging open, the world moving as if he were underwater. Phillip was flying backward from where James had shoved the table hard at him. The rounds had already peppered the table and turned the laptop into nothing more than scraps of plastic and circuitry instantly before James had sent it and Phillip airborne. Phillip got to his feet; his gun aimed as he opened fire on the agent. The man caught a round in the shoulder and spun on Phillip, his own weapon aimed. James swung in a haymaker motion, his open palm slamming into the side of the shooter's head so hard the guy did hands-free cartwheel. He maintained his shooter's stance, unaware that he'd been hit, his body fully upside down and in midair before instinct took over and he flailed and hit the bed and floor in an unconscious heap.

The second gunner opened fire on James, the rounds smacking into his side and chest, stinging and burning slightly before his flesh pushed the bullets back out. James looked at the gunman and growled. *Should've used silver, asshole*, he thought.

The gunman's face fell, and he tried to backpedal into the hallway. James reached for him, snatched him up by the shirt, and slammed him down onto the floor. Phillip closed the door and shoved what was left of the table in front of it, keeping his gun trained on the now-disoriented assassin.

Lacy's voice sounded from underneath the bed as the dust began to settle. "I'm going to guess that wasn't room service."

"Don't worry, we got it," Phillip said with a sarcastic edge.

"Yeah, I have faith in you," Lacy responded. "That, and the whole sunlight thing. What happened? Shoot me a pic?" James watched Phillip pull his phone out and snap some pictures of the two men. A second later, he heard Lacy from under the bed again. "Damn. Friends of yours?"

"Never seen 'em," Phillip said. "James, stay in wolf form in case they brought friends."

The agent stared at him, his face hardening as he spoke through grit teeth. "Fuck you."

James picked the man up and snarled in his face, his eyes wide and wild and his teeth bared in his well-rehearsed "Psycho-Wolf" look. The man let out a high-pitched scream as James opened his mouth and clamped his jaws around the shooter's head just enough to cause an uncomfortable pinch. The high-pitched scream sounded again, and Lacy called out from her sleeping spot. "Holy shit, you guys got shot at by Jamie Lee Curtis?"

Phillip stepped up to James, putting his gun away as James held his bite on Jamie Lee's head. The man whimpered as Phillip crossed his arms in front of his chest and glared at the man. "Okay, asshole. We're gonna play a game. It's called 'Who is Your Daddy, and What Does He Do?'"

"What?!" Jamie Lee squeaked.

Phillip blinked. "You don't get that reference? Damn, I should let James eat you on principle. Let me clarify: who the fuck sent you and why the fuck did you just try to kill us?"

"I can't tell you that," Jamie Lee cried, his voice hysterical. "They'll kill me!"

"Better than being processed werewolf shit later." James reacted to Phillip's response by growling, tensing his jaw as Jamie Lee let out another scream and waved his arms.

"Okay," he cried. "Okay! The FBI! The FBI!"

"What the hell?" Phillip said. "A government agency tried to off two former agents. You expect me to believe that?"

"The SCU has a termination policy," Jamie Lee continued.

"I've read the termination policy," Phillip snapped. "It says agents are debriefed, not killed off."

"I'm just following orders, man. I swear! Let me go!"

"Like hell," Phillip snapped. "Try again, dickhead. The SCU isn't even part of the—"

James's phone rang from somewhere in the room before Phillip could finish his sentence. He and Phillip looked at each other as Lacy spoke. "Someone gonna get that? Little too bright for me."

Phillip moved past James and picked the phone up off the floor. He turned to James, shook his head, and held it up. The caller ID sent James's nerves on edge.

"She can go to voicemail," Phillip said.

"And raise some suspicion?" Lacy countered. "James meets her the other night, talks to her one time on the phone, and ghosts out? Not a good look, Bacon."

"I'd answer it," Jamie Lee said, his voice wavering as he held his hand up in James's line of sight. "Just saying."

James fought back another urge to bite down on the assassin's head and shot Phillip a panicked expression. Phillip grumbled as he hit the answer icon on the screen and put it on speakerphone. Molly spoke before Phillip could say anything. James could hear the worry in her voice.

"Hello? James? Are you alright?"

"Uh, hi Molly." Phillip cleared his throat. "Um, this is Phillip. James's friend."

"Oh," Molly said with some surprise. "I—hello. Is James available? Is everything okay?"

James's eyes were wide, his body frozen. Phillip looked around at the trashed room, then back at James. "Yeah, we're good. James is in the bathroom. We're…about to head to a meeting."

"A meeting? Phillip, I heard shouts and gun fire. What's going on?"

"Oh, we were watching a movie. Resting up before the meeting. Did you need to talk to James? Is it important?"

"James called me," Molly said. "I answered and I heard the commotion before the call ended." She sighed. James could hear a small amount of disappointment in that sigh, and he mentally kicked himself for it. "Must have been a pocket-dial, then. Tell him I called?"

"Sure, no problem," Phillip said. "I'll have him call you after we're done."

"Thank you, Phillip. Ciao."

"Yeah, bye." Phillip ended the call, and James felt some relief just before his guilt started back up again. He wasn't intentionally trying to avoid Molly. Having Lacy around wasn't helping.

Neither was the terrified man with jaws wrapped around his head.

"She sounds cute, Jimmy," Lacy said. "British chick? Love the accent."

Phillip moved closer and spoke to Jamie Lee. "I'm gonna tell James to let you go. We're going to have a nice little chat."

"I told you everything I know," the man said, sobbing.

"James? Eat him."

Jamie Lee Curtis began screaming again as James put pressure on the man's skull with his teeth. "Okay! Stop-stop-stop-stop!"

"James, let up," Phillip said, tapping James on the shoulder. "I think we...oh *shit*."

James's ears perked up at the sound Phillip had probably recognized. Sirens in the distance, vehicles pulling up outside, boots on the ground as men shouted orders.

"Is that what I think it is?" Lacy asked. "I can't see any-damn-thing but box springs. What the hell is going on?"

"Cavalry," Phillip said. "Rocky and Bullwinkle probably cleared the hotel before their little sting and had back-up on standby just in case." He went to the window. "Shit, they aren't even staging, they're coming right the fuck in!" He turned to James. "We've gotta move."

James pulled Curtis's head out of his mouth and shoved the man back onto the bed as he shifted to human form. "Go where? It's broad daylight."

"Anywhere but here," Phillip said.

"What about Lacy?"

"I'm fine," Lacy said. "I can manage. Just get the hell out of here before these guys come in with some actual firepower. I'll call you tonight and we'll meet up."

"They blocked my car in," Phillip said, glancing out the window again. James moved to the window and saw at least ten heavily armed agents scurrying across the street, their weapons aimed. "MP5s. Shit, they plan to light it up in here. Place must definitely be empty."

James shifted into wolf form, picked up Jamie Lee Curtis, and toss him over his shoulder in a fireman's carry as he moved out into the hallway. The armed agents stepped out of the stairwell at the end of the hall and shouted, all of them taking aim with their guns. James dropped Jamie Lee to the floor as Phillip caught up to them and grabbed the man, dragging him out of the way.

James heard more agents come out of the stairwell behind them. He turned, saw five more enter the hall with their guns aimed at him and Phillip both. One of the men shouted at the others. "Kill the human, but we need the werewolf alive!"

Helmets, James thought. *I hope they have earplugs.*

James opened his mind, not hesitating to let the wolf forward.

The James stepped back in Wolf's mind, nodding as it spoke. *You know what to do.*

Wolf stood tall, ears scraping the ceiling as it spread its arms wide. It heard the Phillip shout at the squealing man to cover its ears just before the voices of the spirits began to whisper, drowning out other sounds. Wolf called to Fenrir, asking the Wolf God for strength and guidance as men screamed and dropped the things the James called guns and fought with the shells on their heads. Wolf heard glass shatter, walls crack and pieces of the building fall as Wolf pushed the call out further to reach Fenrir's ear, to ask the father for his savage gifts.

That's enough, the James said from inside. *We don't want to kill anyone.*

Wolf pulled the call back, feeling Fenrir's grace come with it bringing the peace of victory. It stepped back. The James came back to his place in the forefront, taking control once again.

James looked around the hall at the damage. Plaster had fallen away from the slatted lathe in the walls, light fixtures were shattered, and debris cluttered the floor around the piles of unconscious men at the stairwells. The doors to the rooms had been blown off the hinges, and he could see the windows in each room had all exploded outward.

"I wish you could talk when you're in dog mode," Phillip muttered behind him. He looked down as Phillip got up off the floor and brushed the dust and pieces of plaster off of his shoulders and chest. "Be easier for you to warn me when you're gonna do that shit." Jamie Lee Curtis was unconscious on the floor. James saw the trickle of blood coming from the man's ear. Phillip reached down and searched the agent until he managed to find his phone. "Can probably crack this and scope at his email."

James heard the commotion in the stairwells, the telltale sound of more trouble headed their way. He crouched down and woofed at Phillip, who shook his head. "What?" His eyes widened. "Oh, *hell* no."

James woofed again, more forceful.

"You ain't a damn horse!"

A voice shouted from the stairwell ahead. "Up here! Cover the door! You in the other stairwell take down Brown first!"

"Shit," Phillip muttered as he swung himself onto James's back and wrung his hands into the thick fur in a death-grip. He squeezed his legs around James's ribs and gave him a kick. "Giddy-up, asshole!" James felt another kick accompanied by a sound smack on his rear, and he took off down the hall toward the far window just as more gunmen stormed out of the stairwell. Phillip leaned forward, wrapping his arms around James's neck and gripping the fur in the front. "Do it!"

James was in full wolfen speed as he blew through the group of agents and out the window, his ears full of nothing but Phillip's screaming. He hit the ground, Phillip still screaming as he zipped through town and took a corner before darting down the highway. Phillip was still shrieking something to Jesus and the Lord as they blurred past cars and trucks on the highway with no clue on where they were going and only James's intent of putting as much distance between them and the SCU as possible.

19

acy, it's me. I'm on Phillip's phone. Call me as soon as you get this." James ended the call and handed Phillip's phone back to him. "She'll likely call when she gets settled and out of sight. We'll need to watch for it."

"Yeah, no shit," Phillip said.

James had sprinted at wolfen speed until he'd reached the Victory Square shopping center just off of the Harry S. Truman Highway. He'd hidden behind Target while Phillip had gone inside to purchase him some clothing. Once he was clothed, they made their way out into the open and walked through the parking lot as if searching for their vehicle. The lot was busy, cars and people moving up and down the lanes as the two looked around to get a lay of the land. They made sure to wander between cars, particularly trucks and SUVs that could provide cover if necessary. "They're probably already coming for us," Phillip said as he glanced around the lot. "Damn. Someone could get hurt."

"Why?" James asked. "What did we do?"

"We got fired," Phillip said, still staring at his phone. "Looks like Jamie Lee Curtis was telling us the truth. Hoyt's sayin' here there's a kill order on me."

James didn't hold back the snark. "Does the Federal government always eliminate the people they no longer wish to associate with?"

Phillip grunted. "You have no idea. But no, not typically. There would have to be some really bad circumstances. Like National Security-level threats. And they're just trying to kill me. They want you alive."

"Best of luck to them," James said. He pointed back toward the shopping center. "There's a Starbucks over there. Coffee?"

Phillip gave him a bewildered look. "Are you fucking stupid? We just got shot at. We're being hunted."

"And I would like a Café Mocha," James said. "As well as a place where we can sit and not be as likely to have someone do the same thing with quite so many people around."

"You've been watching the news lately, right?" Phillip sighed. "But that would also draw some attention they might not want. Maybe it's not such a dumb idea. Good thinking."

James shrugged. "The Café Mocha was my larger priority."

"Shut the hell up."

They made their way back across the parking lot and into the Starbucks without incident. James ordered the drinks while Phillip found a corner in the back of the place that was largely hidden from view, a sort of nook that college students would've likely used as a study area. It had four comfortable-looking chairs placed around a small coffee table. The windows made up two of the back walls, but Phillip had already closed the blinds. James brought the drinks over and sat down in the chair across from Phillip. He began sipping his drink while Phillip typed furiously on his phone screen. "I dunno how Hoyt is getting this to me without them seeing, and I don't give a damn. This shit is hot, James."

James raised an eyebrow. "Do tell."

"Okay, so we pretty much figured out the SCU isn't under the FBI umbrella. It's painted that way, it operates that way, but they don't get any funding or resources from them. It's more like a front."

"So then why is the FBI after us?"

Phillip shook his head. "They're not. My guess is that any of the guys we've seen wearing FBI gear are fakes." Phillip looked up from the phone screen. "But something isn't adding up. An organization like the SCU ain't gonna stay out of view of the FBI for long. They're too big. Too many moving parts. And impersonating a Federal agent is a crime."

James was about to take a sip of his coffee when he paused, looking at Phillip. "I'm inclined to think that would mean you were also breaking the law."

Phillip blinked. "Say what?"

"How many times did you say you were FBI?"

"I didn't know. Plausible deniability is a thing."

"Still could be a problem."

"You were doing it too."

"You started it."

Phillip tensed and raised his hands as if he were about to grab James by the neck, glaring at him as he visibly clenched his jaw. "*Why* do you do that?!"

"The levity helps me think," James said as he casually sipped his coffee. "I don't operate well under stress. And you are a fairly easy target."

"Am not."

"Are too."

Phillip bristled again, his tone warning. "James."

"And I believe it makes sense that someone in the right place is telling the FBI and any other branch of our illustrious government to ignore our friends."

"Good job, Sherlock," Phillip said. "I'll file that under 'obvious' in the idiot section."

"Which means that the police departments are unaware. And also looking for us."

Phillip started to speak again and stopped, blinking. He covered his face and rested his elbows on the table. "I didn't think about that." He dropped his favorite sentence enhancer, dragging it out in a long groan.

"It means that they might also be looking for Lacy," James said. "We'll need to warn her."

Phillip pulled his phone out. "I'll shoot her a text now."

"It also means we're stuck here. We *have* to finish this now."

"We talked about this, James. That hero stuff is bullshit. We march Agatha in there, *if* she's really the necromancer, they'll take her *and* us down. And that's *if* they give a shit about her at all. They might just cut her loose and tell her to have a nice day. Who the fuck knows?"

"Or she's someone of importance to them and could be used as leverage."

"What makes you think they give a shit about her?"

"It's that tattoo she's got behind her ear," James said. "I still can't place it, but I know I've seen it before."

"Just no idea where."

"Exactly."

Phillip shook his head again. "I doubt she's got anything to do with those assholes. I think her deal is more with Noble Jones. Which would only involve her indirectly since he's caught up in the vampire politics shit."

"He might be our leverage then," James said. "He's been reasonable with us so far. We may be able to get him to help us."

"He's probably already out." Phillip paused again. "Or not. They've got to keep up appearances. They'll keep him in there long enough to keep the locals in the dark. Mimic the process. That would've taken until the wee hours of the morning. The sun was coming up by the time we got back from the bureau after our exit interview. I'll bet he goes loose tonight." He looked at his phone. "That's weird."

"What?"

"Lacy's still at the hotel. I thought she said she was bailing ass."

"How do you know?"

"I snuck her phone onto the same app I use to track you. All I needed was her number." Phillip said. "Hell, I'm showing your phone too. Looks like no one cleaned up. *Damn* weird."

James tensed, worried. The wolf grunted and began pacing in his mind. "We may need to go back to the hotel."

"Hell no," Phillip said. "I promise you they've got the place locked down. We go back, I'm dead and you're their bitch. Besides, we don't have a car."

James raised an eyebrow. "We don't need a car."

"I'm not riding you again."

"It would be easier."

"*Hell*-to-the-no. And they're probably looking for that anyway. Kinda hard to miss a big damn dog loping down the road with a screaming black dude on his back."

"It's Lacy," James said. "Besides, they're looking for us knowing we ran. If they do have someone watching the hotel, it'll be minimal."

Phillip rolled his eyes. "Fine. But if I get killed, I'm kickin' your ass."

The trip back to the hotel was slower, but James still maintained enough speed to make reasonable time. The sun was setting, the sky starting to turn its orange evening hues as he moved down the back roads that ran along the highway, Phillip on his back once again with a grip on James's fur that would rival any vice or clamp one could find in a car garage. They eventually made it back into downtown Savannah, and

James ducked into a small alleyway so Phillip could disembark. He shifted to human form, dressed, and they made their way out into the busy evening streets and sidewalks, cutting through the parks like a couple of tourists whenever the wolf sent a warning to James that someone was watching them. His wolfen senses were on red alert, his vision just sharp enough to not be yellowed and his hearing enhanced to the point where he could hear conversations from yards away clearly. An occasional police car would drive by, or an officer would wander through on horseback. James and Phillip would take a corner or turn and walk the other way, re-routing their trip back to the hotel. The sun was completely down by the time they made it over to the Olde Harbor Inn. Lacy's Mini Cooper was parked in a space behind the hotel.

"That's worrisome," James said. "I would think she would've left the minute the sun was down."

"She said she was going to try and leave when we did," Phillip said. "Ain't like she couldn't find a place nearby before the sun cooked her. All the buildings on this strip are pretty close, and most of them have cellars."

James saw a figure move in the dark near the back walk. The wolf shifted his human eyesight into his wolfen night vision, and he saw the man wandering aimlessly around the back entryway. He was dressed as a construction worker, pulling a hammer from his tool belt and using it to tack up a sign indicating that the hotel was under renovation. James spotted the handgun at his side. He searched with his eyes until he saw the large toolbox a few feet away. "I'm fairly certain the tools in that toolbox are not meant for hanging drywall."

"SCU agent," Phillip said. "If they're doing that, it means they're trying to keep people out. Place is probably empty."

"Or it's a trap," James said.

Phillip shook his head. "I seriously doubt they would think we're stupid enough to come back here."

James smiled. "They underestimate us."

Phillip grumbled as James crossed the parking lot and moved behind a large van. He looked around to make sure he wasn't being watched, stripped, and shifted. He made his way closer to where the agent was finishing the last nail for the sign. Bob the Builder took his tool belt off and moved to open the toolbox, his back turned. James moved in and swung, clapping Bob on the side of his hard hat. Bob's hard hat went flying, and his head smacked into the wall before he crumpled to the ground and lay still.

Phillip caught up to James and opened the toolbox to reveal a set of small machine guns and SWAT gear. "That ain't no screwdriver. C'mon, let's get inside. And bring Chuckles with us." He searched the unconscious agent and pilfered a hotel key from the man's pockets. James lifted Bob the Builder and threw him over his shoulder, then followed Phillip inside. Only a few lights were burning, just enough to not need the ability to see in the dark. Phillip turned to James as they passed the front desk. James hefted Bob the Builder off his shoulder and casually tossed him over the desk and into the floor with a loud thump. Phillip startled and spun on his heel. "Are you serious?! We don't know for sure the place is empty. *Try to be quiet.*"

James crouched down and tried to look forlorn. Phillip snorted. "Knock off the guilty puppy shit. You just look drunk and stupid."

They made it to their room floor in a few minutes. The debris hadn't been cleaned up, and the area wasn't taped off. None of the lights were working, likely having been shot out during the attack. The wolf pushed James's vision again, and he crept down the dark hallway toward the room, glancing into each of the other rooms along the way to make sure they were alone. The area was still filled with the smell of spent gunpowder and dust from earlier, and James felt some relief at the slight hint of vanilla in the air. *She's here.*

Phillip pulled his phone out of his pocket. "Let me call Lacy and see if it rings."

James's ears perked at the sound of the Dragnet television show theme coming from their room. He moved in, glancing around the trashed space as he followed the sound. The wolf mewled inside. *I know,* he thought at the beast. *It's dark. Why is she still here?*

The ringing stopped as Phillip stepped into the room behind James. He could hear the tinny sound of her voicemail message coming from Phillip's phone. Phillip canceled it and redialed. Lacy's phone started ringing again. James moved to what was left of his bed, crouched down, and gave a low *"Woof!"*

Phillip came over and crouched down next to him. He reached underneath the bed and pulled the ringing phone out. The pink case had Lacy's name written on it in glittery calligraphy, and the screen displayed Phillip's number overlayed onto a wallpaper pic of a plate of bacon.

James stood, his stomach a knot as Phillip ended the call and sighed. "This just keeps getting better."

James shifted to human form. "Where would she have gone? She wouldn't have left her phone behind."

"The SCU probably got to her before she could bail," Phillip said. "They turn into ash when you kill 'em, right?"

James nodded. "I would've smelled it when we came in. I very much doubt she's dead."

Lacy's phone chimed loudly. James sniffed it, saw the text message notification on the screen just before Phillip held it up. "The hell?"

"What is it?"

"Text message. Someone asking for a status update on Noble Jones."

20

With surprising ease, James and Phillip left the Olde Harbor Inn and crossed over to the parking lot where Phillip had parked his car that morning when they visited the Waving Girl. No SCU agents were around that they could recognize, though they still kept their heads down and tried to blend in as they went. The sun was down completely, and Savannah was alive with the tourist nightlife of shopping and dinner out. The massacre at Abercorn hadn't made the news since the SCU and FBI took major steps to clean it up and keep it quiet. Both the house and the hotel where James and Phillip had been staying were now disguised as historic buildings under renovation. The air was filled with the smells of all the various foods being cooked from the restaurants on the strip, though James also had the wolf forward to pick up any other smells as well, such as gunpowder or the stench of sweat in plastic armor.

Or burning cloves from Agatha's cigarettes. Or Lacy's vanilla scent.

Phillip drove out of town and headed in the general direction of Butler Island Plantation, getting off the highway as soon as he could and hitting back roads and neighborhoods. "I turned off the GPS in the car's programming," he'd said as he took the exit and started taking turns at random. Soon treed swamplands replaced houses and neighborhoods. "Set the phones up too. Got a scrambler app from a friend on the Richmond, Virginia police force. Guy's not a conspiracy nut, but he does love that tech. Here we go." Phillip pulled the car off onto a small dirt road that led into the woods. He turned around and parked with the car facing the road, then killed the lights and double-checked that the doors were locked. "Let me know if the mutt hears banjos."

The wolf huffed in James's mind, sending a feeling that James swore could've counted as the animal's version of the middle finger. "What makes you think they won't track Lacy's phone?" he asked, holding it up and waving it at Phillip.

"They don't have a reason to. They acted like they didn't even know she was there. And none of the emails Hoyt sent me mention her." He took the phone from James and started tapping on the screen. James saw the "Invalid Password" error pop up a few times, and Phillip muttered. "Well, there goes that idea."

"What idea?"

"Most people use someone's birthday as their passcode. Or a phone number. Looks like I gotta do it the hard way." He pulled his phone out and opened a screen James had never seen before. It was bare bones, much like what Phillip sometimes referred to as a DOS shell. The screen was black with green text on it that appeared as nothing more than random numbers, letters, and symbols to James. Phillip pulled up the onscreen keyboard and began typing furiously while James watched.

Phillip had always had a knack for computers. He'd taken a few courses in college on coding as well as a computer forensics class for the easy A, and he'd also done a fair amount of training during his time in the Army. James, on the other hand, was often doing good to check his email. Texting and Google was the extent of his knowledge. Not that he was computer-illiterate, but he'd never had the need to go as in-depth as Phillip when it came to networks and gizmos and other things that would give James a headache if he tried to wrap his head around it. James was more into books and movies, though he never begrudged Phillip for his geeky nature and the regular trip to Comicon.

The screen on Lacy's phone changed, and James saw a cluster of apps on top of a pic of a kitten. "I'm in," Phillip said. "Damn, she's got a lot of text messages and emails."

"I see Candy Crush."

"It's a white girl with a cell phone. Why wouldn't she have Candy Crush?" He pressed on the small icon at the bottom of the screen that looked like a dialogue bubble in a comic. The app opened with a list of text messages from various contacts. "Damn, she's even got me in her *phone* as 'Bacon.'"

James saw his contact scroll by, the name "Jimmy" next to his last text message. The rest of the contacts were not as telling. "What cruel mother names her offspring CheezeWizard94?"

"It's a handle," Phillip said. "Same shit you've seen before when I play online. Like a gamer tag. It's what people use as ID when they don't want to give their real names. You never give your real name on the internet." He shook his head. "I don't know why the hell she wouldn't have real names in her contact, though. Some people are like that. Seems weird and confusing to me." He stopped scrolling. "What the fuck?"

"What?"

Phillip shook his head, blinked a few times, and looked at the screen again. "Damn. Check this."

James took the phone. The name on the screen was another tag. His chest tightened as he read through the text thread. The first message was from a contact only entered as V1@DD.

Status update.

I'm in Savannah. Butler's. They're here.

Make sure they get the documents. The rogue?

Idk. I'll find out what they know, but she's been active.

Take care of it.

James scrolled and saw more messages back and forth between Lacy and V1@DD that were similar in nature. All short and sweet, but obviously someone checking in on Lacy and what she was doing. He clenched his jaw slightly, the knot forming in his stomach only adding to the tightness in his chest.

"James?"

James barely heard Phillip say his name. Phillip spoke again, this time a little louder as he stared at the phone, not seeing the device in his hand. He kept replaying all of his moments with Lacy, everything that she'd said to him that he could remember. She'd always been closed when it came to her reasons behind things, often just waving her actions off with a smart remark or deflecting and moving to a different subject. He tried to think about the short amount of time he'd known her. Where was she from? What was her life like a hundred years ago before she'd been turned? He thought back to that night in the cabin at Westenra Island, that moment when he thought they'd finally broken the barriers between them. He thought he'd be able to be with her, acting on his feelings. He remembered her touch, the coolness of her skin against his, her kiss firm and passionate. He remembered...a mark? Something on her neck. Behind her ear. A birthmark.

The wolf flashed the image in his mind again, but it faded. He couldn't see the shape beyond it being a dark spot as his memory replayed the moment she broke away and left him standing in the room alone, bewildered, and frustrated.

Had it been real?

"James," Phillip said, jarring him out of his fugue. "Hey, let me see the phone."

James held onto the phone as Phillip reached for it, moving it away from his grasp. "No, I've got it." The phone chimed as a new message appeared from V1@DD.

You haven't checked in. Respond.

James paused, the onscreen keyboard in place waiting for input. It chimed again.

Phone will deactivate in thirty minutes unless you respond.

"Dude, give me that," Phillip said. "I gotta get the SIM card out so they can't fuck with it."

James swatted Phillip's hand away and pulled up the onscreen keyboard. Phillip sputtered. "Wait, what the hell? James, don't."

James ignored him as he typed a message back to Lacy's contact. *Sorry, had a situation. I'm here.*

Phillip fumed next to him. "You. Fucking. *Idiot.* They can pinpoint the *exact* location of that phone. They figure out you ain't Lacy, they'll—"

"Quiet," James said, surprising himself with the firmness of his tone as he cut Phillip off. He kept his eyes on the screen, watching as the mark on his message changed from *Delivered* to *Read.* A dialogue bubble popped up on the screen, three dots dancing in the center just before it changed into a new message.

Report.

Phillip breathed out slowly. "Oh, fuck."

James started typing again, making sure to first glance at some of the most recent texts to try and prevent himself from being inconsistent with whatever Lacy had already told the person on the other end. *They got fired from the SCU.*

Good. The human?

Tried to kill him, but Coldstone got him out of there.

We need them both.

James sighed, closing his eyes for a second. *How would Lacy respond?* He started typing again and hit send. His message blinked up into place on the thread. *What do I do?*

The three dots came back and stayed for longer. "Shit," Phillip said, his voice low. James ignored him, waiting for what seemed like an eternity until the new message finally popped up onscreen.

Same thing you did last time. Stay with them, help keep them alive, and use them to help you take down the rogue. Keep the SCU away from them. Keep Jones in prison, he'll be safe there.

James handed the phone back to Phillip, the lump in his chest now in his throat as he kept his jaw clenched to keep himself from shouting in anger. He stared out the window in the dark and tried to piece together some sense of what he'd just read. He replayed his interactions with Lacy again, especially since they'd run into her in Savannah. The more he thought about it, the more he realized that there was something he couldn't pin down. She was off. She seemed less spirited than usual, more focused and secretive. He'd never seen her nervous before they'd pointed the finger at Noble Jones for the slaughter at the Abercorn house. She'd denied that he would've been capable.

Then she flipped. She'd accepted it. She'd taken part in his arrest with no question, only with a seriousness and worry he'd not seen in her before.

If Phillip had committed a crime, James would've gone to the ends of the earth to prove his innocence. He knew he'd make sure Phillip had the best defense, had every shred of evidence he needed to prove that he was not guilty. And if it was undeniable, James would've gone to every length in his power to find out what made Phillip do it and get him whatever help he needed. Or prove that Phillip wasn't under his own control. Lacy hadn't done any of that until after they'd hauled Jones in. And as angry as Agent Smith had been about Jones being in custody, Lacy seemed more determined to give them a reason to keep him under lock and key.

The necromancer was still at large. It was all pointing to Agatha. And now it looked like she could certainly control a vampire. A long-dead human under the control of the necromancer was bad enough. A vampire could be a hellishly deadly weapon. Which meant that Lacy was also vulnerable.

And she was missing.

"We have to go back," James said.

"Dude, *hell* no," Phillip said. "It's nighttime. The city is probably crawling with SCU agents by now since the supernatural activity will be up. And I'd like to *not* get popped while we're here."

James turned and looked at him. "Lacy's missing. She's in trouble."

Phillip held the phone up. "Lacy lied her ass off about why she's here. Fuck, James, she lied about every-damn-thing if you think about it. We don't know who the hell she is, or who the hell she's working for." He held the phone up and pointed at it. "And thanks to you, I can't pull the SIM card out now. I'm sure they're trackin' her, and they'll notice the signal pop out if I do. Probably not an alarm we wanna trigger."

"If she was going to cause us problems, she would've done it already," James argued.

"She's *already* caused us problems," Phillip shot back. "Christ, man. The most powerful vampire in Georgia knows who the fuck we are, and I'm pretty-fuckin'-sure he doesn't like us. We arrested his ass on his own property in front of his minions. We fucked with his ego. Last time we fucked with someone's ego, I ended up with a broken leg and you almost got offed by a sea monster with boobs." He rubbed his face and breathed out deeply. "Look, man. I get it. I do. You care about Lacy. I'm not stupid. But she's obviously wrapped up in all of this somehow. And now I'm wondering if she ran into us in Charleston on purpose."

"Even if she did," James said. "Even if she's been conspiring against us, or *for* us, that doesn't negate the fact that she almost died fighting for us on Westenra Island. She almost died in Charleston fighting with me on the beach." He looked at Phillip. "We owe her the benefit of the doubt."

Phillip held the phone up. "I don't doubt at all that she's been lyin' like hell. James, when you found out I kept the fact that I was a Fed…sorry, *fake* Fed, you went apeshit and pushed me away."

"You're different."

"I don't have boobs and blue eyes."

"It's not that. I've known you longer. After all these years, I wasn't expecting that kind of secret," James said. "We need to find her. If nothing else, she'll have answers." He bristled and felt the chill up his spine as the wolf tensed inside. Phillip started talking, but James held a hand up to quiet him as he listened with heightened hearing. Rustling in the brush, something moving and shuffling around. A low grunt. "We have company."

Both of them got out of the car. Phillip pulled his gun and flashlight and pointed them around the area while James stripped and stood in the dark. He shifted and sniffed the air for rot and soil. There was something else. He shifted back to human form. "Vampire."

Phillip looked over his shoulder. "You sure?"

The sound of something rushing in, the intensity of rotted blood and pine mixed with the stale stench of body odor, all of it hit James's senses at once as his muscles braced. He was in wolf form only a split second before something slammed into him, sent him flying away from the car. He hit a tree, the pain spreading from his lower back down his legs, fading away just before he hit the ground. The wolf snarled inside, the act causing James to do the same as he got to his feet. Phillip fired at the thing that had attacked him, ducked as a draugr lurched from the trees, and jabbed a pitchfork at him. James collected himself and rushed in. He had the draugr in his grip before the thing could react, and he smashed its skull against the ground before wrenching what was left off the shoulders and throwing the husk off into the woods.

"Well," a voice said in the dark. James recognized the underlying Georgia drawl it carried, but it was different than what he was familiar with. As if it was a forgotten aspect of the accent. "I must say that your recoverin' from that blow is just damned impressive, sir."

21

James stood, putting himself in between the voice and Phillip as he showed his true size to the speaker. Phillip moved around just beside him and pointed the gun and light in the direction the voice had come from. "Let's go, dickhead," he said, his tone authoritative. "Step the fuck out here where I can see you with your hands up."

James didn't need Phillip's flashlight to see the man standing there, staring at them with a smirk on his face and a draugr slave on either side of him. His hair was slicked down against his scalp, his old-fashioned clothing was worn and dirty. His eyes flickered red, bright enough for James to see the color in his yellowed vision. The vampire shook its head, chuckling as if about to reprimand a child. "I do believe that one of your station has no business hurling insults at one of my status, boy."

"You watch who the fuck you're callin' *boy*," Phillip snapped back, his tone dark.

James recognized who he was looking at, but he couldn't put his finger on the name. He'd seen the photo, but so many of them from back then were similar and generic. The fashion back during the Civil War was to look so much like everyone else. The slicked-down short hair, the collared shirts, and overcoats, yet this man stood out in his mind.

Suckhead McSimilar grinned. He snapped his fingers and the two draugrs attacked. Phillip opened fire on one as James plowed by the other and ran at the vampire. He lashed out, but Suckhead dodged and shot past him. James felt a blow to his back and careened off balance, his own momentum fighting against him as he slammed into a tree and hit the ground. He shook the blow off and got to his feet. The larger draugr was already after him, swinging his scythe, and barely missed James's face. Two shots rang out from Phillip's gun, and the draugr fell headless to the ground. James saw the other draugr behind Phillip, a double-headed axe raised to strike down on Phillip's skull. James darted at the attacker and had it by the neck instantly. He lifted it and squeezed until his fingers curled inside his palm and the head rolled over his knuckles and hit the dirt. He heard the footstep and whirled around to attack. Suckhead McSimilar landed a punch hard enough to send James staggering. Another punch whipped his head to the side, and a final blow to his chin clacked his teeth together and sent him backward and onto his rump. James recovered as Suckhead pounced on Phillip, knocked his gun away, and pinned him to the ground. He snarled in Phillip's face as he shook him and shouted at him. "Where is it, boy?"

Phillip pushed back, struggling against the vamp's impossible strength. "What?!"

"You got somethin' of mine!"

James rushed Suckhead and shoulder-checked him off of Phillip. The vampire rolled, and James put himself between Phillip and his prey. He barked and snarled at him, braced for another attack.

The vamp stood and brushed himself off. James saw his head jerk slightly as if something pinched a nerve in his neck. He grit his teeth and glared at them. "Another time."

James blinked, and Suckhead McSimilar was gone from sight.

"Shit," Phillip said, breathless. "The hell did he go?"

James growled, the wolf pushing at the front of his mind, heightening his vision and hearing to its limits. Only a nudge would give the animal control as James searched the area, trying to see or hear any trace of where their attacker might've gone.

Besides the disintegrating husks of two dead draugrs, the area was clear. James shifted to human form and turned to Phillip. "I didn't see him run off."

"He's a vampire," Phillip said. "Don't they move faster than the speed of light?"

"No, I can usually see Lacy run off. Even if it is a blur."

"The fuck," Phillip muttered. He looked at James. "You know who that was, right?"

149

Phillip was about to answer his own question when something rustled in the brush. James shifted to wolf form, taking in the scents as Phillip picked his gun up and aimed at the sound. The blood and vanilla hit James's senses just before Lacy stepped out of the dark. "Pierce Mease Butler," she said in her trademark casual tone. "He's an asshole. And sorry I'm late. Girl problems." James felt his heart skip a beat, saw something in her eyes. Something was off. She was acting like her normal self, but that was just it. It was like she was acting.

James shifted, and Phillip holstered his gun. "Nice," Phillip said. "What the hell happened back at the hotel?"

"A lot," Lacy said. "And Butler's place is right over there, though I doubt he's still hanging around. Saw him head the other way."

"Where would he be going?" Phillip asked.

Lacy shrugged. "Dunno, but I wouldn't hang around the most obvious place I could be found if it was me."

It seemed like several minutes for James, the anger in his chest mixing with the hurt in his gut as he glared at Lacy. He replayed that night at Westenra again, holding her close to him, kissing her, wanting her. He still wanted her. The wolf mewled in his mind and stepped back. James could feel its confusion, could feel it going through the same emotions he was. But here she was. The same Lacy he'd once thought cared for him. The one he'd fallen for. The one he'd felt he'd betrayed in some way when he'd slept with Molly.

Now she was the one who'd lied to him.

Walking to the car without a word, James opened the door and got his clothes out to start dressing as Lacy continued to talk.

"I was tracking Butler, but he's way older than me. It means he's got me on everything. Speed, strength, all of it. Kind of a slippery shit, but I managed to follow him here. Looks like I just missed him."

James finished dressing and spotted Lacy's phone sitting in the passenger seat. New anger welled, and he picked the device up and went back to her. He shoved it at her. "I believe you left this in the room."

Lacy took it and smiled. "Thanks, Jimmy!"

"Yeah," Phillip said. "Might want a different password."

Lacy paused, and James saw her face fall slightly. Her entire demeanor changed. James could almost hear a door shut between them, could feel her close off from him.

It hurt.

She pursed her lips and stared at the phone as she sighed.

"Who are you working for?" James asked.

She shook her head and looked at him, all traces of her smile gone. "Can't tell you that."

"Why are you here?" Phillip said. "You leave right after we get back from Florida, ghost us, then just happen to show back up in Savannah-damn-Georgia of all places?"

She gave Phillip the same expression. "Can't tell you that, either."

"Goddamit, Lacy," Phillip said. "After everything we went through?"

She raised an eyebrow at him. "Funny coming from you, Bacon. How long were you lying to Jimmy about who you were working for?"

Phillip fumed. "Listen here, you hemoglobin-munchin'—"

"She does have a point, to be fair," James said automatically, cutting him off.

Phillip whirled on him. "You're *defending* her?!"

"Not necessarily," James said. "Just pointing it out." He spoke as he turned to Lacy. "You need to explain—" He stopped short, his eyes on the spot where Lacy had been standing. The wolf zipped to the forefront, his sight and hearing wide open, his sense of smell picking up everything. The bloody vanilla trailed off toward the road, the sound of sneakers beating on the asphalt fading as Phillip cursed loudly. James didn't register what he was saying, his mind focused on the direction Lacy had gone. He started to strip off the new clothes. "Stay here."

"What?!"

James shifted and gave the wolf everything he could without giving the beast full control as he moved from the woods and blasted down the road at wolfen speed in the direction Lacy had gone. Her scent began to grow stronger, the sound of her running growing closer as trees and the occasional car went by in a blur. He saw a shape in the distance, and it shifted to the side to avoid a truck. James took the cue and did the same, the move barely slowing him down. His muscles began to burn, his joints aching as he and the wolf both pushed harder, his body picking up speed. He could see Lacy's pink t-shirt in the distance, the color distorted slightly in his yellow night vision. He could see her hair blowing back in the wind, her arms and legs moving at impossible speed. He pushed even harder, closing the gap between them just before she bolted down another road. James took the corner as well, the space between them widening only slightly as the trees eventually turned into marshlands. He pressed himself again, the wolf taking only the slightest amount of control to dull the pain in his body from taxing himself. He drew closer to her again, this time almost enough to reach out to her. Nipped at her feet, startling her enough to slow her down. He kicked with his right foot and launched himself into the air, sailing over her head and landing in front of her. She stopped on the spot as he blocked the road in front of her. They stared at each other for a minute, both breathing heavily from running. He'd never seen her winded before. She'd been pushing herself too. But why?

"Jimmy," she said between breaths. "Get the fuck out of my way."

James barked twice. *No.*

"James, I mean it," she said, her breathing slowing. "I'll kick your ass all over this place. *Move.*"

James shifted to human form and approached; his face twisted in anger. He hadn't meant to loom over her before and felt bad about it. He often forgot his size. He meant it this time. He wasn't trying to intimidate a woman.

He was staring down a possible opponent.

"Then do it." He leaned in closer, his nose almost touching hers, his eyes locked on her icy blues. "Hit me."

Lacy stood her ground, glaring back at him, her jaw clenched and her body rigid. He saw the fury in her eyes, the anger.

The hurt.

He shouted at her. "*Hit me!*"

His heart jumped; the wolf inside braced for combat as she grabbed him by the face. It took him only a second to register her cool lips pressed hard against his. He returned the kiss just as aggressively, pulling her close. He pressed his hand to the small of her back, ran his other up her back and through her hair, and found her bra strap. His mind spun, the mixture of anger and want dizzying. Her scent and need intoxicated him, his heart pounded in his chest as he moved his hand away from her bra strap and rested it on the back of her head, not wanting to let her go. He didn't want the kiss to end, not even long enough to move to the next step as he felt her arms around him. His chest ached slightly when she ended the kiss and rested her head against his chest. He held her, wanting to protect her from whatever it was that was causing her so much pain and conflict.

"I'm sorry, James," she said, her voice a whisper. "I didn't have a choice. I still don't."

"You always have a choice," James said without pause.

She pulled away enough to look up at him. She shook her head slightly, tears in her eyes. "No, no I don't. Please understand that."

He could feel his jaw clenched, his nerves on edge and his body tense as if he were physically trying to push back against the heartbreaking wall between them. A wall that he'd built. One he knew he would likely not ever fully tear down. She'd lied to him. She was still lying to him, only now by refusing to open up to him rather than misleading him.

A breeze whipped through the night, the coolness against his skin not as comforting to him as Lacy's touch, but still refreshing in its own way. It moved her long, thick chocolate curls with it, exposing her pale and lovely neck. James's eyes instinctively focused on a small mark behind her ear, and his mind whirred. The wall between them still hurt, still took his breath, but he realized then that it was a necessary wall. It had to be there. He had to make sure that it didn't come down. Not yet. Not until he had answers.

"I'm not asking you to trust me on anything else," she said. "Walk away from this, James. Let it play out."

James had never been one to lie. Now, he hoped he was good enough at it to keep things from getting any more complicated than they had just gotten at that very moment. "Okay," he said automatically, nodding. "I'll talk to Phillip. We'll leave in the morning."

She smiled at him, reached up, and kissed him gently and briefly on the lips. "Thank you." She pulled away and zipped off into the night, her vampiric speed leaving only the faint trace of her scent behind.

James stared in the direction she'd gone as Phillip pulled up in his car. He heard Phillip speaking, but he couldn't take his eyes off the dark road Lacy had taken. "Goddamn, you two were *movin'*," he said as his window rolled down. "If I didn't have Lacy's phone on my tracker, I'd still be..." He trailed off. "Oh hell, what'd I miss?"

22

H ave you heard anything I've said, or are you too busy brooding?"

James kept staring out the window as Phillip guided the car along the highway. Phillip decided that heading back in the general direction of Savannah was the only option they had if they planned on taking down Agatha. "We can ditch the car and hole up in the Abercorn house," Phillip had said. "They've already cleaned it, so they've got no reason to go back in there. And get dressed. You ain't sittin' your naked ass on my upholstery."

"James," Phillip said, firmly this time. "Seriously."

"I apologize," James said, not looking at him. "I may need you to repeat yourself."

Phillip sighed, not hiding his annoyance. "Dude, you gonna have to let that girl go. She's messin' your head up."

"It's more complicated than that."

"No shit. You're tellin' me she's got the same damn tattoo on her neck that Agatha has. Fuck, James. They're working together."

James looked away from the window and at Phillip with a hard glare. "No, they aren't. Of that, I am certain."

"What, because she planted one on you before she ran off?" Phillip shook his head. "Not trying to be insensitive here, but it's hard to believe you're not thinking with your dick."

"She wants us to leave," James said. "She's afraid for us. For me."

Phillip nodded. "Yeah, I get that. But she's also wrapped up in whatever shit Agatha's doing. Christ, man. Both these chicks got Dracula's mark tattooed on their necks."

"That text message said something about a rogue," James said. "It's entirely possible that Agatha is their rogue, and Lacy is here trying to find her and stop her."

"Ain't ruling that one out, either," Phillip said. "But what the hell does Noble Jones have to do with it?"

"Alma sent us there if you'll recall," James said.

"Yeah, she did. Now she's dead as hell. And her coven. Grab that file out of the backseat."

James reached into the back and pulled the file out from underneath the empty bag he'd brought for his clothes. He spoke as he opened the file. "Butler said we have something of his. The only thing we took from the house is that deed signing everything back over to Noble Jones."

Phillip nodded. "Yup."

"But why go to such lengths? You said Butler died a pauper. He squandered his entire fortune twice."

"Doesn't mean third time's not a charm," Phillip said. "Money makes people do stupid shit, and that place is rolling in income now with all the tourism. It's still in the family." Phillip clenched his jaw and shook his head. "Slaves when they were alive, still slaves after they're dead. Fucked up shit."

James looked at Phillip. He could see the anger in him, could see the hurt it was causing. Phillip had been through it, there was no question. He was sensitive to oppression against others, and he had every right to be. Phillip's record was spotless outside of the occasional speeding ticket when he was younger, nothing that almost one hundred percent of the population had against them. He'd been pulled over more than once for what he'd referred to as "Driving While Black." There were times when they would be in class working in groups, and the other students would ignore Phillip's points and ideas. "Being Educated While Black." James couldn't imagine what Phillip was going through, seeing people who'd lived and died as property now being controlled by someone else who only saw them as tools for use. And he'd had to put so many of them down since they'd been there. Did he see it as giving them peace? Freeing them? Or was there a chance that they were only adding to their torment?

"Kathleen Wilson is the key to all of this," James said, getting the subject back on track. "She found something she wasn't supposed to find."

Phillip nodded in agreement. "Then let's see what else Miss Wilson might've found."

D ude, you're lucky I work late," Hoyt said, his voice sounding canned from the speakers on Phillip's phone. "And you're lucky you're blocking the tracking on your phones. They're out everywhere looking for you two."

"They'll never take us alive," James said, unable to keep his tone from being bitter.

"Okay, that was kind of funny," Hoyt said.

"Kathleen Wilson's place," Phillip said, pushing the conversation forward. "You got the report on the search?"

"Yeah, but it doesn't really go into what you guys are looking for." Hoyt leaned closer to the screen, and James could hear the tinny sound of typing from the other end. "Looks like they found the place a wreck, though. Like it was searched or something."

Phillip rolled his eyes. "Pretty good guess they got what they were after. Hello again, Square One."

"The CSI guys didn't find anything that stood out to them," Hoyt continued. "Nothing that pointed to her being anything other than an above-average college student. She graduated and was trying to go back for graduate work. Looks like she was on track to get more scholarships for her historical research. Got her emails and phone records here, though, and you guys might find this interesting."

"Do tell," James said.

"Looks like she reached out to a professor about something she found at work while she was in the archives. She didn't want to go into it over email, so she set up a meeting with the guy. He teaches night classes on Southern Heritage at the university."

Phillip sighed. "His name ain't Butler, is it?"

"Good guess."

James put it together in his mind and spoke. "I'm also going to guess that she set up a meet for the night she was murdered."

Hoyt nodded onscreen. "That's two for the win."

"And Butler insisted on meeting her at Butler Island Plantation."

"Wow, three for three. You two are a lot smarter than that Agent Smith guy says you are."

James saw the opportunity for some much-needed levity and took it. "I like to think I'm quite brilliant."

Phillip looked at him sidelong. "Says the guy who drinks out of the toilet."

"It has a better flavor."

"Blue water is bad for you, James."

Hoyt interrupted them, laughing as he spoke. "Okay, guys, knock it off. Time's wastin'. You said you have that paperwork she was looking over?"

"Yeah, I've got it here," Phillip said, holding up the folder.

"Keep that safe. I'm looking through her hard drive now, and her cloud accounts. She didn't digitize it. Probably wanted to ask her professor first."

"Wait, hold the phone," Phillip said, turning to James. "Didn't Kimble say that Kathleen's hard drive was wiped?"

"I believe the term she used was 'destroyed'," James said.

"Yeah, I got a computer here that says different," Hoyt said.

"Why would Kimble lie about that?" Phillip wondered.

Something clicked in James's mind. "We were sent here to be a distraction."

Phillip nodded. "Yeah, I can see that. Send us down here to look left while they go after whatever it is on the right."

"Makes sense," Hoyt said over the phone. "Chances are you two weren't even supposed to get as far as you did. Probably why Smith ran down here like he did when you brought in Noble Jones."

"We're dead in the water here unless we can get back into Savannah," Phillip said.

Hoyt gave him a sly smile. "Well, I'm pretty sure an interdepartmental memo just now went out telling everyone to hold off on looking for you two. It won't stick long, but it'll buy you some time. Day at the most." His smile quickly turned into a frown as he looked away from the camera. James heard him type some more, then saw him sit back in his chair. "Oh, shit."

Phillip blinked. "Oh shit? I don't like oh shit. What's oh shit mean?"

Hoyt looked at the camera. "Noble Jones just got busted out of lock-up. By force."

I t was shortly after eleven when Phillip and James pulled into the dirt driveway in front of Hoyt's place. Hoyt's neighborhood was actually a small trailer park just outside of the Savannah city limits and tucked away from the main road at the end of an unpaved road that would've been missed had Hoyt not sent his address to Phillip via text message. There were eighteen, maybe twenty trailers total on the short stretch of road that comprised the park, Hoyt's being on the very end. The place was well-kept, the yards clean and the single-wide homes on either side had a variety of hand-built porches and decks at the front doors, most of them covered and screened in. James saw a few yards and driveways with the innocent clutter of tricycles, big-wheels, and sports toys intended for use by small children. Inhabitants sat under low porch lights in groups, stopping to look over their shoulders at the newcomers driving so slowly through the place. The wolf kept James sharp, allowing him to feel the unease and suspicion coming from the residents around him.

"We need to do what we're gonna do here and leave," Phillip said. "We act right, make it obvious we ain't here to cause trouble, and we'll be fine."

James raised an eyebrow. "I doubt they're dangerous, Phillip. Though the wolf can feel their ire at us being here."

"Ain't no different than the hood, James," Phillip said as if explaining a simple fact. "These people have seen enough trouble. They don't want any more of it here, and they'll defend their homes and think of anyone else as outsiders here to start shit. We're cool, they're cool. We bring trouble, they'll make sure to handle the trouble and us along with it."

James remembered the neighborhood Phillip had grown up in. Phillip was born in Kansas and grew up in a place he often referred to as "Hidden Valley." Though the police often cited it as crime-ridden and dangerous, James got a much different experience when they'd gone there the first time to visit Phillip's mother.

"Pretty simple, James," Phillip had said during the drive. "White folk have brought problems in the past, and black folk don't want it in their yards anymore. So don't be surprised if you get stared down. You don't go there unless you're with someone, related to someone, or know someone."

"Sounds exclusive," James said, trying to keep the levity. He wasn't often fond of heavier conversation.

"These people are just trying to survive, and that's enough to deal with on its own without strangers coming in and causing problems," Phillip had said. "You show up and act right in my neighborhood, I'll give you a bit to make sure you're cool and you know someone, then we're cool. But everyone here is family either by blood or by community. You show up and act an asshole to Miss Essie down the street, I'm gonna come talk to you. You show up and get cross with Little Billy's momma, I'm gonna come talk to you. It's how we kept the peace here all these years. They wanna be afraid of the place and call it a crime-zone? Fine. Keeps 'em out and leaves us in peace."

The residents had stared down Phillip's car as they drove through, most of them acknowledging Phillip once they saw him behind the wheel. Some of them nodded to James, still regarding him warily. By the time they'd arrived at Phillip's house, several people from the houses nearby were already outside watching them. They'd been met at the front porch by Mrs. Brown, a short overweight Black woman with strong arms and a welcoming personality. She'd hugged Phillip and kissed him on the cheeks chanting "My baby! My baby!" over and over before moving to James and embracing him as a son. "Phillip told me all about you! Thank you for takin' care of my boy!"

That scene had obviously been the catalyst for James to be welcome in the community during Thanksgiving and Christmas visits to Phillip's mother, the same people who had stared him down before now sending him home with a plate of food and a clap on the back.

Hoyt opened the front door as James and Phillip climbed the steps up onto the porch. He wore a Born of Winter band shirt and jeans, his long black hair still tied in a single braid rather than the two he normally wore. James could hear the sound of hard metal music mixed with acoustic guitars coming from inside the trailer. "Thanks for coming out, guys," Hoyt said. "I was live-streaming the video at the time. Otherwise, I'd have sent it to you. Takes time for that stuff to get archived so I can get to it without the man seeing me in there."

"No problem," Phillip said. "I thought you said you lived on a reservation?"

"I used to before I moved here," Hoyt said, motioning them to follow him inside. He spoke over his shoulder as he led them into the small home. "The government doesn't officially recognize any of the Native American nations in Georgia, so there aren't any Federally recognized reservations. We're a community. That's all that matters." He went to the fridge and pulled three beers out, popping the tops and handing them over to Phillip and James before leading them down the short hallway to the bedroom that Hoyt had apparently converted into what looked like a high-tech superhero's lair. Four computer towers sat on the floor under a long desk against the far wall of the room. Six monitors sat on the desk while two large flat-panel televisions hung on the wall above them. Each monitor displayed a different image, some of them maps and websites, others nothing but waterfalls of binary code.

"Looks like the Matrix in here," Phillip mumbled under his breath.

"*Voooom!*" James said, also keeping his voice down. Phillip shot him a look.

"Since when did they teach people how to run a secret lair at med school?" Phillip said, turning back to Hoyt.

"Got my fingers in all kinds of stuff," Hoyt said. "The Medical Examiner thing is my main gig, but I've been doing code and hacker bullshit since I was a kid. More of a hobby, really. I got a degree in computer forensics. Ended up getting hired by the FBI after I hacked into their database."

Phillip blinked. "They hired you for being stupid and a threat to national security?"

Hoyt laughed. "Nah, I just wanted to mess with them. Ordered like six hundred pizzas on their dime and sent them to the office. Most of the agents loved it, the brass was not amused."

"Yet they hired you," James said. "Interesting."

"Amused and impressed are two different things," Hoyt said as he sat down in a tall-backed chair in front of the desk and typed a few things on the keyboard. "Went back to med school and I've been looking at corpses ever since." A desktop window opened on one of the large televisions on the wall as he spoke. "I'd have told you over the phone, but I figured it would be better if you two saw it for yourselves."

"You told us Jones got busted out," Phillip said.

Hoyt glanced over his shoulder. "Didn't say by who." He hit a key on the keyboard and the video began to play. James watched the screen intently, the black-and-white security camera footage playing without sound as it displayed the holding cells that ran on either side of the brightly lit hallway. A door opened at the far end and a guard stepped into the area. He walked toward the screen, keeping his pace slow enough for him to glance into each cell as he went. The lights flickered, and the guard stopped and looked up and around.

"This isn't the interesting part," Hoyt said.

James felt his stomach knot as Lacy appeared in the hall with the guard, zipping into the frame as if coming out of her vampiric speed. The guard startled, then relaxed as she approached him. James could see her eyes sparkle, even in the black-and-white picture. She moved like a predator approaching her prey, keeping the stunned victim in an intense state of shock. She reached up and stroked his cheek, smiling and saying something to him. She put her other hand up, holding his head and drawing him closer as if to kiss him. The wolf stayed quiet, sending no urges, James's tension and dismay his own as Lacy jerked the guard's head almost completely around before dropping him to the floor. She pulled a badge off of the man's belt and opened a nearby cell.

Noble Jones stepped out, looking down at her. He and Lacy both ran down the hall, gone in a couple of blurs that the camera was barely able to pick up.

23

Trying to keep his thoughts and emotions organized and manageable was possibly the hardest thing James had ever done up to this point. The wolf was sending waves of anger and determination at him, feelings of betrayal mixed with a sense of doubt.

Yet, its anger wasn't directed at Lacy. Not entirely.

"They're headed to Wormsloe," James said. "It's the only place that would make sense."

Phillip turned to Hoyt. "We'll leave the file with you. They won't think to look here."

Hoyt held his hands up. "No offense, guys, but you two gave your real names out like a couple of fuck-ups. The only way I'll be safe is if you guys leave and take that folder with you. Kill off the one you revealed yourselves to, and we'll talk." He turned fully to James. "That's how you shut the door you opened with the spirits. At least that's what my Grandpa always told me."

James had his phone out, watching the replay of Noble Jones's jail-break over and over as Phillip drove out toward Wormsloe. "This doesn't make any sense," James said. "She wouldn't do something like this without an explanation."

Phillip grunted. "Still blowin' my mind that you're trying to justify anything she's said or done, man."

James looked up at him. "It's Lacy, Phillip."

"I know," Phillip shot back. He breathed before speaking again. "She was against arresting Jones off the jump. She chilled out when she saw him on the street cam, but she wasn't all that thrilled with it. She's made the conscious effort to fuck with your head every time you've asked a question that gets a little close to whatever it is she's up to. And you can't deny that tatt she and Agatha are both rockin'. James, too much of this points to them working together. The bigger question is who in the *hell* they're working for."

James pinched his fingers together against the phone screen and spread them out to zoom in on the paused video. The image digitized and blurred, trashing any of the quality it'd had before. "Damn it," he muttered. The wolf gave a small bark in his mind. *If I could just see her face,* he thought at the creature.

"You good, man?" Phillip asked.

James caught the sincere concern in Phillip's tone and looked up at him. "Yeah, I'm good." Phillip nodded, and James went back to staring at the phone screen. He startled when something smacked him on the shoulder. "Hey!"

Phillip stared ahead, focused on the road, one hand on the steering wheel while the other gripped the makeshift taped grip he had created for his customized newspaper. "Imma ask you again: you good?"

"I said yes," James said.

Phillip shook his head. "I don't believe you." He kept his eyes forward as he smacked James with the rolled paper again. "How 'bout now?"

"I'd be better if you'd stop hitting me."

Smack!

"Now?"

"Phillip, I said stop!"

Smack!

"Gonna keep happening until you quit lyin', Snoopy."

James stopped himself from snatching the newspaper from Phillip and hurling it out the window, the realization of what Phillip was doing hitting him harder than the newspaper had. He sighed, staring out into the night as Phillip turned onto the road leading the way to Wormsloe Plantation. "I may need another."

Smack!

Phillip spoke again, still watching the road. "Better?"

"Quite." James looked at him. "Thanks."

Phillip nodded, then smacked him again.

"I said I was good," James snapped. "Why'd you hit me again?!"

Phillip tossed the paper into the backseat. "That one was for the pile of werewolf shit you left next to my car, you dick."

P hillip pulled up to the front gate of Wormsloe and stopped the car. He sighed and shook his head. "Here we go again."

James tensed, keeping his face neutral as the two large guards from earlier stared back at them, standing in front of the gates like before and armed with the huge .50 CAL Brownings. One of them smirked and motioned for Phillip to roll the windows down, shifting the large gun to one hand in order to make the gesture. James looked at Phillip, who sat with his hands gripping the steering wheel so hard his knuckles had gone white. "I believe he would like a word."

Phillip grunted. "Yeah, that's what that seven-foot vampire fucker has his damn handheld turret gun loaded with. Words."

James rolled his window down and leaned his head out. "Good evening, gentlemen. We believe Mr. Jones and Miss Faulkner came home a bit ago."

"Yeah, they did," the guard said. He looked at his partner and nodded before looking back at James. "They're expecting you."

"I'm sure they are," James said. "My friend would like assurances that you will not use your considerable firepower on us as we enter."

"No promises, but we'll think about it." The guards chuckled as they stepped aside, the one on the left who hadn't spoken making a motion to someone on the other side of the gate.

"See?" James said as he turned to Phillip. "He'll think about it. They aren't all bad."

"I'm going to fucking die tonight," Phillip grumbled as he reluctantly pulled forward. James kept his eye on the two as they moved past, making sure he didn't see them raise their guns and point them at the car. The gate was closing behind them, James looking over his shoulder to take a last glance at the guards when Phillip hit the brakes hard.

"Okay," James said, startled. "That was necessary because?"

Phillip kept his eyes forward, still clutching the wheel as if his life depended on it. "Because I didn't wanna run your psycho-vampire girl over and fuck my car up."

James looked forward and saw Lacy standing in front of them, her stance tense, her eyes glowing bright red as she glared back at them. The headlights on Phillip's car showed small traces of blood spray on her pale legs, and her pink Hello Kitty shirt was also spattered in blood. Her mouth was covered, red running down her chin and soaking into the shirt collar. Her face was sallow, her hair a tangled mess matted with blood.

Phillip spoke with an even tone. "James, please tell me why Lacy looks like she's feelin' cute and might break into the mall and eat brains later."

James got out of the car, ignoring Phillip's panicked protests as he closed the door behind him. He approached Lacy cautiously, the wolf tense and prepared in his mind. "Lacy? It's me. I was worried about you." He motioned at the car. "Both of us were. We thought they'd gotten you back at the hotel."

She stared at him, not speaking or responding other than following his every movement with her eyes. James couldn't help noticing that she seemed off, her eyes hard as she stared at him like a paranoid animal on the defense.

"James," Phillip called from the car. "Dude, something's up with her!"

"I know," James said over his shoulder.

"Get your ass back in the car and leave that girl alone," Phillip called. "She ain't right!"

James moved closer to Lacy, reaching for her as he spoke. "Lacy, let's talk about it. Let us help." She just stared at him with the same expression, blankness with anger seething below it, her body rigid and tense as if she might lash out at him. James put his hand on her cheek, felt her cool skin against his. She looked up at him and blinked, the glowing red in her eyes fading slightly as her lower lip trembled. *She's in there*, James thought. The wolf urged against his body's automatic response to relax, sending a warning bark through his mind. Lacy reached up and put her hand over his. "That's right. We're here to help."

She gripped his hand and jerked, pain shooting white-hot up James's arm and through his shoulder and back as his forearm snapped. He barely had time to shout before Lacy slammed her hand into his chest and sent him flying across the parking lot. He hit the asphalt and rolled until his lay on his back, his chest locked and airless as he tried to take in a breath, his stomach churning from the nausea the pain was causing him.

The wolf came to the forefront, pushed away his pain and forced his body to shift and heal his human wounds.

The James tried to fight Wolf, but Wolf pushed the James away and held it down, kept the body. The Lacy had to die. She was traitor. Attacked pack.

The Phillip was out of the car, gun aimed. The Lacy moved at it, but Wolf was faster. Grabbed the Lacy by the nape of her neck and moved to throw her away from the Phillip. The Lacy caught Wolf's arm. Smacked it away, punched Wolf in face before grabbing Wolf's head and slamming it to ground. Wolf recovered quickly and went for prey again, yearned to feel the Lacy's dust in fur. The Lacy was on the Phillip, pinned him to the ground, and bared his neck. Canines long as the Lacy reared back, hissing, ready to feed. Wolf felt fury, rivaled only by hatred of the betrayed. Rushed the Lacy, jaws open to crush skull.

James surged forward, broke free of the wolf's oppression and took control as he shoved the beast back. He moved his jaws clear of Lacy just as he felt some of her hair brush his tongue and lips. He tackled her off of Phillip, rolled with her as she fought against him and grappled with him. She flipped him onto his back easily, pinned him down, began to swipe back and forth as she slashed at his chest with her long vampire nails. James heard the telltale sound of the gate opening and large guns being locked and loaded. He barely heard Phillip's shout before the air was filled with thunder, bullets, and the stench of gunpowder.

"Oh, fuck *me!*"

James slung his arm over and yanked Lacy down and rolled as massive rounds slammed into the ground and sent chunks of stone and dirt airborne. Lacy fought against James, struggled beneath him as he rolled over top of her and dragged her in front of Phillip's car. He tried to pin her down and fell back when she dug her claws through the flesh of his jowl, scraping his molars through the meat. He yelped uncontrollably, the pain like fire as she pulled herself free and ran off into the night.

He looked up and saw Phillip duck behind a parked car and return fire at the two large vampires firing their turret guns. He felt the impact through the front bumper as .50 CAL rounds tore into the backside of Phillip's car. The gunpowder stench mixed with gasoline, and James heard Phillip scream *"James! Gas tank!"* just before the back end of the car exploded. James heard the two vampires shout to each other, the guns silent, and took his chance.

Fire dried the blood on his face to the fur as he ran up the front end of the car and kicked off, blew through the wall of flames like a curtain, and landed on one of the gunmen before he could react. James crushed the vampire's head on the ground, picked up the machine gun, and slung it around to club the other guard in the head just as he was trying to take aim. He staggered, and James smacked the gun out of his hand and rammed his fist into the vampire's chest, the bone cavity caving in and the spine snapping as James's fist exited through the other side.

James pulled his arm out of the vampire and let the newly re-killed thing drop to dust on the ground. He looked around and saw Phillip standing next to the car he'd hidden behind, staring at the burning remains of his blue Honda Civic. He started to shift, but the wolf surged forward and stopped him, barking with a sense of warning. James touched his face where Lacy had clawed him open, felt the tendrils of meat that used to be his cheek healing slowly, the pain like fire and increasing as he was healing from his other injuries that weren't inflicted by a vampire. *Good call,* he thought at the wolf. *That may have been a bit unpleasant.*

"James," Phillip called. "Get over here! James!"

He moved over to Phillip as the wounds on his face started to heal quicker. He felt the still-tender flesh connect, cutting off the outside air drying out his gums and teeth on that side of his mouth. The pain was subsiding, but he was still hesitant to shift into human form. He'd learned a long time ago that mildly annoying pain in wolf form was agonizing and dizzying in human form. He noticed that the car Phillip was standing beside was a black current-model Corvette, the same model that Phillip had once described as "a damn Batmobile."

"What the hell happened," Phillip said as James approached. "Why'd she attack you?!"

James barked and followed it with some slight mewling, the signal they'd established years ago as *I don't know.*

Phillip shook his head as he pulled his ringing phone out. "Damn car blown up, two motherfuckers shooting at us with guns that level damn buildings, and now psycho vampires. Who gives a shit about the necromancer anymore?" He answered the call. "Hoyt, you're on speaker."

Hoyt's voice squawked from the phone's speakers. "You guys are in serious shit."

"Oh," Phillip said, not holding back the sarcasm. "Hadn't noticed. Been kinda quiet on our end."

"A call came into the bureau from Wormsloe about five minutes ago," Hoyt said. "It places you guys out there. You're not there are you?"

Phillip and James looked at each other, then back at the phone. Phillip cleared his throat. "Uh...maybe?"

"Okay," Hoyt said, dragging the word out slightly. "At least tell me you're keeping your heads down."

James and Phillip looked at the burning Honda, then at the two piles of dust around the two .50 CAL Brownings before looking back at the phone. "Yup," Phillip said quickly. "Pretty sure they don't know we're here."

"Wow," Hoyt said. "Smith's an asshole, but he's not wrong about you two being able to fuck up a wet dream."

James's cheek had just finished healing. He shifted, wincing slightly at the sharp pain in his face, and kicked himself for assuming it was a hundred percent. *At least it isn't still open,* he thought. "Hoyt, what's going on?"

"The SCU just sent their tactical guys out. They're coming to Wormsloe looking for you guys *and* Lacy. They plan to write it off as you guys holding Noble Jones hostage."

"How long?" Phillip asked.

"They're about thirty minutes out now," Hoyt said. "They're hauling ass."

"Shit," Phillip said, looking up at James. "Hoyt, I'm standing next to a black Chevy Corvette XR1."

"Sweet ride," Hoyt said. "Not going to help you against a bunch of heavily armed dudes. They didn't find you at the hotel. What the hell happened there anyway?"

"I'm fairly certain I've lost my room deposit," James said.

"They didn't cover your room when they sent you guys down?"

"I upgraded."

"Pretty sure this thing has a remote computer," Phillip said, rolling his eyes at James. "Can you access it?"

"It'd be nice if you challenged me," Hoyt said. "Can you see the VIN number?" Phillip found it and read it off to Hoyt. The car doors unlocked, the engine roaring to life suddenly as the headlights turned on. "You two get the fuck out of there."

"No time," James said. He looked at Phillip. "I've got to go after Lacy."

"James, are you fuckin' kidding?!" Phillip snapped. "She almost killed your ass! Those two assholes you smoked at the gate weren't the only walking tanks Jones had around here."

"It wasn't Lacy," James argued. "She wouldn't have attacked me like that. Not to injure or kill me."

"The necromancer would have to be in some proximity of whoever they're controlling," Hoyt said. "At least on the same property. She was probably there those times at Butler's."

"I can end this," James said. "You know I can."

Phillip clenched his jaw, shook his head as if about to explode into a tirade, then looked at James again. "You're an idiot. Okay, let's go." He opened the car door.

"No," James said. "It's too dangerous. Can you keep the SCU away from here?"

Phillip patted his hand on the roof of the Corvette. "In this baby? Shee-it." He paused. "James, this is stupid, you going in there alone. You get killed and I'm kicking your ass."

"Buy me the time," James said. "I'll be fine."

Phillip nodded. "You'd better be, dumbass." He got into the car, and James moved out of the way as Phillip kicked it into reverse and pulled out of the spot. The engine revved, the tires screaming on the asphalt as Phillip peeled off through the gate and down the road, the sound of the engine fading into the night.

James stood tall and sniffed the air, catching the last remnants of Lacy's scent as he looked in the direction she'd gone. The wolf gave a low *woof* in his mind. *I know*, he thought at it. *But we can't leave her behind. I won't.*

The wolf shook off and barked, sending a sense of determination through James that matched his own. *That's more like it.* He shifted and blazed off in Lacy's direction, not holding back his speed as he made for the home of Noble Jones.

24

James wished he still had the collar Phillip had given him earlier. He wanted to be able to check in and make sure Phillip was okay. He also wanted to check in with Molly, though that would involve a little more than a dog collar with a radio and a GPS. He didn't know why he cared so much about her. Not that he was in love with her by any means. He'd had one-night stands before, but he found them dissatisfying in that nothing else would ever come of them. James had never been a "casual sex" kind of person. He cared about Molly. But he'd been through so much with Lacy, and had developed feelings for her, which only deepened his sense of guilt. And he knew she felt the same, but what was holding her back?

He didn't care. She was still Lacy and giving up on her was not an option.

Gunshots jerked his mind away from the jumbled musings and emotions, his charge toward Noble Jones's estate no longer mechanical. He heard shouts, more gunfire, and an explosion as the night sky lit up with a plume of fire. His stomach dropped as he pushed himself harder, faster. *They're already here,* James thought. *The SCU. How'd they get here so fast?*

He burst from the trees just as a legion of draugrs charged, all hissing and growling, armed with scythes and rakes and every other imaginable farm tool. The small gazebo at the end of the stairs leading up to the house lay in fiery ruin, the staircase wholly inaccessible now as Noble Jones and his army of vampires held their ground at the top. They opened fire on the draugrs, undead slaves dropping to the ground under another hailstorm of bullets. Something exploded from behind the house, and more draugrs emerged from the trees. A group of Jones's men broke off the frontline to counterattack and were overwhelmed. Draugrs tore the humans apart quickly while the vampires were able to take a few down with them before succumbing to dismemberment and beheading. Their attacks weren't wild or feral like he'd seen in zombie movies. The groups were coordinated, organized.

Holy shit, James thought to the wolf. *It's a literal army of the dead.*

The wolf huffed in agreement and pushed out, giving more focus and strength to James's wolfen vision and hearing. There was a grunt, high-pitched and female. She snarled and hissed. James knew that hiss. He bolted in as the draugr army reached Jones and his men, gunfire only cutting down the first row of dead as the rest swarmed them. James sent several draugrs flying into the air as he plowed into combat, bullets whipping by him and connecting to any draugrs he'd missed. He glanced at Jones as automatic fire barely drowned out the groans, gurgling, and rasping around him. He heard Lacy grunt again, heard her cry out. He darted in that direction as the two men continued to open fire from their position in the windows on the upper floor. He rounded the corner just as Lacy was tearing the head off of a draugr. She tossed the body aside and spun around, her eyes widening when she saw James. "Jimmy, no!"

A draugr lunged at her from behind. James shoved her aside, grabbed the attacker, and tore him in half. Another came at them. Lacy attacked him, took him down easily. More poured out from the night, all of them gnashing their broken teeth, their glowing eyes fixed hungrily on James and Lacy.

James shifted to human form and grabbed Lacy's arm. "We've got to get inside!"

She nodded and motioned for him to follow her. He shifted back into wolf form as she led the way to the back porch of the giant house. She around to the side and pulled open a set of doors that faced upward and shouted over her shoulder. "Here! Let's go!"

James followed her down, moved past her as she turned and closed the door behind them. She threw a latch and backed away as the doors started to shake and twist from the draugrs trying to get them open.

"That's not going to hold long," Lacy said as she moved down the stairs and into the cellar. "This way."

James followed her, staying in his wolf form just in case as they moved past aisles of wine and old tools. He followed her up a set of stairs to a door that opened into the downstairs foyer beneath the staircase leading up to the second floor, stepping out just as the front doors burst open. Noble Jones was shouting at his men to fall back as they peppered the oncoming crowd of the dead with machine gun fire. A draugr took several rounds to the chest before falling, a machete raised high about to strike the shooter. It swung down as it fell to the floor, burying the machete deep into the soldier's face. Very human blood poured from the wound as the man went down. Jones ordered his men to move the body and get the doors shut, but more draugrs were already coming onto the porch.

My turn, James thought as he charged in. He swung his arms left and right haymaker style, the attack sending them flying off the porch in multiple directions. He gave the wolf full control, screaming at it in his mind as he stepped back. *Now! Do it now!*

Wolf stood, felt the grace of the All-Father, and called out to Fenrir for aid and strength. The James was braced, ready to come forward again, but Wolf knew better than the James. Knew to push. The Lacy had betrayed. The James was too trusting of the cold ones, too ready to embrace those who had slaughtered hundreds of Fenrir's children at the behest of their master. The James tried to fight, but Wolf kept it back as the call grew louder, the man-made ground beneath Wolf's feet shaking and rattling. The dead things staggered away, many of them thrown by Fenrir's might as the windows in the house all shattered at once. The Lacy screamed, and Wolf felt itself thrown back as the dark vampire, the one the James called Jones, shoved Wolf off balance and into the staircase. The James took the opening, seized control, pushed Wolf to the side as it shouted. *What the hell has gotten into you?!*

James felt the wolf growl at him, defiant, stubborn. It barked at him, sent warning urges about Lacy and Jones, sent the sense of betrayal at him with images of Lacy. *I know*, he thought back. *But it wasn't her. You know that.*

"Little overboard, Jimmy, don't you think?" Lacy snapped as she moved past him and looked out through one of the broken windows. "Shit, they're regrouping. He bought us some time, but not much."

James shifted into human form despite the wolf's urges not to. "We have to get out of here. Now."

"We'll do no such thing," Noble Jones said, rounding on James.

"The SCU is on their way," James said, going back at him. "You won't just have the dead to worry about."

Jones got in his face, his eyes red and flaring, his fangs out completely as he roared. *"This is my home!* I will *not* back down!" He turned away from James and shouted at a small group of men working to seal the front doors. "Take position! Be ready to lay down fire! Hold the line!"

"Sir, there's only a few of us left," one of them said over his shoulder. "The humans are dead, and the others have retreated."

Jones and Lacy looked at each other, then Jones turned his surprised glare to James. "Vampires don't retreat easily."

"The necromancer," James said. "Agatha. She's controlling them. She's controlled you both. That's how you were freed from prison." He looked at Lacy. "And why you attacked me at the front gate."

"Then why not have them turn on me?" Jones said.

James heard the telltale sound of a gun being readied, saw the three men at the front door stop and point their weapons at Jones. The one who'd spoken earlier smiled. "Because we haven't had a chance yet."

He shifted into wolf form and shoved Jones aside as two of the three vampires rushed in. He swatted their guns aside, grabbed one by the head and yanked it free while he bit down on the second one's head, the skull collapsing under the pressure from his jaws. They were nowhere near as strong as Lacy, possibly just out of their Youngling phase. He tossed the crumbling bodies aside and made for the last one who opened fire. A bullet barely grazed James's face, the burning white hot and dizzying as he lost his footing and collided with the shooter. He fought through the blurred vision, the searing pain as he tore the vampire's throat out brought his fist down onto the vamp's chest like a hammer. The ribcage caved in completely, and the body went to dust as he stood and turned to Jones, then looked up at the top of the stairs where Pierce Mease Butler stood, clapping slowly as he smirked down at him. "Nicely done, Fido. Could've used you in the fields back in the day." He stopped clapping and sneered at Jones. "Might still have need of you."

James tensed to strike just as Jones stepped in front of him and growled at Butler. "Get the hell out of my house!"

"My house," Butler said without pause. "See, right now the only thing

keepin' them dead negroes out there from comin' back up here is me. I'd mind my manners, boy."

A flash of rage hit James hard. He made for the stairs, for Butler. The gun was out before he knew what was happening. James barely registered the sound of the flintlock pistol going off, his collarbone the only thing stopping the silver bullet from entering his chest cavity. He hit the stairs and rolled back down to the floor as Lacy cried out.

"Heel," Butler said as he tossed the flintlock aside. He moved down the stairs toward Jones, who stood in place fuming, his eyes wide with hatred and fury. James's vision blurred slightly from the pain as he looked around and saw Lacy standing in place, her face suddenly stoic and emotionless like it had been at the gate as she stared at him. Jones stood his ground as Butler moved closer to him and looked him up and down. "The matter, boy? You not gonna try to hit me?"

James saw Jones's hand balled into a fist, saw his arm shaking, his muscles strained as if he were trying to lift a hand that was now too heavy to move. The pain hit him again, and he felt the tendrils of silver moving out from the wound. The wolf barked inside and staggered around in James's mind before its legs gave. It slumped down, the silver taking hold. James moved his arm around, reaching up to where the round had hit him. His claw scraped over something hard, the stench of cooking blood wafting from the wound.

"What do you want?" Jones said, his voice strained as he struggled against whatever force was holding him.

"My rightful property," Butler said. "My status, son."

"That's what all of this has been about?" Jones asked in a disgusted tone. "The wealth you squandered away years ago?" He grunted; his mouth turned up in a smirk. "Guess I shouldn't be surprised at a Butler being petty."

Butler laughed at him. "Quit actin' like you can talk to me on the same level. My God, Jones. Actin' like you're all educated and holier than thou."

"This is about the contract that girl found," Jones said. James saw Butler's face twitch, his smug expression faltering as Jones's smirk turned into a grin. "Oh, I know all about that. Butler Plantation is supposed to revert back to the Jones family. To me."

Butler's hand moved in a blur, the sound of the slap sharp in James's ears as his vision blurred again, the pain from the gunshot wound more intense as he worked a claw into the flesh around the bullet. He heard

Butler's tone lower to a growl as he spoke. "I'll die before I let some negro from the field take my grandfather's legacy from me."

"You died years ago," Jones said, still grinning at Butler despite his face being slapped. "We're the same now, Butler. Both just a couple of blood-drinkers who can't stand the sun." He grinned at Butler again. "Welcome home, brother. Brandy's in the cabinet."

James saw Butler's face twist in pride-driven fury as he lunged at Jones, punching him hard enough to knock him down. Jones laughed loudly as Butler straddled him, swinging over and over again and shouting slurs at him while Lacy looked on with her blank stare. *Shit, he's going to kill him,* he thought as he closed his eyes and breathed deeply. He pressed his claw hard into the meat around the wound, his body spasming as the bullet moved around in its fleshy nest. He made a scooping motion and let out a small mewl as the round popped out and hit the floor followed by an impressive flow of silver-specked blood. He felt his strength start to come back, the wolf slowly getting to its feet in his mind as he worked on doing the same himself. Butler still wailed on Jones, still shouted at him while Jones laughed maniacally at him, which only seemed to enrage Butler more. James got to his feet, his legs still moderately weak, and he looked again at Lacy. She still stared off into space, her shoulders slumped as she swayed slightly in place. The necromancer had to be close by. He had to get her out of there.

He moved at the two struggling vampires, more strength returning to him as the silver poison worked its way out of his system. He grit his teeth and growled as he began to pick up momentum. He grabbed Butler by the neck and lifted him, the vampire struggling against him as he yanked at James's hand on his throat. He was weak, his struggle no more effective than if he'd been human. James slammed him down to the floor hard enough to split the wood, his grip growing tighter as thick cold vampire blood seeped between his fingers and poured from Butler's eyes, nose, mouth, and ears. James kept squeezing until his fingers met his palm, the loud crack of Butler's head separating from the crushed spine followed by the body going limp and turning into dust.

James didn't have to look up to recognize the sound of Agatha's voice as she spoke casually.

"One on his way to Davy Jones's Locker. Now, about the other two."

25

Butler had gone completely to dust, particles of what had once been a vampire from before the Civil War sifting through James's fingers as he rose to face Agatha. She stood just inside the doorframe where the large front doors had once been. Parts and pieces of draugr littered the floorboards behind her, and James could hear the sounds of those who'd survived his sonic howl rallying in the yard beyond.

He clenched his teeth, a low and threatening growl in his throat as he glared at her. Agatha chuckled as she motioned at what used to be Pierce Mease Butler. "Man was dumb as a lead sail in life, and bein' a vampire made nary a difference by his condition." She spat into the ashes at James's feet. "Good riddance to the rapscallion piece of seagull shit."

James took a step forward and went to charge Agatha. Arms wrapped around his waist, Noble Jones's scent in hitting him just before the vampire lifted him easily and slammed him to the floor. He put a foot on James's back, keeping it pressed firmly enough to keep James in place on the floor.

"There you go," Agatha said, laughing. "That a little more familiar to ya? Butler didn't even know I'd commanded him to not resist." James was able to look up at her as she motioned between Jones and Lacy. "Just like these two got no idea I'm playin' 'em both like a fiddle."

James growled at her, tried to get up, but Jones pressed harder. James's spine strained under the pressure. He heard and felt the creak of bone and cartilage at the same time. He chuffed, ran his claws lightly over the floor in three distinct scrapes.

"That means he wants you to let up."

James blinked at the sound of Phillip's voice. He moved his head and was just able to see Phillip step up on the porch behind Agatha and point a pump-action shotgun at the back of her head. Agatha said, as if someone pointing a twelve-gauge shotgun at her skull was just another day, "Nice one, boy."

Phillip pumped the shotgun, chambering a round. "Watch who you're callin' boy, blondie."

James saw Agatha nod and wave her hand nonchalantly. He felt Jones's foot lift from his back. He got to his feet as Jones backed away. Lacy still stood off to the side, still swaying as if she were both half-asleep and drunk. He shifted into human form and turned to Phillip. "You were not supposed to come here."

"Yeah, I'm not supposed to do a lot of things," Phillip said. "Like let your dumb ass get killed by Goldilocks and the three bloodsuckers. Hoyt made a few calls. We got a small window, but it's something."

"And here I thought I'd have a normal evenin'," Agatha said, her tone still casual. "Instead, I get a boomstick against my head and a nekkid man with doggy issues."

Phillip gave her a perplexed look, then spoke to James again. "She always talk like a pirate?"

"It's her charm," James said, focusing on Agatha. "Let Lacy and Jones go. It's over."

"Oh, it be *far* from over," Agatha said. She motioned to Jones and Lacy again. "These two be just a means to an end."

"What end?" James said. "Butler's estate?"

Agatha snorted. "That damned fool? Everything he had he got from his scallywag grandfather."

"Another tool," James said. He shook his head. "This is all so pointless. Why the body trail then? If he was worthless?"

"Yeah, he's got a point," Phillip said, chiming in. "All that power and all you can think of to do with it is raise the dead and kill the shit out of people who don't deserve it?"

"Butler caused me problems," Agatha said. "But he served his purpose. Kept you off me until I could get where I needed to be."

"We had you figured early," Phillip said. "Just a matter of findin' your scrawny little ass." Phillip squinted at something, then looked at James. "Dude, you can't draw for shit."

James raised an eyebrow. "I'm sorry?"

"That tatt you told me about? I'm lookin' at it now. Seriously, you can't even draw a damn bat?"

"I've always been more literary."

"Then you should've recognized that symbol."

"I'm afraid not."

"That's Count Dracula's crest for damn sure," Phillip said. He turned his attention to Agatha. "Why the hell would you have something of Dracula's on you like that?"

James heard Lacy speak, her voice low and her speech broken. He looked at her as she spoke, her lips barely moving, her words slurred. "T... Tepes. Not..."

Agatha grunted. "Didn't tell her she could talk."

James went to Lacy, putting his hands on her shoulders. "I know you're in there," he said, looking into her eyes, speaking gently as he tried to get his face level with hers. "Fight her. Come back to me."

"Save your breath, mate," Agatha said. "She don't care 'bout you no more than I do. And she's a loyalist wench who'll be wantin' to take heads off the minute she's got the chance. Or when I tell her to."

James wheeled on Agatha and moved closer to her, clamped his hand around her throat. "Stop this," he snarled in her face.

Agatha laughed back at him. "Spare me," she said. "If you intended me harm, your friend would've removed my head by now." She spoke to Phillip over her shoulder. "Too soft to kill a pretty lass like me?"

"James, get clear," Phillip said. "Unless you want a brain bath."

James started to move away, dropping his hand from Agatha's throat. He knew Phillip would put her down if he needed to. After what he'd seen her do, James was ready to do it himself. The wolf licked its chops inside, urging hunger at him. Human meat had a different taste, he was sure. He'd accidentally tasted human blood during plenty of fights.

He couldn't put anything together. It was all so random. He tried, looking back over everything he'd seen since they'd gotten to Savannah. Butler seemed to have his own agenda. But Agatha had been controlling him? And now Wormsloe House was under siege, but Noble Jones and Lacy were still alive. They could've easily killed off the draugrs and driven them back with the amount of firepower they had. But they didn't. Jones's own vampires had turned on him. But their efforts had been weak, ineffective. Smith had been angry about Jones being arrested. James could tell the man had been doing everything in his power to keep from blowing up when he'd fired them.

Tepes? Vlad Tepes? What did he have to do with any of it?

"Don't," James said, raising his hand at Phillip, signaling him to wait.

"You kidding me?" Phillip said. "James, she can still command these two vampires *and* the dead things outside to kill us."

"My slaves are just waiting," Agatha said over her shoulder. "All they need is my word."

"Word of the day is brought to you by the phrase 'shut the fuck' and the direction 'up.'" Phillip said through gritted teeth. James heard the sudden fury in Phillip's tone, the way his voice shook slightly as his body visibly tensed. There had been only one other time James had seen that reaction from Phillip, and that was a bad memory. "These were people. *People!*"

Agatha nodded, her casual tone quickly tinged with a layer of acidic threat. "Aye, they were. Now they're not. An' they don't be needin' anything more than a wrinkle of my darlin' little nose to come swarmin' in like a horde of locusts."

James motioned to Phillip to lower the shotgun. Phillip's eyes narrowed, his head shaking as he pressed the shotgun against her head again, bit his lip, then shoved it against her scalp before moving it away. Agatha left her head in the position Phillip had shoved it, then settled her eyes on James as she spoke. "I was a slave, too, James Coldstone." She gave Lacy and Jones a disdainful look. "Vampires. Bastards. Humans be only one of two things to these parasites: tools or food. I was the former." She moved her hair aside, fully brandishing her tattoo. "House Tepes. The most powerful vampire house in this world." She nodded at Lacy. "Just like that bonny lass over there."

James felt his heart sink as he glanced over at Lacy. She still looked listless, unaware of anything. Lacy Faulkner, a vampire with no house.

Yet another lie.

"Why kill the Abercorn witches?" James asked, turning his attention back to Agatha.

"They were in my way," Agatha said with a shrug. "Little Alma knew somethin'. Pointed you right to me."

"She pointed us to Noble Jones," Phillip said.

"Because she wagered I was under his employ," Agatha said without pause. "I went to her when I first came to Savannah. Dark witchcraft is only a breath of wind in the sails away from necromancy. But she turned me away. Said I was an abomination."

James stepped forward again. "But why?"

"The vampires have controlled it all for too long," Agatha said. "They feed on us, use us, manipulate us into doing their bidding. And when one of us presents as a threat, they try to turn it in their favor. If they can't?" She made a slicing motion across her throat with her finger. "Just like me." She pointed at Lacy. "Just like her." She nodded and James and Phillip. "Just like you."

James started to speak when something plowed into him, knocking him to the floor. He shifted as Lacy pinned him down, her vanilla and blood scent intensified by her sudden rage. He pushed back against her, his strength close to hers, but not enough to shove her away. Phillip shouted and James heard the shotgun go off, plaster and debris raining down from where Noble Jones had knocked the gun away before the buckshot could hit Agatha. Jones lifted Phillip by his shirt and tossed him to the side like an old doll as Agatha laughed and clapped her hands. James bucked as Lacy tried to slash at him with her nails, sending her off balance. He rolled on top of her and tried to pin her under his immense weight, but she got her foot underneath him and kicked out, sending him into the stairs hard enough to crash through them before hitting the stairs that led down to the cellar.

James recovered quickly and charged through the debris as Phillip shouted for him. He saw Noble Jones pick him up, the vampire's eyes wide and red as his fangs elongated. James made for him and swung his arm out as Jones moved to plant his face into Phillip's neck. Phillip dropped as Jones's teeth sank into James's arm, the fangs penetrating thick bluish-silver fur and the flesh underneath. He felt his blood flow into Jones's mouth as if his life was being sucked away. He hammered Jones in the face until the vamp tore free, a large chunk of James's arm still in his mouth. Jones staggered back but didn't fall down, his eyes glowing redder as he spat the piece of werewolf meat aside. His eyes widened, a guttural sound coming from him as he attacked. James swung at him again, but Jones ducked and grabbed James around the midsection in a football grapple before picking him up and slamming him down onto the floor. James struggled, but Jones put his boot on his neck and pressed until James could feel his windpipe start to strain.

"Well, ain't that mighty interesting?" he heard Agatha say. He saw her saunter up beside Jones and put a hand on his shoulder, leaning against him as if he were a post. "Never knew what would happen if a vampire drank from a werewolf. Learn somethin' new every day." She looked over her shoulder. James followed her gaze and saw where Lacy stood with Phillip pinned against the wall by the throat. He struggled against her, but she barely moved from his efforts. "Aye, ye' just proved yourself useful, James Coldstone." She looked back down at James. "Your friend, not so much."

James felt his consciousness yanked backwards and locked away in the dark recesses of his chaotic mind as Agatha turned to Lacy and spoke. "Don't need that one. Eat up, lass."

26

The James was easy to push back, still dumbstruck by the shock. Wolf took control, no time for human weakness. The cold one called Jones pressed against back harder with foot. Wolf bucked, forced new strength into body as it took over fully. The James did not resist this time.

Could not resist.

The Jones fell away as Wolf rose and made for the Lacy. She snarled at him and tossed the Phillip aside as she made to counter. She ducked the first swipe, kicked out and struck Wolf in knee. Wolf went down, and the Lacy grabbed Wolf and slammed him against the wall hard enough to cave it in, wood and man-stone falling away as Wolf hit the floor in the next room.

She's never been that strong, the James said from inside. *Be careful.*

Wolf felt bloodlust grow, gnashed its teeth as it rose, growling at the Lacy.

Don't kill her, either. She's still in there.

Betrayer. The Lacy was a betrayer. A liar. Wolf wanted to take the Lacy apart.

The Phillip's firestick barked, the Lacy crying out as the fire cut her shoulder. The Phillip made the stick click again, pointed it at the Jones. "James! Agatha just bolted!"

Wolf made for the Lacy, anger making its blood run hotter. The Lacy looked at him, holding her bloodied arm as she shouted the James's name. The James reached out, pulled itself forward. *No, go after Agatha! Lacy's okay!*

Wolf ignored. The Lacy betrayed pack. The Lacy was liar.

James felt the wolf push against him, fight for control as he clawed his way to the forefront, took control of the body. The wolf snarled and writhed inside, angry and murderous, urging a need for vengeance against Lacy. *We'll deal with her on that later.*

"Jimmy," Lacy said as she slumped to the floor, her back against a wall. She wavered, weak, the blood running from her arm tinged with lines of silver. "She...what's going on? Why the hell am I here?!"

"James," Phillip said, still pointing the gun at Noble Jones. Jones held his hands up, his expression grim. "Agatha took a round to the shoulder. Went through and hit Lacy. She's hurt bad. Go get her so we can end this. I've got these two."

"I don't know what's going on," Jones said, still looking at Phillip. "But I do not mean you harm."

"James," Lacy said, her voice shaking. "Was I under her control?"

James let out a slight mewl.

"Break my legs."

James barked twice. *No.*

"Damn it, Jimmy! If she can control me, I'll come after you after I'm done with Phillip. Break my legs. It'll take longer for them to heal if it's you doing it. Especially with silver poisoning."

"She's right," Jones said. "If the necromancer is controlling us, you won't make it out of here alive." Jones nodded at Phillip. "Right kneecap, please."

Phillip obliged with a round to Jones's knee, the silver shot turning the complicated joint into pulp. Silvered blood spattered as Jones cried out and hit the floor, holding his bleeding and destroyed leg.

James looked back down at Lacy, heard the wolf bark at him. He breathed deeply, leaned down, and clamped his jaws around her leg. Her cool skin tasted of her rich vanilla, the blood scent mixing in as his teeth penetrated her flesh. She screamed in agony as her femur snapped under the force of his teeth, vampire blood filling his mouth and staining his facial fur. He released her, stepped back as she slumped over and held her mangled leg, gasping and heaving as shock began to shake her body. She looked up at him, her breathing panicked and quick as she took an insane moment to choke out a quick laugh. "Not the...worst I've been hurt. Go!"

James was out the door, clearing the porch in one leap and landing on grass. Draugrs surrounded the area, some taking the time to shove the bodies of Jones's men and their own fallen aside as they made for him with their weapons ready. A shotgun report sounded only a split second before a draugr's head exploded and the dried husk dropped to the ground.

James heard Phillip pump the shotgun and dove to the side, tackling a group as four broke off to make after Phillip. James took down the first one by pouncing on him and landing with all eight hundred pounds of his weight, the draugr's body breaking under the force. Another came at him, a second shotgun blast removing its head just before it attacked, the decapitated body in mid swing with its axe before it fell to the ground. James turned just in time to see a few of Jones's vampires come after Phillip, who back-pedaled away from them as he fired three more rounds at them, the silver sending three different vampires to their knees screaming in pain. James rushed in, shoving a group of draugrs aside as he reached Phillip, then collided with the last two vampire guards.

They were far weaker than Jones or Lacy, far weaker than James, but still strong enough to tear Phillip to pieces if they got near him.

James put his clawed hand through the chest of the first one before he grabbed his victim's arm and tore the struggling vamp in half. The other still tried to counterattack despite seeing his comrade fall. James grappled him, held him in a sleeper hold as he slowly forced the vampire's head around, twisting until he heard several loud and distinct pops of vertebrae completely separating from cartilage. He dropped the dead vampire and looked at Phillip, who was reloading as he surveyed the yard. "Fuck me, we'll never find her like this. There's too many of them." He looked at James as he finished reloading and pumped the assault shotgun. "She's human and she's hurt, she couldn't have gotten too far."

James hunkered down and motioned for Phillip to mount him.

Phillip's shoulders slumped. "Shit. Better than stayin' here." He climbed onto James's back and grabbed two large handfuls of fur, his legs squeezing James around the ribcage. He leaned forward and spoke in James's ear. "We're never talking about this. Now be gentle this time."

James took off, minding his wolfen speed as he mowed through a group of draugrs and leapt over a cluster of bodies. He caught the smell of Agatha's clove cigarillo and moved in that direction, taking care to make sure Phillip stayed in place on his back as he tried to make sense of which direction he was going, crossing over a street and passing through a small, quiet neighborhood. He stopped once he reached a wrought-iron fence that surrounded the Bonaventure Cemetery. The gates had been blown open, and Agatha's scent was strong the closer they got.

"Great," Phillip muttered as he dismounted. "Another fuckin' grave-yard. Figured she'd go somewhere she could get some back-up." He readied the shotgun and checked the satchel he carried for more rounds. "Good thing this puppy was bangin' around in the trunk of that 'vette."

James went low and sniffed the ground, tried to see if he could get a more specific direction on where she'd gone. There was no denying she was there. *This could get ugly,* he thought to the wolf. His ears perked and he stood to full height as Agatha's voice echoed through the dark grave-yard, carried by the breeze, headstones, and monoliths that populated the fenced-in area.

"You two be needin' an engraved invitation?" She laughed. "Or an escort?"

The ground stirred near one of the headstones. Phillip took aim while James growled at the violet mist that moved up from the soil. It began to take shape, the dirt loosening as a shadow pulled itself free and melded with the floating aura. The figure took form, a rotted skirt and blouse hanging in tattered rags from the decayed woman that stood before them. Her skin was putrid, wrinkled and dry, her eyes the familiar glowing diamonds of a draugr. One of her breasts would've been exposed had it not rotted away over a century ago, bare ribs filled with soil and dust where the woman's top would've once maintained her decency. She rasped at them, gave a hollow and croaked grunt before pointing off into the dark cemetery. She put her hand down and began to walk slowly, her steps calculated and balanced for a dead woman.

"Think she wants us to follow her," Phillip said. "Damn. Stay frosty, Coldstone."

James let Phillip take the lead, staying close behind him. He had the advantage Phillip didn't: size and strength. If Agatha or one of her draugrs wanted to start something, Phillip and James both would see it coming, and James was more likely than a human able to take the hit from behind and not go down.

The walking corpse led them deeper into the cemetery, the tombs and crypts lonesome and haunting in the dark, the statues seeming to watch the odd trio as they made their way to a darker part of the area. James saw a light in the shadows, the flame a deep violet hue even in his yellowed dark vision. Agatha stood on a monument occupied by a concrete angle, a single cross marking a small grave next to it. She smiled at him as he approached, laughed when he stood to his full size. "Your size doesn't cause me fear, James Coldstone. I've felled bigger men and stronger creatures at the behest of a master I no longer abide."

Phillip took aim, planting his feet as he stood his ground next to James. "Got a silver buckshot in this motherfucker with your name on it," he said.

Agatha waved her hand lazily, and the dead woman that had led them to her turned on Phillip and stood in front of him, staring down the barrel of the shotgun now aimed in her face. "That one was all of fourteen when she died. A young lass just at the age of courtin' and marriage." She grinned at him. "Or should I call on more of Butler's and Jones's slaves? Greater number o' them."

James felt Phillip tense next to him, heard the waver of pained fury in his voice as he spoke. "Those people died slaves. It was the only way they could be free. And you go and enslave them even after they're dead." James saw Phillip's grip tighten on the shotgun, his knuckles going pale. "You're an evil bitch."

James shifted to human form. "Then what?" he said to Agatha. "You've taken control of Wormsloe House. Noble Jones is one of your slaves now."

"Got my sights set on Charlotte," Agatha said. "A few stops along the way, but House Tepes is my aim." She spread her arms out to her sides and tilted her head back, facing up into the night sky. "But let's not leave loose ends here in Savannah."

James and Phillip looked at each other, then around the area as the soil over the burial plots began to shift and move. Crypts opened, purple mist and shadows coming together in the form of those who'd once occupied the graves, the Southern upper class of old Savannah now draugr slaves to Agatha. James shifted back into wolf form and stood back-to-back with Phillip, who trained his shotgun on the dead that surrounded them. "You think James and I can't take out your dead-heads?" he called to Agatha. "Nothin' but smart zombies. James takes 'em apart like easy!"

James saw her rise from the ground, hovering several feet in the air as the draugrs moved closer. They walked by him, not seeming to notice him and Phillip, their glowing eyes locked on Agatha as they encircled her and stood still. They began to deteriorate, the shadows flowing out of their eyes, noses, and mouths and up Agatha's arms like tendrils and vines until she was wrapped completely in blackness. She opened her mouth, and the thick cloud began to flow in like water into a drain until none was left. The draugrs around her crumbled away as she settled back down to the ground. She breathed out slowly, then flicked her eyes open, staring at James and Phillip with an evil smirk on her face. "So, this be what a god feels like."

Phillip fired at her. She jerked, the round smacking her in the chest and blowing open her ribcage from the back as it exited. The bones immediately pulled back in, the skin returning to its healed state as she chuckled. "Can't hurt me with yer fancy musket, lad," she said. "Ain't gonna kill me. The dead make me stronger, and the souls make me immortal." She thrust her arms at them, two columns of shadow flowing out as James and Phillip dove to the side to avoid the attack. Phillip fired again and missed. James came out of a roll and charged, but Agatha fired another smoke column at him, hitting a large tombstone next to him and causing it to explode. The debris caught him off guard and he stumbled, but he recovered quickly as he reached out to grab her. She disappeared into the darkness, and James felt a blow to his back that sent him forward with his own momentum. He crashed into a nearby statue and fell over it before hitting the side of a nearby crypt hard enough to crack the stone.

Another shot rang out, and Phillip cursed as the round slammed into a nearby tree. James saw Agatha stumble, then laugh as the back of her head healed up immediately. "Keep firin', lad. Makes you more entertaining." James saw shadow leak from the wound just before it healed up.

The bullet needs to stay inside her, James thought. The wolf barked inside in agreement.

The round went through Agatha and hit Lacy, Phillip had said earlier. Lacy had dug the round out, and she had to dig deep to get it.

James sighed. *This is going to suck.*

The wolf whined and mewled inside.

Got a better idea?

The wolf huffed and barked at him, standing firm and ready.

That's better.

"Gonna finish with you two gents," Agatha was saying as she approached Phillip. "Then I'm gonna take that darlin' lass you two been chasin' back to Charlotte with me. Gonna march her right into House Tepes, and when she stands before her master, she's gonna get the urge to kill him on the spot. And I'll be makin' sure I be the last thing he sees before House Tepes burns to the ground and sends him to the pit where he fuckin' belongs!"

James pushed off from the ground, the world slowing around him as he hit his wolfen speed, his eyes locked on Phillip as the shotgun was pointed at Agatha's head again, a look of determined fury on Phillip's face. James passed her, and he threw his hand out as the fire blasted from the barrel, the silver round already moving. His head spun from the pain as the round tore through the meat and bone in his palm, the silver sending waves up his arm and shoulder and across his chest. He dropped to his knees, holding his wrist, squeezing to stop the flow as silvered blood poured from the wound in his hand. Agatha stumbled, her hand over the growing patch of black on her chest. She coughed, her eyes wide in bewilderment.

"Shit," Phillip said. "James, what the hell?!" He fished in his pouch and pockets and cursed as he turned the shotgun around and held it like a club.

Agatha's body went rigid, her head back and her arms out as she screamed to the stars above. James watched as black shadow poured from every orifice and flowed from the wound in her chest. A hand burst from her chest and grabbed her throat, another following it and grabbing her jaw, forcing her to keep her mouth open. Another hand punched through her lower back and grabbed her by the hair, yanking her head back further as the hand clenching her jaw pulled against the force. She swatted at the hands, but more burst free and caught her by her arms, held them in place as two grabbed her by the top of her mouth. The sound of bone and meat tearing and breaking was accompanied by the sound of her scream turning into a high-shrill that sounded like glass as the hand on her throat tore at the skin, shredding her vocal cords. Her body fell to the ground as the hands that had sprouted from her became black smoke and joined with the rest of the cloud spreading in all directions, each tendril finding a grave and pouring into the soil like black wine.

James stood, his wound beginning to heal slowly as Agatha's bloodless, mangled corpse stared back at him with lifeless eyes, her face broken into a rictus and overexaggerated smile where her jaw had been torn open. Phillip stepped up beside him, looking down at her body as he spoke in a casual tone. "That's the most fucked up thing I've ever seen."

There was a new sound. Something off in the distance, coming at them fast. Sirens. Horns. James looked down at Phillip, who shook his head and cursed before looking up at James. "Yeah, this just got worse." He tossed the shotgun aside. "We gotta move!"

James shifted to human form. "Lacy and Jones are back there. We have to go back!"

"*Fuck*," Phillip spat. He ran a hand over his bald head and sighed. "Damn it. Okay, I've got a plan, but we better fucking move *now*."

27

The sirens were still in the distance, but James could hear them getting closer as he ran through the woods, his wolfen speed not affected when he had to jump over one fallen tree and dodge another on occasion. He could smell the stench of gunpowder mixed with dried soil and mildew, and could hear Jones shouting to his remaining men to be ready. He burst through the trees and into the yard as a small group of Jones's men took aim at him. James halted, and Jones gave the gunmen the order to stand down as Lacy ran past them, her leg now fully healed.

"Jimmy," she said as she came to a stop in front of him. "All of those things just crumbled to dust. You killed her, didn't you?" She looked around. "Where's Phillip?"

More like Agatha did it to herself, thought James. *But who's keeping track?*

The wolf chuffed in agreement in his mind, then gave a low growl at Lacy.

Not now, James thought at the beast. He shifted to human form and spoke. "He's waiting on us. Dropped him off at the front gate. The SCU are coming. Those sirens are getting closer."

"We hear them," Jones said from the porch. "We mean to stand."

"They aren't coming for you," James said to him. He looked back down at Lacy. "It's us they want. You, me, and Phillip."

"Then go," Jones said. "I'll have my men cover your escape." His phone rang in his pocket. James kept his voice low as Jones answered the call.

"Your leg?"

"It's fine," Lacy said. "Healed up, just a little bruised now."

His concern for her was mixed with his anger. She'd lied to him. She'd been lying the entire time. Had Marianne been her niece? Had it been an accident that they'd met in Charleston?

He couldn't deal with it. Not now. "Phillip has a plan, but we have to get to the front gate."

"They're here," Jones called from the porch. Scattered gunfire rang out in the distance as if on cue. Jones ordered his men to take their positions. "We still have rounds for the Brownings. Use them if they reach the house." He turned to James and Lacy. "Go now."

"Thanks, Noble," Lacy said.

"You can thank me by never coming here again," Jones said, his tone cold. "I thank you for freeing me from the witch, don't misunderstand. But the mess I have to clean up because of you is monumental, and this will not be kept silent from the Southeastern houses regardless of any efforts on my part. Go."

James shifted and barked at Lacy, motioning her to follow him as he tore down the road toward the front gate, the sounds of gunfire growing louder and more sporadic. He pushed harder, and Lacy closed behind him as the entrance drew closer. A large, armored truck blocked the gate, several men in tactical gear firing at the nearby stone sign welcoming visitors to Wormsloe Plantation. The rounds had chipped away at the brick and concrete, Phillip huddled on the back side of it reloading as he waited for another chance to fire. James saw two agents already laying on the ground. Others were coordinating, reloading in phases to keep the rounds flying in a constant flow. The barrier wouldn't hold much longer, and he could see the look of realization on Phillip's face; that brief moment one had when they knew that they'd come to the end of the line and accepted it for what it was.

James licked his chops as he focused his fury on the others firing at Phillip. It would hurt. It would break him. But the injuries wouldn't be supernatural. He'd heal quickly. He laughed on the inside as he quoted one of Phillip's comic book superheroes to the wolf. *It's clobberin' time!*

He yanked the wolf into place in his mind, his speed increasing even more as he made a direct line at the SCU truck. A few of the men dove to the side, the slowest one having no time to make a sound before James collided with him and then with the armored truck with enough force to cave the vehicle in and send it across the road, the tires screeching on the asphalt cut short as they shredded from the rims, sparks flying up from the road. The truck stopped when it hit the trees on the other side of the highway. Waves of pain covered his body, the unnatural shifting of broken bones in his shoulder making him nauseated as he slumped to the ground. The bones kept shifting around, trying to heal as he managed to look up at his handiwork, the smashed remains of what was once an SCU SWAT member still stuck to the side. The man's body was pulp, a few ribs sticking out from the sides of what was once his torso, one of his arms missing. His head was smashed, his tongue hanging out of the remains of his jaw and down to his collarbone since nothing was left to hold it in.

Wolf smash, James thought without a beat as he rounded on the other gunmen. Lacy had already taken two of them out. James saw two more still trying to get to their feet from where they'd avoided his attack on their transport. A third was missing his leg, possibly having been too close when James hit the truck. He screamed in agony as the other two took aim. Phillip's gun went off, and one of them dropped, his head jerking to the side as the round smacked his helmet. James took advantage of the distraction and pounced, his shoulder showing its displeasure by aching more as the bones finished fusing back together. He grabbed the man's gun, broke it in half, and brought the stock down on the guy's head hard enough to knock him out cold. Lacy was on the last one, knocking his helmet away and burying her face in his neck before he could react, his eyes wide with shock as she drank. She pulled away; her face covered in blood as she sighed deeply. "Yeah, I needed that." She jerked her victim's head completely around and tossed the body aside as she looked at James. He cocked his head to the side, and she shrugged. "What? I was hungry."

An engine roared to life, and the black Corvette Phillip had left in earlier sped over to where they stood, tires screaming on the asphalt as the black car whipped into place. The passenger door opened, and Phillip looked out at them with a dark, serious expression. "Get in."

Lacy and James glanced at each other, then back at Phillip, and Lacy burst into hearty laughter as James started panting, his mouth turned up in a huge doggy-grin. Lacy calmed down enough to speak, tears streaming down her face as she nudged James. "How long has Batman been wanting to do that one?"

James stopped panting and held his hands out wide, palms facing each other.

"Fuck both y'all," Phillip said with a grunt. "Don't hate. And Alfred says you can suck it."

Bullets peppered the ground where James and Lacy stood. Phillip screamed at them over and over to move. Lacy dove into the passenger seat, and James slammed the door behind her and climbed on top, gripping the roof on either side and thankful the windows were rolled down. Phillip gunned the engine and peeled off into the night as sirens blared behind them. Two black SUVs came at them followed by what looked like another sports car.

"A Dodge Charger?!" Phillip shouted from inside the car. "Really?!"

"Relax, Bacon," Lacy called to him. "It's not as aerodynamic."

"They also don't have Lassie Lard-Ass riding on top like a fuckin' luggage rack!"

"Good point."

Bullets sang as they whipped by, submachine guns rattling from the two SUVs behind them. Phillip swerved sharply to the left, causing James to hold on for dear life as the quick motion threatened to hurl him off in the opposite direction. The Corvette swerved again, this time to the right, but James was ready and held on as bullets flew by. He barked at Phillip a few times, hanging on as Phillip moved into the opposite lane.

"Hell no, it can't go faster," Phillip shouted at him. "It's a goddamn sports car. It ain't made to haul your fat ass on the roof! Hang on!"

James heard the clicking of the parking brake couple with the tires against the asphalt as the car whipped to the right and around a corner, moving sideways several feet before Phillip disengaged the brake and shifted hard. The car darted forward, James's stomach still trying to process the maneuver as Phillip howled with triumphant laughter. "Hell yes! Let's see 'em top *that* Tokyo bullshit!"

"Movie was overrated," Lacy said in response.

"Yeah, they shouldn't have tied it to the series," Phillip said in return, his tone just as casual. "Better as a stand-alone offshoot."

James looked over his shoulder as the SCU vehicles tried to make the turn while keeping pace with the sports car. The Dodge Charger pulled the stunt off easily, the engine roaring as the driver regained control and started to close in. One of the SUVs tried the same move and flipped over, rolling twice before heading off the shoulder and into the brush. The other SUV slowed to avoid the botched stunt and managed to take the corner before continuing the pursuit, falling just behind the Charger as more automatic fire came from the passenger-side window.

"This is it?!" Lacy shouted at Phillip. "This is your plan?!"

"My plan was to lure them off while you and James made a run for it," Phillip shot back. "I didn't count on their fucking ice cream truck being parked at the front gate the minute James dropped me off!"

"These guys are kicking their own asses and we still can't shake them," Lacy shouted. "Give me your gun."

"I'm out of ammo," Phillip said back. "That damn shotgun was the only thing in the car, and there wasn't much ammo left."

Lacy cursed as James looked over his shoulder again. The shooter had stopped, possibly to reload. The Corvette struggled under his weight but maintained speed. The Charger was closing in as Phillip cursed from underneath. "God damn, would it kill them to put some fucking lights out here?!"

"You're in the deep South, sweetie," Lacy said. "Lighting isn't historically accurate. Get with it, Bacon."

James could see clearly as the Charger reduced speed, moving to the side and allowing the SUV a clear path. He could also see someone pop up through the open sunroof. The man was dressed in black tactical gear and wore what appeared to be night vision goggles.

The bazooka he was carrying was also quite visible.

James smacked Lacy's door and barked at her. He saw her glance in her rearview mirror and saw her eyes widen. "Um, Bacon. Think you could avoid a bazooka?"

He heard Phillip groan. "Please tell me you're just asking. I know better, but just lie to me."

James looked back again and saw the man take aim as the SUV maintained its distance. Phillip wouldn't be able to dodge something like that, even if it impacted near the car. Not with eight hundred pounds on top. James breathed and got his feet underneath him. Thinking would slow him down. He couldn't afford to rationalize, make a plan, consider the factors. There wasn't time to think about whether or not it would work, whether or not he would make it before the rocket fired.

No time to think about how much this was going to hurt.

He kicked off as one thought crossed his mind, accompanied by Phillip's annoyed cursing and reminders of how dumb James could be simply because it was a force of habit at this point.

Voom!

He laughed hysterically inside as he flew through the air, the Corvette driving off and the SUV coming at him no faster than a golf cart on a low battery. He opened his arms, ready to grapple the vehicle, feeling some panic as he began to fall. He wouldn't make it. It was too far away. He knew why it was all moving so slowly, his senses stalling the inevitable pain that would come with the impact, stretching the split second of time it was taking to close the gap.

He laughed again at his initial comparison of the SUV to a golf cart, and at his own stupidity, the humor quickly turning to feral rage as his eyes widened, his teeth gnashed, the impact interrupting his snarl with a surprised yelp as the front end caved in. The windshield shattered, the driver screaming and swerving the vehicle as the man standing on the console struggled to maintain his footing. The shooter in the passenger seat fired wildly, bullets peppering the ceiling as James fought through the pain and swatted at the driver. The SUV swerved again, and the guy with the bazooka shouted as he was thrown out of the sunroof and over the side while James was flung in the opposite direction. James heard the bazooka click and rolled off to the side of the battered SUV as the thing fired, the hard road scraping and bashing his already bruised and cut body as he tumbled. He pushed through the pain and forced his body to work, ending the roll in a runner's stance as the Charger blasted by him. He saw the rocket shoot under the front end of the sports car as the SUV turned and flipped on the highway. The explosion came from where the gas tank probably would've been on a Dodge Charger, the car flipping rear-over-front into the air before the sliding SUV crashed into it. The two vehicles exploded, shrapnel and debris flying out as the blaze and smoke plumed into the night.

James heard the Corvette coming toward him from up the road and stood as Phillip pulled up next to him and rolled down the window. James shifted to human form; his body healed but still sore from all the self-inflicted battering. "I'm stating for the record that I did not intend to make them explode."

Phillip shrugged. "Probably had more rounds for that bazooka and some hand grenades with them. Fuck 'em, let 'em cook."

"Now what?" Lacy asked from inside the car.

"They sent a shitload of people after us," Phillip said. "Probably only the first wave. We'd better move before the reinforcements show up."

"Yeah, but where do we go? It'll be daylight soon."

"The trunk is big enough for you to fit in," James said. "Phillip and I can sleep in the car."

Lacy gave him a look and spoke to him the same way his kindergarten teacher used to talk to him when he made an uninformed decision not unexpected of a four-year-old. "Sweetie, let's look at that for a second: a black guy and a naked white guy are sleeping in a stolen luxury sports car with a dead chick in the trunk." She cocked her head to the side. "You okay, Jimmy? You sure you don't have a concussion?"

Phillip shook his head. "Nah, he's always that stupid."

Another thought came to James' mind. "I think I know a place. And I'll be able to get some clothes there. Is there enough room for one more?"

"It's only a two-seater, James," Phillip said.

"Lacy can sit in my lap." James winced as soon as it was out, realizing what he'd just said and wishing he could run away and hide.

Lacy guffawed as she got out of the car. "I'll get in the trunk. Not the first time. You can stop blushing, Jimmy, I'm not offended."

James helped Lacy into the trunk, closed it, then got into the car with Phillip, who was looking at him with a raised eyebrow. James blinked. "What?"

Phillip shook his head again as he sighed. "Just tell me where we're going. Dumbass."

28

The sun was just coming up, the air cool and still rich with saline despite how far inland they were. James breathed it in deep, letting himself relax a little for the first time since they'd gotten to Savannah. The sky was relatively clear, thin white cirrus clouds stretching across purple and blue as the sun made its slow ascent to its early morning position. James had already tuned himself in to the steady growl of the engine, letting himself be numb for a while as Phillip drove them back toward Hoyt's place.

"How hard did you hit your head when you plowed into not one, but *two* large vehicles?" Phillip had said when James had proposed calling Hoyt. "He *works* with the FBI. Do you really think the SCU isn't watching his every move?"

"Considering he can start a car with his computer at home, I'm sure he can avoid the SCU," James said.

Phillip sighed. "You really don't know how technology works, do you?"

"I can use a phone."

"It does more than texts and calls, James."

"Yes. It also has the Google."

"*The* Google?"

"Though I do miss Jeeves. He was more personable."

"Christ."

Phillip called Hoyt, who told them to come on over and that he would have clothes for James as well as a new cell phone with James's contacts and data already loaded. There were no cars parked near the trailers and campers. James noticed the stillness of the place right away, the dark windows of the domiciles indicating no life on the inside, not even a nightlight or a television running. The morning sun was just high enough to turn the sky blue when Phillip pulled the Corvette into the small drive next to Hoyt's trailer.

The place was empty, every trace of evidence indicating that someone had lived there gone as if the home had never been occupied. Not even the obligatory wire for cable television stuck out of the floor. The cabinets and refrigerator were completely bare, and there were now only holes in the walls of the room that had once housed the various computers and screens to make up Hoyt's makeshift command center. Everything had been wiped clean, and even James's wolfen senses could only pick up the smell of bleach and cleaning chemicals. A set of clothes hung from the ceiling fan in the living room, and James noticed right away that they were his laid-back style of a collared button-up casual shirt and cargo shorts with sandals, all his size and complete with tags attached. The new cell phone was in one of the pockets along with a note from Hoyt with the password to log in. James got dressed while Phillip booted the phone up.

"Huh," Phillip said as James finished dressing. "You already got a text message from Hoyt." He handed James the phone.

Guess you guys have noticed the place is empty. SCU headed this way as soon as you hung up. We barely got out of there before the raid. They can't trace this phone, but Phillip's phone is all over the map. Might want to trash it. I'll have a backup ready for you soon. The whole rez cleared out. We have friends at an actual Federally recognized reservation in another state. I'll hit you up as soon as we're settled. Keep your heads down.

"Funny," Phillip said without a trace of humor. "Tells two dudes driving around in a stolen luxury sports car to keep their heads down. I see what he did there."

"All of my contacts are still here," James said as he scrolled through the phone. "I didn't think he was serious about that."

"Yeah, he probably hacked your cloud account. Dude got skills."

James looked up, raising an eyebrow. "Cloud?"

"Online storage? Can access it anywhere?"

James shook his head. "Still not following."

198

Phillip blinked. "Goddamn, James. The cloud. *The* cloud. How do you not know about the damn cloud?"

"I've never needed to worry about it."

"How the hell are you this technologically behind?" Phillip said with a sputter. "What the fuck, Coldstone? It's damn basic technology. It's—" He stopped short, and James knew that Phillip had already noticed the smirk on his face. He narrowed his eyes at him. "You're clowning me, aren't you?"

"I needed the levity."

"You need a kick in the ass."

P hillip decided it would be better for them to drive to Hilton Head Island instead of finding a place to stay in Savannah since the city was likely still crawling with SCU agents. Given that the full moon was happening that night, they would know to be looking for a large target with a lot of fur and no way to shift back and blend in.

They found themselves at the same house on Blue Heron Point they'd stayed at back when James had initially began hunting the group that had kidnapped Mindy Robertson from her home. It was an older, sprawling single-story home with cedar shingles and a large set of oak double doors that served as the front entrance.

The side door entered into a laundry room with a small room off to the right that served as an office for whoever needed it during their stay at the time share. The floor of the laundry room and office was a dull yellow linoleum that extended into the large kitchen and stopped at the hallway to the left and the main room straight ahead. The kitchen was dominated by an island with a wicker-mesh countertop, and the wood cabinets matched the color of the high-end wood paneling that made up every wall of the house. A large screened-in porch took up half of the rear of the house and was accessible from both the kitchen and the dining room that shared half of the main area with the living room. The back wall of the living room was made up of sliding glass doors that accessed the open section of the back deck and gave the occupants a clear view of the marsh and the intercoastal waterway that separated the island from the mainland. Two bedrooms and a bathroom occupied the long hallway that ran the length of the kitchen and the dining room, and the open foyer separated that hallway from the other that led to the master bath-room and bedroom.

Outside of the kitchen, the rest of the house was beige carpet, and all of the lighting in the house was recessed except for the chandelier that hung over the large oak dining table. James liked the smell of the place, the scent of rich foods of meals past mixed with the pleasant sweetness of wood polish and marsh mud. The lot was large and populated with a mixture of palmetto trees, pine trees, and oak trees with large tendrils of moss that hung down and moved in the breeze.

"You and this place," Phillip said as he looked around the kitchen.

"I find the atmosphere soothing."

"It's a time share."

"It is."

"And you're willing to risk someone showing up and busting us squat-ting here because you like the place?"

"Watching the sun come up over the marsh is worth the risk." James smiled at him. "Besides, they have cable."

"I'm serious, James," Phillip said, looking at him sidelong. "The hell's wrong with you? Do you *want* to get found and dragged off?"

"The people who own this place aren't around anymore," James said in a more serious tone. "The family is trying to figure out what to do with it, and right now it's just a rental. I paid them in advance until the end of the year because I didn't know how long we'd be here when we were tracking down Mindy. Better?"

Phillip rolled his eyes. "You could've led with that," he said as he went into the hallway and opened the door to the first bedroom. "I got this room. Need to grab a shower later and get some clothes." He motioned over his shoulder. "You know, since all my shit is still in Savannah."

"The original owner's clothes are still here," James said. "I believe he was your size, and the family kindly asked me to make sure I do laundry and put things back in place if I borrow anything."

Phillip turned and walked back into the kitchen. "Damn, James. You covered the bases, didn't you?" He paused. "Why not just stay here? Fuck it. You hate your family home in Rock Hill, this place would be pretty easy for Hoyt to take off the grid, and no one would think to look for you in a spot full of retirees."

The wolf grunted inside in agreement with Phillip. James felt a weight on his shoulders, the idea of leaving Rock Hill both tempting and painful at the same time. Phillip was right. He had the means. He could contact the family, make Hilton Head his new home, disappear. Had Phillip said something only a few months ago, he likely would have. But so much had come to his attention over the summer, all brought to the surface when Wade Anderson had started killing people responsible for his incarceration and had used Dracula's ring to separate the wolf from James's consciousness, making the beast its own entity inside. Or had it always been there, and the ring had just brought it out of hiding?

And then there was House Tepes. Charlotte was only twenty minutes north of Rock Hill, and a sprawling thirty minutes to the north side of the city from the South Carolina state line. Lacy had lied to him, had claimed that she was a vampire with no allegiance to a house. Yet she and Agatha had shared the same mark on their necks. And why had a vampire house had anything to do with a necromancer in the first place? Someone who could have easily taken them over, enslaved them, and brought the house down? Agatha could have just razed the entire organization to the ground, crippled the entire Southeast. Why go to the trouble she'd gone to? Why over-complicate things when, given her power, she could've just controlled the vampires in the house and turned them on each other? None of it added up, and she'd given no real answers before her own power had killed her. The idea of enslaving Lacy and sending her in to kill the master was overblown and overthought.

But she'd made the plan anyway. And why Lacy? Did that mean that Lacy had a higher standing in House Tepes than most other vampires? Was she closer to the master? She had to be.

"James?" Phillip said, his voice interrupting James's thoughts. "Earth to James? You home, McFly? You in there?"

"Sorry," James said. "I'm tired. Guess it's caught up with me."

"Right," Phillip said. "Dude, I can smell myself. I need a shower. And we all need a rest."

"Right," James said. "I'll let Lacy know where we are." He turned to go back outside, putting his thoughts aside as he prepped himself to talk to Lacy in a situation that didn't involve prioritizing survival over talking about her secrets.

"Hey, James?"

James stopped and looked over his shoulder. "Yes?"

"You did good, man," Phillip said. "Back in Savannah. Just wanted to tell you that."

"Thanks," James said. "So, I'm not an idiot after all?"

"Oh, you're dumb as hell."

"Then my secret is safe."

"What secret?"

"I can't tell you. It wouldn't be a secret."

Phillip sighed. "James, I'm not in the mood for this shit."

James looked over his shoulder at Phillip, a sly grin on his face as he gave Phillip a determined stare. "Like I said: it's a secret. Just know that Super Wolf will always be there to protect the innocent and uphold justice."

Phillip just stared at him, his expression humorless and defeated. He shook his head and groaned as he spun on his heel and left the kitchen muttering under his breath as he went. "I hope they have soap that washes off stupid. I'm damn near covered in it."

James knocked on the car's trunk and told Lacy where they were. He was met with silence and figured she was probably completely wiped out from being under the control of a necromancer, having her leg broken, being shot at, and ending the night in the not-so-spacious trunk of a sports car after riding along during a high-speed car chase.

He went back inside, set an alarm on his new phone, and made it to the small bedroom midway down the hall before the exhaustion hit him hard and he couldn't fathom making it all the way to the master bedroom. He opted for the smaller guest bedroom and picked the twin bed on the left wall to fall onto and was asleep before he realized that he was laying down. His dreams were vivid, covering the events of everything that had happened, even the most disturbing parts.

The wolf was also tired, but it still stepped in and put itself between the memories and James's subconsciousness, forcing dreams of seeing Mindy Robertson playing with other children on the playground without a care in the world mixed in with dreams of walking in the pastures at Coldstone Keep with Molly as they talked and laughed.

Another dream hit him, finding him walking on the shore with Lacy at some non-descript beach during the earliest hours of the evening, the sun low enough not to harm her but still present enough to cause her to sweat. The moisture made her skin glisten as her flowing chocolate curls moved with the breeze that swept in off the ocean, the water washing over her feet as the tide drifted in.

It was evening when James's alarm went off, the setting sun still high enough in the sky to fry a vampire to ashes. His mind still held onto the image of Lacy on the beach, his chest hurting as memories of her lies came back in a flood.

After all they'd been through. After all they'd done together. Why lie to him? If she was caught up in something bad, he would've gone to the ends of the earth to help her, done anything necessary to pull her out of trouble. But the lingering thought still stayed in his head, stationary rather than random and rattling.

What if she *was* the trouble?

He got up, rubbed the sleep from his eyes, and went outside. The humidity was still high, but the air was clean and easy to breathe. He took a deep breath, letting the various aromas of the marsh flow over the glands in his mouth that came with being a werewolf, letting the beast inside fill his head with images of weather and wildlife in the lower Southern marshlands.

The Corvette was still in the driveway.

He looked to the sky, the sun almost completely set as he stepped down off the small porch and made his way over to the rear of the vehicle. Hoyt had uploaded an app into James's phone that acted as keys to the car and had done likewise to Phillip's. James didn't ask how the ME had done it, knowing that the end result would be a mountain of tech jargon he didn't understand or care about. It worked. That was what mattered.

He took another deep breath before he spoke to the back of the car. "It'll dark enough to come out in a few minutes, and I know you're hungry. It's a full moon." He paused, gathered his nerves, and spoke again. "We need to talk. Now. Before you leave. Before I shift. Because I don't trust you to come back. I want answers, and you're going to give them to me. If you are in trouble, I want to help. I have to help. But if you still feel like you need to run, that you need to push me away, I won't stop you." He paused again and took another deep breath to calm the knot in his chest and the lump in his throat. "I'll always let you come back. I'll always help you. I don't care what you're wrapped up in. But you can't lie to me anymore. I have to know the truth. Otherwise, I cannot possibly know what to do to help. But it won't stop me from trying. I'll always be there." He paused, waiting for some sort of response, even a denial from her. A sigh. Something.

Nothing.

The wolf stepped forward, his sense of smell deepening. Pluff mud, mildew, saline, gasoline, oil.

Blood. Vanilla. But weak.

"Lacy?" James opened the app on his phone and tapped the screen and watched the trunk lid pop open. He gritted his teeth, standing still and stoic as he processed the frustration and disappointment, the hurt that was bundled in along with the sight of the empty trunk still carrying the remnants of Lacy's scent in the interior fabric.

29

I guess you guys have figured out that the SCU called off the kill order on you," Hoyt said, his voice squawking from the small speakers on the phone on the table. James and Phillip had gotten a text from Hoyt to call him as soon as they got up that morning. They'd gotten back to Coldstone Keep just as the sun went down the night before, and both had taken the opportunity to get a full night of sleep. They'd left late so James could recover from his full moon run.

He'd managed to bag a deer for his trouble, so at least he wasn't hungry.

James had woken feeling refreshed for a change, though he still felt the weight of Lacy bailing out on him again. He pushed his feelings back, pressed them down. The wolf chuffed at him as if scolding him but kept itself calm otherwise. It didn't like it when he suppressed his feelings, but it also knew that it was a pointless argument.

"That doesn't make sense," Phillip said, shaking his head. "They're a government outfit. They don't just shrug off the kind of damage we caused the other night and decide their target gets to live."

"They're *not* associated with the Federal government," Hoyt said, correcting him. "Remember? And they can do whatever they want. Or do whatever they're told by whoever is pulling the strings. Oh, and I have your new phone ready, Phillip."

Phillip blinked. "Um, thanks?"

"No problem." James heard the sound of rapid typing on a keyboard before Hoyt spoke again. "Looks like I'm playing Doctor Dead in your hometown, guys."

"I didn't know they were looking for someone," Phillip said.

"They weren't. Not until the other guy figured out he could retire since his house is paid for. And his car. And his student loans. And his credit card debt. And he may have won the lottery."

James blinked. "When did this happen?"

"About an hour ago."

Phillip thunked his head on the table and groaned before sitting up and rubbing his face. "God. Damned. *Illegal*, Hoyt! Jesus *fuck!*"

"You guys are going to need someone who can do what I do," Hoyt said.

Phillip glared at James. "What?"

James shrugged. "You've always wanted to play superhero, and I have a feeling we've only seen the beginning of something much larger."

Phillip nodded. "Damn right. And Super Wolf has a badass car, now." He clapped James on the shoulder. "See you in the Wolf Den."

James laughed a little as Phillip left the room. Hoyt spoke after a moment over the phone. "Really? He doesn't know?"

James looked back down at the phone. "Know what?"

A high-pitched shriek sounded from the garage. James bolted from the kitchen, heading to the garage as the wolf readied itself for a shift.

He found Phillip standing at the door leading from the house interior into the garage. Phillip was staring at the brand-new blue Honda Civic Si Type R, his lip trembling as he clutched a piece of paper in his hand. James pried the paper from Phillip's fingers and read it.

Gentlemen,

I will assume that you appreciate my lending you my car. I have taken the liberty of replacing your other car with a newer one, my pleasure. This will be my payment for your assistance in the matter of the necromancer, and I will overlook the damages caused to a rather expensive vehicle as they were accrued while you were defending my home. I hope that we do not meet again, as those circumstances will not likely be ideal for either of us since you tend to bring trouble like most bring clothing and toiletries.

Best,

Noble Jones.

James put a hand on Phillip's shoulder. "At least it's newer."

"It's not a Batmobile," Phillip muttered weakly.

James looked at it. "It still looks fairly sporty."

"It was so pretty."

"I'm sure you'll move on."

"It was the one, James."

"There are others out there. And I think you may really like this one."

Phillip sniffed loudly as a tear rolled down his cheek. "I need time to process this."

James suppressed a grin and nodded. "Let me take you to breakfast. You're driving."

They'd ended up at a small diner nestled in a strip mall across the street from the Winthrop Commons shopping center. The place was known for serving meals made from local produce and farmers, and the owner prided herself on serving foods with no artificial ingredients. Phillip was a fan of the chicken and waffles in particular while James stuck with pancakes, sausage, and scrambled eggs.

"The Civic suits you better," James said after the waiter, a young effeminate man with glasses and large hooped earrings, refilled their coffees and went to turn in their order "And why do you need to find another job?"

"I have bills, James. A mortgage." He huffed. "At least I don't have a car payment."

James shook his head. "I can't imagine."

"Imagine what, you entitled bitch?" Phillip said. "Working for a living? Some of us didn't inherit billions of dollars. Dick."

"That isn't what I meant," James said. "I mean I can't imagine juggling what we do with a full-time job."

"What do you mean 'what we do?'"

James sat his coffee cup down and clasped both hands around the mug. "This is the second time we've run into a situation that proved to be more than human law enforcement can handle. I can't imagine that the Rock Hill police will enlist the use of silver bullets and holy water any time soon."

"So, you wanna play Sam and Dean Winchester?" Phillip said. "Cruise around the country and hunt monsters and shit? Find cases from our bunker here and have angsty conversations in the car?"

"We do have a decent car," James said, nodding.

Phillip rolled his eyes. "They have a badass muscle car. We *had* a badass muscle car."

"You had to know we wouldn't have been able to keep it."

"I just wanted more time."

"You ate all of my ice cream."

"Shut up."

"And binge-watched Gilmore Girls."

"It's a good show."

James shrugged. "I got fairly bored with it after season 2. We have also come across something larger. House Tepes."

"You think they had something to do with Agatha?" Phillip said. "She said she was trying to bring them down."

"Precisely," James said with a nod. "She wasn't stupid. One human cannot possibly bring down an entire army on their own, even with magical powers. She was running a suicide mission. That was why she was using Butler to access Wormsloe. If she could destabilize Noble Jones's ownership of so much property in the lower part of Georgia, that would be a step closer to destabilizing the state. Even if she was killed, the dominoes would already have started. There would be conflict in the houses."

"What makes you say that?" Phillip asked. "Houses seem pretty close-knit to me."

"Personalities and opinions still clash," James said. "Even among supernaturals. Just because a group has power doesn't mean there won't be factions. If someone was looking to usurp Jones's status and position with the Southeastern houses, Agatha would've given them a prime opportunity. While Jones was busy trying to fend off murder accusations and draugrs, another group could slip in and take control quite easily." He paused. "She was trying to start a war."

"You think she wasn't on her own?" Phillip said. "Huh. I didn't think about that."

"I think she was lured away from House Tepes. Probably quite easily as she was only valued because of her powers. Whoever sent her after Noble Jones wants to rattle the cage." James took a sip of his coffee. "This is far from over. And so, I rest my case. I do not believe you will be able to work a full-time job and continue our current lifestyle."

Phillip looked at James, his face twisted as if he'd just heard James say something in a foreign language. "Wait, you just spouted all that bullshit because you don't want me to work? You seriously want to do this bull-shit full-time?"

"Who else will?" James asked. "If my theory is correct, and a vampire house is behind what just happened, then they won't expect us to act on our own. And the SCU won't be effective in stopping them, either. Not with Agent Smith so intertwined with the politics."

"Yeah, that's cute, James," Phillip said with a laugh. "And who's gonna cut us a paycheck? Kickin' dead things in the balls ain't gonna pay the bills."

"True," James said. "Wouldn't it be helpful if you had an incredibly rich friend who lived in what amounts to a small castle in the country and would like a roommate?"

Phillip blinked. "Are you serious?"

"Quite."

"You're asking me to move in with you?"

"I believe I am."

"That's a big step."

"I feel it's where our relationship has been heading for a while."

Phillip sat still, his eyes suddenly darting to the side. James followed them, looking up to see the waiter standing next to the table holding a pot of coffee. He looked from James to Phillip and back again before speaking. "Oh, my god! I'm so, sorry, I didn't mean to interrupt, but this is so exciting!" He refilled their coffees, talking rapidly over Phillip's sputtering denials. "This is so romantic, and I'll bet you two's parents are so excited!" The last word came out in a gleeful high pitch.

"It's not like that," Phillip managed.

"Oh, don't be shy," the waiter said, putting his hand on his hip and giving Phillip a knowing grin. "There's always one in the couple who's a little more modest than the other." He patted Phillip on the shoulder. "He's a catch, sweetie, go for it." He turned on his heel and went back to the kitchen, calling out "Congratulations!" in a singing voice as he went.

Phillip glared at James. "I hate your ass."

James grinned. "I know, Sweetie."

J ames and Phillip had returned to Coldstone Keep after breakfast and spent the day working on the house. James had called Molly, who was immediately apologetic for not calling him over the past few days. "I was so wrapped up in work. We just got set up in the new com tower, and I've been sitting in front of flight navigation systems for days. I actually slept in a hotel one night because I wouldn't have time to sleep between shifts otherwise. It's been hectic."

James was just glad that her work woes had happened to coincide with his own chaotic trip. "Do you like going to the movies?"

James looked around the movie theater lobby, the smell of popcorn mixing with the scent of nachos and candy as people purchased their snacks at concessions. A large television screen played a rotation of trailers for upcoming films, the sound from the speakers around the lobby mixing with the thrum of crowd conversations. He felt Molly squeeze his hand. "James?"

He blinked, looking down at her. "Sorry, I spaced out for a minute."

"Try sleeping sometimes," Molly said with a smile. "It does wonders."

"Right. Sorry again for not calling you right away when I got home. Work wore me out."

"No worries, I get it," Molly said. "Sometimes I just need a day to decompress too. I am glad you called, though."

James nodded. "I felt the need to give you a more normal evening out than our last encounter. Though I'm not complaining in the least about our introduction to each other."

Molly laughed, and James smiled at the musical sound despite the small ache in his chest as Lacy's face flashed through his mind. He put it aside immediately, forcefully redirecting his thoughts to Molly and their night together that seemed like eons ago. He'd told himself to move on, and that was what he intended to do.

The line moved again, and James ordered a large popcorn and two drinks. The girl behind the counter was young, James guessed mid-teens and working her weekend job. She smiled at him, asked if there was anything else, rang out the order, and handed James a receipt as another kid placed the popcorn and drinks on the counter. "Enjoy the movie," the girl said in a spirited and happy tone.

James and Molly made their way to their theater and found their seats. James always sat in the exact center, a habit he'd picked up from Phillip.

"You get the best audio that way," Phillip had once said. "And the screen is just the right distance away."

"Huh," Molly said as she picked up a few pieces of popcorn. "They forgot the butter."

"Oh," James said. "I'll get it fixed." He grabbed the bag and stood.

"No, it's fine," Molly said. "I don't mind. Probably don't need to be eating it anyway."

"I don't mind," James said with a smile. "Besides, eating movie theater popcorn without butter is a crime in quite a few countries. I'll be back." He made his way back out to the lobby, pulling the receipt from his pocket as he approached the concessions stand. He waved to the kid who'd filled his order earlier. "Excuse me? I'd ordered butter."

The kid nodded. "Sorry about that, sir."

"No problem. Thanks," James said as the kid took the bag. He glanced down at the receipt, looking over the items as he waited.

He saw the small mark down by the note on the receipt to "please take our survey." It was stamped, the red ink already faded, but not enough to make him think he was seeing anything other than the House Tepes crest.

His blood ran cold, his skin gooseflesh as the wolf snapped to attention inside, growling at him. He looked up and around the lobby, then down at the register where the young girl had rung out his order. A tall, thin, gangly boy with acne stood in her place, his voice cracking as he rattled off his scripted greetings and up-sell pitches. James looked around the lobby again, trying to find the girl. His phone buzzed in his pocket. He pulled it out and looked at it, the lump in his throat back as he read Lacy's text message.

It's bigger than we thought.

END OF BOOK TWO

ACKNOWLEDGMENTS

Great big special thanks to everyone who has stuck with me for an insane ride these past couple of years! Shoutout to my editor, Erin Penn, for doing a great job with the edits on book 2, and big shoutout to Susan Roddey for an amazing book cover. Special thanks to Nirvana Jane Briarwood for being patient with me during the process because I tend to disappear from life while working on edits and such. And the biggest special thanks to my fans. You guys make these books possible. Enjoy!

ABOUT THE AUTHOR

Jason Gilbert Bio

Jason is the author of *The Clockworks of War* series, *The Rifle Chronicles*, and urban fantasy series *The Coldstone Case Files*. His stories are Alternate History with an Urban Fantasy and Horror element set in worlds of the supernatural. His favorite pastimes are reading, video games, horror movies, beer, and heavy metal music...but on the weekends he is his own boss!

facebook.com/jasongilbertauthor
instagram.com/jasongilberauthor
amazon.com/author/jasonhgilbert

ALSO BY JASON GILBERT

FRIENDS OF FALSTAFF

Thank You to All our Falstaff Books Patrons, who get extra digital content each month! To be featured here and see what other great rewards we offer, go to www.patreon.com/falstaffbooks.

PATRONS

Dino Hicks
John Hooks
John Kilgallon
Larissa Lichty
Travis & Casey Schilling
Staci-Leigh Santore
Sheryl R. Hayes
Scott Norris
Samuel Montgomery-Blinn
Junkle

www.ingramcontent.com/pod-product-compliance
Lightning Source LLC
Chambersburg PA
CBHW030424120726
47903CB00003B/794